Praise for Portia MacIntosh

'Smart, funny and always brilliantly entertaining, every book from Portia becomes my new favourite romcom.'
Shari Low

'I laughed, I cried – I loved it.'
Holly Martin

'The queen of romcom!'
Rebecca Raisin

'This book made me laugh and kept me turning the pages.'
Mandy Baggot

'A fun, fabulous 5-star romcom!'
Sandy Barker

'Loved the book, it's everything you expect from the force that is Portia! A must read.'
Rachel Dove

'Fun and witty. Pure escapism!'
Laura Carter

'A heartwarming, fun story, perfect for several hours of pure escapism.'
Jessica Redland

PORTIA MACINTOSH is the bestselling author of over 30 romantic comedy novels.

From disastrous dates to destination weddings, Portia's romcoms are the perfect way to escape from day-to-day life, visiting sunny beaches in the summer and snowy villages at Christmas time. Whether it's southern Italy or the Yorkshire coast, Portia's stories are the holiday you're craving, conveniently packed in between the pages.

Formerly a journalist, Portia has left the city, swapping the music biz for the moors, to live the (not so) quiet life with her husband and her dog in Yorkshire.

Website: portiamacintosh.com
Instagram: @portiamacintoshauthor

Also by Portia MacIntosh:

Off The Record
Love On Tour
Always The Bridesmaid
Drive Me Crazy
Truth or Date
It's Not You, It's Them
The Accidental Honeymoon
Here Comes the Ex

Marram Bay series:
Falling For You
Snow Love Lost
Met Your Match

Honeymoon For One
My Great Ex-Scape
The Plus One Pact
Stuck On You
One Night Only
Faking it

Life's a Beach
Will They, Won't They?
No Ex Before Marriage
The Meet Cute Method
Single All The Way
Just Date and See
Your Place or Mine?
Better Off Wed
Long Time No Sea
Fake It or Leave It
Trouble in Paradise
One Wild Night
Ex in the City
The Suite Life
It's All Sun and Games
One of the Boys
You Had Me at Château
Wish You Weren't Here
Too Hot to Handle

Never the Bride

PORTIA MACINTOSH

ONE PLACE. MANY STORIES

HQ
An imprint of HarperCollins*Publishers* Ltd
1 London Bridge Street
London SE1 9GF

www.harpercollins.co.uk

HarperCollins*Publishers*
Macken House, 39/40 Mayor Street Upper,
Dublin 1 D01 C9W8
This edition 2026

1

Previously published in Great Britain as *You Can't Hurry Love* by HQ, an imprint of HarperCollins*Publishers* Ltd 2017

Copyright © Portia MacIntosh 2017

Portia MacIntosh asserts the moral right to be identified as the author of this work.
A catalogue record for this book is available from the British Library.

ISBN: 9780008802691

This novel is entirely a work of fiction. The names, characters and incidents portrayed in it are the work of the author's imagination. Any resemblance to actual persons, living or dead, events or localities is entirely coincidental.

All rights reserved. No part of this publication may be reproduced, stored in a retrieval system, or transmitted, in any form or by any means, electronic, mechanical, photocopying, recording or otherwise, without the prior permission of the publishers.

Without limiting the exclusive rights of any author, contributor or the publisher of this publication, any unauthorized use of this publication to train generative artificial intelligence (AI) technologies is expressly prohibited. HarperCollins also exercise their rights under Article 4(3) of the Digital Single Market Directive 2019/790 and expressly reserve this publication from the text and data mining exception.

Printed and bound in the UK using 100% Renewable
Electricity by CPI Group (UK) Ltd

For my boy, my family and my dogs.

Chapter 1

I don't know what hits me first: the smell of meatballs or the fist of an impatient child who, having clearly spent too much time in IKEA, is flailing around like a maniac in the hope his embarrassed parents will get a move on and take him to Toys R Us. I wonder, only for a second, whether adopting a similar tactic might work on my boyfriend, except I've probably done much worse to embarrass him in the past.

Trips to IKEA are a regular event for us since we bought our house – partly because we spent most of our money actually buying a house and this is now our number-one social activity, but mostly because said house is what you'd euphemistically call a 'fixer-upper'. What I call it is a building site, but it was cheap, and my boyfriend, Leo, loves doing DIY, so it's perfect for him. To be perfectly honest, I'd go as far as to say he loves IKEA too. Why else would we be here, dashing in through the exit door (something that is highly frowned upon, but is undoubtedly the most efficient way to work the place), the day before we're set to go on holiday? Like, I don't know what it is, but something about flat-pack furniture just makes him come alive – get yourself a man who looks at you the way my boyfriend looks at the instructions for an IKEA coffee table.

'OK, let's split up to save some time,' Leo suggests. I pull a face, because even I know you never leave a man behind in IKEA, especially when you're going against the tide. IKEA is a signal dead zone so, if we separate, it will be hard to find each other. 'I'll get most of the things we need; all you need to do is grab a trolley and get a white SÄVEDAL door, 60x40.'

I feel my face contort with pure confusion.

'Seve . . .'

'SÄVEDAL,' he repeats himself. 'Make a note in your phone.'

'Leo, I'm not an idiot. That . . . word you just said . . . 40x60.'

'No, *60x40*, Mia,' he corrects me. 'Grab one of the little pencils and write it down.'

'Yeah, fine, go, go,' I babble.

I watch Leo disappear into the crowd before turning my attention to the task at hand. I need a seve . . . seve . . . dal? I'll just use one of the little computers dotted around to tell me where they are.

As I walk past the showrooms, I feel like I'm strolling down the street, peeping in people's living-room windows. Couples are sitting on the sofas, chatting like they would in the comfort of their own homes, as they deliberate which lamp to buy. There's even a couple arguing in one of the dummy rooms, who both shoot me a filthy look for looking inside – the very thing the fake room is here for. In one of the dummy kitchens there's a kid sitting under a worktop, visibly contemplating whether or not to take a bite out of a plastic apple, like a less bright Sir Isaac Newton. He decides it's a good idea and raises it to his mouth, but his dad stops him just in time, scooping him up and planting him on his shoulders, six feet in the air where he can't get in too much trouble.

I patiently wait my turn to use the computer, because IKEA is expert-level busy today. I mean, it's always busy, but today it is bank-holiday busy, and everyone and their spouse and 2.5 kids are here to get their hands on furniture and pieces of Daim cake.

The only problem is, by the time my turn comes around, I've completely forgotten what I'm looking for. I type S E V, hoping it will suggest something. He said it was a door, right? And we're shopping for things to build the kitchen. There's no way he'd send me for an actual door, so it must be for a cupboard or something.

I glance behind me, only to see the queue growing longer, and increasingly more impatient. I try again, typing S A V, but I'm still not getting any hits. Defeated, I give up and try to find a yellow-and-blue-striped employee to help me out.

'Excuse me,' I say to a man sitting at a computer. 'I wonder if you can help me? I'm after a door, for a kitchen, I think.'

'Sure, what's the product name?' he replies helpfully.

'Sev . . . sav . . . something, I don't know, sorry,' I reply apologetically.

A few punches of the keyboard and a quick look through their products and the employee knows exactly what I'm after.

'SÄVEDAL?'

'Yes,' I reply, a little too excitedly. 'I need a white one, please.'

'What size?' he asks.

Shit. Leo was right — I should have written this down.

'Erm . . . So, I think it's 60x40 or 40x60. So, whichever one of those is a real size.'

'We actually do both of those sizes, miss,' the employee points out.

Double shit.

'Erm . . .'

Come on, Mia. You've got this. Just think about what numbers he said — he even said them twice.

'Erm . . . 40x60?' I tell him, although it sounds more like a question than an answer.

'Are you sure?' He laughs.

'Positive,' I reply.

With an unconvinced laugh, he tells me where to find what I need and, as I walk there, I can't help but think about how much

3

my life has changed since I moved back to the UK. If you'd told me four years ago, when I was living in the Hollywood Hills, hanging out with movie stars, and playing the dating game to the best of my ability, that I'd be living in Canterbury, in a house that needs a lot of work, spending my days procrastinating and my nights watching Netflix, I would have laughed in your face – and probably threatened to do something drastic to save myself from such a life.

Don't get me wrong. I love Leo so much, and I'm so lucky to have him, but my life has changed so much and I'm really starting to feel it. My day-to-day life has changed, my hobbies have changed – even my looks have changed, which I can't help but notice, standing here in front of this full-length ISFJORDEN mirror. Gone are the days I'd spend hours at the gym, eating clean and tanning regularly to maintain my 'LA body', and since I stopped dropping triple digits on my long, blonde locks at a swanky salon, instead going to a cheaper, local place, I've had what's known in the trade as a chemical cut, which basically means they've been using such strong peroxide on my hair that it has broken off, leaving me with much shorter locks. As superficial as it sounds, I took such confidence from these things, and now I feel kind of unremarkable by comparison. I don't look bad; I just don't look like me.

Finally through the checkout, I spy Leo standing over by the door, finishing up a hotdog. It took me all this time to find one item and here he is, his trolley piled high with things, finishing up his dinner. This is further proof that he's some kind of IKEA wizard. He just seems to know how to manipulate the place, to bend it to his will, whether he's modifying furniture or taking the little shortcuts he knows to get from sofas to plates in a matter of minutes.

'There you are,' he says as I approach him. 'I was just about to come looking for you – I half expected to find you curled up in a bed somewhere.'

'What would you have done then?' I ask, adopting a more flirtatious tone.

'Probably napped with you,' he replies. 'Or something.'

I see that little glimmer in his eye that I love so much.

I laugh to myself. Sex in an IKEA bed, *in* IKEA, is probably Leo's number-one fantasy. It would probably make his day to find me in one of the fake bedrooms, whispering sweet Swedish nothings into his ear before some postcoital meatballs.

'OK, we need to go if you're going to get to Boots before they close,' Leo says with a clap of his hands.

I absolutely need to get to Boots before they close. It might feel like it's been a really long time since we had sex, but there's no time for flirting if I'm going to get the things I need for my trip tomorrow. Plus, we're not going to have sex in IKEA, are we? Our naughty days are a thing of the past. Well, when you've been together for four years you don't really do wild anymore, do you?

'Here, I got you one,' Leo says, handing me a hotdog.

'I'm OK, thanks,' I reply. 'I'm trying to eat less . . . like you.'

Leo just laughs, shrugs his shoulders and happily eats it himself.

Everyone told me it was easy to put a bit of weight on when you were happy in a relationship, but I thought it was a myth. Well, how can happiness weigh anything? It turns out, what actually happens is, your palate changes. You start eating what your partner eats and, turns out, grown men often eat like fussy children. I rarely ate meat when I met Leo. Now, honestly, it's alarming how many chicken nuggets I put away per year.

Of course, as is always the case, it's all so much easier for men. My super-sexy boyfriend is just as hot as the day we first met. I suppose being a fireman helps with that. He has to keep fit, and the uniform still lights a fire in my downstairs. I, on the other hand, work from home, so I'm not as active as I used to be. I'm a healthy-ish weight; I'm just nowhere near as toned as I used to be (but, if I'm being honest, life is a lot better with chicken nuggets in it).

Finally at our car, Leo begins loading things into the boot as I plonk myself down in the passenger seat, exhaling deeply, relieved to have survived another trip to IKEA.

'Erm, Mia,' Leo calls from behind me.

'Yeah?'

'You've got the wrong size,' he tells me.

I massage my temples. 'Can't you make it work?'

'I mean, it would be better to just have the right one. Shall I run back in?'

'Leo, I need to get to Boots,' I tell him.

'I know, I know,' he calls back. 'But I really wanted to do some work on the kitchen today. Aren't you sick of eating microwave food and takeaways?'

'Well, yeah, but we're going away tomorrow,' I reply.

'To Cornwall,' he reminds me. 'Where they have plenty of Boots . . . I'll make sure we stop at one on the way to the beach house and you can even give me a list of what you want and I'll get it . . . and I'll buy you some Daim chocolate.'

'OK, fine, go,' I tell him. 'I'll stay here.'

Leo gives me a kiss on the cheek before dashing off back inside, leaving me sitting in the car. I know he just wants to get the house finished so that we can get on with living a happy life in it. I guess I'm impatient and growing tired of the constant DIY.

Perhaps the kid with the helicopter arms was on to something. That's why he's probably in Toys R Us right now getting whatever toy he wants, and I'm still stuck here, in IKEA purgatory, waiting for a kitchen door.

Chapter 2

Isn't it weird how, when you visit somewhere you haven't been for a while, it seems so familiar and yet so alien. Like it's something you saw in a movie once.

Being back in Cornwall, back at the beach house where my sister got married, is making me feel exactly that. I want to say it hasn't changed at all, because it hasn't, but what happened here during her wedding week feels like something that happened to someone else.

My sister, Belle, and her husband, Dan, tied the knot here four years ago and thought it might be nice to celebrate their wedding anniversary here, with the family and friends who were there on their special day.

It was at Belle and Dan's wedding that I met Leo. I was a bridesmaid; he was the best man – it sounds like something fresh out of romantic comedy, right? *Of course* we were supposed to end up together. It took me a while to realise this, though, and so the path to true love wasn't a smooth one.

You wouldn't think it, meeting me now, but back then I had a real problem with commitment. I arrived at the beach house for Belle's wedding expecting to have a terrible time, but then Leo showed up.

I remember the first time I met him like it was yesterday. The entire wedding party went out for lunch, except Dan, the groom, who was laid up in bed with a bad back, so I wound up staying behind to look after him. There had been mention of a best man who was showing up at some point, but I completely forgot about that. That's why, on my way back to my room,

I didn't think it would be a problem when my bikini top fell off . . . but then I heard this voice behind me. We spoke for a moment before I turned around, and when I finally saw him, I couldn't get over how sexy he was. Sure, he was big and buff, but his swept-back dark hair, and sexy green eyes, and dimples . . . my God, those dimples!

Of course, at the time I didn't know it was love at first sight. I thought it was lust. To protect my modesty I was using my hands as a bra. I remember Leo introducing himself to me and offering me a hand to shake so that I'd remove one of my own from my chest. I loved how cheeky he was, and then he kissed me.

The kiss knocked me for six, so much so that I didn't know what to say afterwards. I think I blurted something along the lines of: 'I've never kissed a fireman before.'

'Neither have I,' he replied.

I assumed he was like me, just after a good time, but he later confessed that he wasn't the ladies' man I thought he was, and that he only wanted me. It took me a little longer to realise this, but I got there in the end.

It's weird, to think that, before, when we met, I thought of his job as the ultimate sexy-man job. I just thought of his big, strong arms and his stripper uniform. These days, all I think about is how dangerous his job is, and how I don't know what I'd do if I lost him.

The beach house is just as beautiful as I remember it: brilliant-white walls, contemporary architecture, with big windows, multiple balconies and an entire beach for a back garden. Thanks to our detour to Boots, judging by all the cars parked on the driveway, I'd say we were the last ones to arrive.

'Of course we're late.' I laugh to myself.

'It'll be fine,' Leo assures me, trapping me in a bear hug before lifting me up off the ground and spinning around a few times. He always knows how to make me feel better. 'Come on, let's go inside.'

I take a moment to glance around the garden. It really is such a beautiful summer's day. The house sits right on the beachfront and, right now, all I want to do is take a walk along the coast. Unfortunately, I've got a family inside waiting for me – probably an angry family, because even though I am consistently late, they're always surprised and offended by it.

'Hello,' I call out as we walk through the large front door. 'Anyone home?'

My voice echoes through the large living room.

'Mia!' my sister squeaks as she charges towards me, seemingly from out of nowhere.

'Hello,' I reply, unable to muster up my sister's level of enthusiasm. 'How's it going?'

'*Amazing*,' she replies. 'We were just about to eat without you. Come on.'

Belle grabs me by the wrist, ready to drag me along, sort of like the way an excited child would drag you downstairs on Christmas morning.

'Who's here?' I ask, wiggling free of her grasp.

My sister greets Leo with a kiss on each cheek and a lingering hug before turning her attention back to me.

'Me, Dan, Mum, Dad, Mike and Rosie, Gran – Granddad wasn't feeling up to it. That's everyone. We thought we'd keep it at close family only, so parents, siblings and their significant others,' Belle explains.

'Cool,' I reply, a little too unenthusiastically for my sister's liking. Belle pulls a face.

'I've put you two in your old room, the one you shared back when you met.' She beams. 'My gosh, doesn't it feel like a long time ago?'

'It does and it doesn't,' Leo replies with a smile. 'I mean, sometimes it feels like we met only yesterday, but I feel like I've known you my whole life.'

As I watch my sister visibly melt, I wonder how I'll clean her off the floor. To be fair, even though I'm not really a mushy person, even I thought that was pretty sweet. Leo is always saying cute little things, reminding me how much he loves me – it's nice.

'Right, dinner,' Belle says with a clap of her hands. 'This way.'

The dining room is just as we left it, the only difference this time is that there are fewer of us, so I don't have to sit at the kids' table.

'Hello, Mia,' my mum says. Her words aren't delivered with the kind of warmth you'd expect from a mother speaking to her firstborn. It feels more like they're uttered out of a combination of obligation and manners. 'Hello, Leo.'

A nice, frosty Harrison family reception, as I expected. When I made the decision to give up life in LA and move back to Kent, it felt like an opportunity to reconnect with the family I'd spent four years avoiding. Instead, I still avoid them, only now it's much harder because I only live down the road. Leo and I stop by for Sunday dinner every now and then, and then there are obligatory family gatherings like this one. Leo lives for family life so he loves visiting our families, but for me it's something I endure as best I can. Today, being back here at this beach house where so much went on, is really going to test my endurance.

We all exchange pleasantries before Leo and I take our seats at the table.

'So, what are we having?' Leo asks excitedly, rubbing his hands.

'Pasta with meatballs,' Belle announces – probably an attempt to appeal to Leo's Italian side and it works. He sits down and grabs a plate, serving himself a generous portion.

I take a seat and serve myself.

'We were just talking about how quickly these four years have gone by,' my mum says, filling us in.

'Yeah, I suppose they have,' I reply. Sometimes it feels like much longer, though.

'It was a great wedding,' Mike, Dan's brother, pipes up. 'It's a shame you missed it,' he tells his fiancée, Rosie, who smiles sweetly.

'It's a miracle it even happened at all,' Belle says.

'How so?' Rosie asks curiously.

'Oh, just, you know, wedding stuff,' Belle backtracks. Well, we did say we'd never talk about it again.

It's fair to say that, even though Belle's wedding turned out great in the end, things were a little bit disastrous. I feel like she still holds me responsible for a lot of what happened, which is probably why my relationship with my sister isn't great.

In fact, it would be fair to say that my relationship with my entire family isn't great. Moving back here was the best decision I've ever made, because I have Leo now, but I still feel like an outcast sometimes. Perhaps it's because I lived away from them for so many years, but as hard as I try to fit in, they still make me feel like a bit of an imposter sometimes. They don't treat me like a black sheep, they treat me like a wolf.

My mum and dad, a middle-class couple in their early sixties, are exactly the kind of people you'd expect them to be. They're so serious and stuffy – just like my grandparents before them, so I have no doubt my sister will end up a similar way. I've always tried so hard to be like anything but the kind of people who raised me, because, for such a tight-knit family, I feel like there's a real emotional disconnect among us.

I've always struggled to remember life before my sister, Annabelle, came along. Beautiful, bouncing baby Belle, who burst onto the scene and immediately became the centre of attention. My only real memory of life before Belle was the night she was born. It was New Year's Eve and we were all at a party when my mum's waters broke sometime during the run-up to midnight. Belle was not only born quickly and relatively easily, but she was the first baby born after midnight, which saw her and my mum's pictures plastered all over the local newspaper. I, on the other hand, came into the world after putting my mum through three gruelling days of labour, so my mum rarely talks fondly about the day I was born, whereas she has a framed photo of her newspaper front page with baby Belle on the wall in her living room.

I was five years old when Belle was born, so I don't really remember being anything but second best. I feel like I was the starter child my parents practised on before Belle came along.

I think my mum gets her coldness from my gran – my Auntie June, my mum's sister, is similar – so I can't really blame her if that's the kind of women she's grown up around. My granddad, on the other hand, is a wonderful man who absolutely worships me. It doesn't matter whether or not I'm in the right or the wrong, he is always on my side, always ready with a funny comment to cheer me up or a piece of helpful advice to help me sort my problems out. I actually really missed him while I was living in LA so I make sure to spend lots of time with him now.

'It won't be long before you two tie the knot, will it?' Belle says to Mike and Rosie excitedly. I've never understood people's hype for other people's weddings, although I suspect she's just trying to change the subject.

'Only a few months to go,' Rosie replies.

I first met Mike, Dan's brother, four years ago in the run-up to the wedding. We had a lot in common back then; Mike was thirty, with no interest in marriage, and had a job his family didn't approve of. He was the Mia of his family, the let-down, the child who never quite lived up to his parents' expectations. Sure, he was happy working in a video-game shop, just like I was happy writing movies in LA, but our parents didn't think we should be doing what we loved. They thought we should be getting married and starting families. It's interesting to see how we've both changed. Maybe everyone does eventually.

'Are you excited?' Belle asks.

'So excited,' Rosie replies. 'All the plans are in place now; it's just a matter of waiting. And the stag and hen parties are next week!'

Rosie squeals with excitement for a few seconds but then stops suddenly – I imagine it's because she's suddenly remembered she hasn't invited me.

'Sorry for not inviting you,' she says to me. 'It's just with your work and stuff, I didn't think you'd be able to make it.'

'You know I work from home, right?' I reply.

'Well, yeah, but I figured that meant you're, like, always busy, busy, busy,' she babbles with an awkward laugh.

I don't care, to be honest. It's not like we're close and I can't think of anything worse than going on a hen party with a bunch of sickly wedding types.

'We'll take you lots of pictures,' my mum says kindly. I love that she's invited my mum but not me.

'Thanks,' I reply.

'Yeah and, er, Leo, buddy . . .' Mike starts.

'I'm working,' Leo replies quickly.

'You don't even know when it is, mate,' Dan replies.

Leo and Mike have never really liked each other. It's a family wedding, so there was never any question whether or not Leo would go with me, but I can understand why he doesn't want to attend the stag do. Still, it's a relief to me, because if there's one thing that fills me with dread, it's stag dos. Mike is going to Magaluf for the weekend with his mates and, as much as I trust Leo as an individual male, I don't trust gangs of lads, full of alcohol, the air around them thick with peer pressure, in stag mode – especially somewhere like Magaluf. Everyone knows that, in places like that, the drinks are cheap, the sex comes easy, and doesn't everyone (rightly or wrongly) believe they can get away with things if no one is ever going to find out?

Trusting Leo has never been an issue, but I'm not sure anyone would be comfortable with their significant other being in that situation, would they? I might be over my commitment phobia, but I still don't think the course of true love runs easy. My sister thinks because she's married it's going to be rainbows and butterflies for the rest of her loved-up life, but I think marriage is work. I think people make mistakes. You don't just have a happy relationship by picking the right person. You both have to do all the right things, every day, to make sure you're both happy.

'I take all the overtime I can get,' Leo replies, ever the tactful diplomat. 'Houses are expensive.'

'Especially rundown ones like yours.' Belle laughs.

I frown. Only I'm allowed to slag off my house.

My mum touches her grey, Nurse Ratched–style bob, which she's been rocking for as long as I can remember (and which makes her look a lot older than she is) awkwardly. You can tell this conversation is making her uncomfortable.

'So, plans for tomorrow. Your morning is yours, but I'm making lunch and I expect you all to be there,' my mum informs the room, putting a stop to our sibling bickering before it can truly get started. She holds her gaze on me for an extra few seconds.

'Sir, yes, sir,' I joke.

My mother rolls her eyes.

'Clean plates all round – that's what I like to see,' Belle announces, making a move to clear the table.

'I'm pretty tired,' I say. 'I might go for a lie-down.'

'Yeah, I'll come with you,' Leo adds.

'Oi oi,' Mike chimes in. Everyone at the table shoots him a look.

'OK,' my mum replies. 'Remember: lunch tomorrow.'

I nod. It's a classic Judith Harrison move to simply demand we all be present for lunch. She's decided we all have to be there, so we must. Because she says so.

I head up the stairs, closely followed by Leo. He gives me a playful slap on the bum, which makes me giggle. He's never struggled to put a smile on my face, even when I'm in a bad mood.

'Well, this room looks exactly how we left it,' I point out.

'Nearly,' he points out. 'Both the pillows are at the top of the bed.'

I laugh. When Leo and I shared this room last time, it was after we'd put our little wedding fling on hold, at the request of my sister, who was worried my sex life might ruin her wedding for some reason. In the interest of keeping things platonic, I slept with my head at the top of the bed and Leo with his at the bottom.

'None of that business tonight,' I point out, running my hands up the front of his body before hooking them behind his neck. I press my body against him and gently place my lips on his, teasing him with my tongue. Usually my eager boyfriend reciprocates but tonight he feels stiff – and not in a good way.

'You OK?' I ask.

'Yeah,' he replies. 'Just a bit tired, I think.'

'You're never tired,' I point out.

'I work long, gruelling shifts as a firefighter, and when I'm not doing that, I'm working on the house – trust me, I get tired.' He laughs.

'You're never too tired for sex,' I point out, narrowing my eyes.

'Tomorrow,' he says, kissing me on the forehead before diving onto the bed.

I nod gently as I think to myself for a few seconds.

It's funny. When you start dating someone, you try to spend as much time with them as possible, trying to work out whether you like them before you sleep with them – all while they're trying to get you into bed. But then, when you're actually a couple, and they can have sex with you whenever they want, it gets to a point where *you're* having to practically beg *them*. At least that's how it feels sometimes. I suppose life just starts getting in the way, especially when your boyfriend works shifts.

'OK. Well, I think I'll take a walk. It's not even really dark yet,' I say.

'You want some company?' he asks.

'No, you rest up,' I reply. 'Save your energy for tomorrow.'

I walk out, closing the door behind me. I bite my lip, like I always do when I'm thinking. I'm not saying I'm irresistible to men, but I know my boyfriend. Something is definitely up here.

Chapter 3

In preparation for renovating the house we just bought, Leo made me sit through a lot of TV shows about buying houses, fixing them up and decking out the interior. While it wasn't exactly my favourite way to spend time, I have to admit I learned a lot. I learned that, when it comes to your home, one thing is very important: location, location, location.

My house in LA was in the Hollywood Hills, and it didn't matter how many times I took in the view from my floor-to-ceiling living room, it took my breath away. This beach house, with its beach for a back garden, is also in a truly amazing location. The house I bought with Leo, well, let's just say the location isn't exactly anything to write home about. We were bound by a few factors, like Leo needing to live close to work, and our financial limits, so when he found us a house that wasn't tiny or expensive, it seemed like the perfect fit. The reason it wasn't expensive is because it used to be a student house, situated in the heart of the student village. I didn't realise a few things when we bought it: one was that the renovations would take so long and the other was that living in a house surrounded by students would be so noisy.

It isn't noisy here, unless you count the lapping of the waves and the light breeze dancing around on the sand. I used to walk this beach back in the day, when everyone was stressing me out and I wanted to clear my head. There's a little café down here called Shell's that I used to go to, but I don't suppose it will be open at this time in the evening.

I don't get too far down the beach before I spot something else familiar: Chris, the lifeguard I met while he was working here four years ago. Not only is he still living here, but his golden retriever, Jay, is still helping him keep the shores safe. They're jogging along the beach, getting closer by the second, and suddenly I feel so self-conscious.

The first time Chris met me I was wearing a tiny nightdress – or maybe it was a tiny bikini. Either way, I had a lot of flesh on show and he had to pick his jaw up from the floor. My long blonde hair was flowing back then and so was my confidence. Now, I no longer have the perfect beach body and the one I do have is hidden under a pair of trackies and a baggy, off-the-shoulder T-shirt. My hair is shorter, darker and scraped up on top of my head, and my easy confidence is MIA.

As Chris approaches I try to psych myself up. So what if I look different? Chris was just some guy I met on the beach who I fancied – I have an incredibly gorgeous boyfriend who loves me now.

I glance up at Chris as he jogs past me with a blank nod of acknowledgement – the kind you'd give to any stranger on the beach. I can't believe it. He doesn't recognise me. I don't look that different, do I? I know I'm not as in shape, and fully clothed, which isn't a state I think he's ever seen me in before, and my hair is different, but I'm still me and I feel like he spent enough time with me that he should recognise me if he saw me again.

That's twice I've received the cold shoulder this evening and it's hard not to take it personally. Chris doesn't recognise me as the girl he knew back then and, now we're back in the beach house, maybe Leo doesn't either.

I consider talking to Leo about how I'm feeling, but by the time I get back to our room he's fast asleep. I climb in next to him and close my eyes.

Chapter 4

I exhale deeply as I wait for Leo out on the decking. When we woke up this morning he told me we were going for a walk, so I scraped my hair back up on top of my head, slipped on my scruffy outfit from last night and sleepily made my way outside to wait for him.

My attention flits between admiring the ocean, playing with the sand with my toes, and picking off the remains of my blue nail polish as I wait for Leo to appear.

'Look at you,' I squeak as he steps outside. 'You look amazing and I look like trash.'

Leo laughs. 'You look great – you always look great,' he tells me in a way that makes it sound like a reminder, rather than a general compliment.

'But you're dressed up,' I point out.

His hair is perfectly blown back, he's wearing a crisp white shirt and he smells delicious, like the Creed aftershave I bought him for Christmas that he usually reserves for special occasions.

Leo smiles that devastating smile of his. I am weak for his dimples, even after all this time.

'Come on, let's go for a walk,' he says, taking me by the hand.

It's a beautiful morning, like something fresh off a postcard. The beach is clear, the sea is calm and the weather is just right. It's not too hot yet, although it's set to be a scorcher later today. Were it not for my mum's compulsory lunch, I could've got the tan my body so desperately needs.

'It's a shame we can't stay longer,' Leo says with a sigh. 'You deserve a break. It might help with your stress.'

'I know,' I reply. 'We'll take a proper holiday soon, when all our money isn't being spent on the house.'

'I know it's taking a lot of time and a lot of work,' he starts, 'but it's going to be worth it.'

'I know,' I reply. I do know – it's just taking *so much* time and money and effort, I kind of wish we'd carried on renting a little while longer.

'I know work is stressing you out too.' Leo stops and turns to face me, suddenly adopting a much more serious tone. 'But you're happy, aren't you? With life and with me?'

'Of course I am,' I say, placing my hands on his gorgeous face. 'Yes, the house is a mess. Yes, work is difficult at the moment. But none of that alters the fact that I love you so much.'

'Good,' he says thoughtfully. 'That's good.'

'Good,' I echo.

Leo looks at me for a second, then he smiles. I wish I could tell what was going on in his head. He isn't always the kind of guy to broadcast his feelings, so I'll often resort to guessing what's going on in there. Of course, being the anxious type, my brain always assumes things are much worse than they are.

Suddenly, Leo crouches down on the ground.

'What are you doing?' I laugh.

'Mia,' he says, pausing to puff air from his cheeks.

'Yes,' I reply in a goofy voice.

Everything clicks in my head a split second before he pulls a ring box from his pocket.

'Whoa, what are you doing?' I laugh.

'Something I should have done a long time ago.'

Leo, who it turns out is down on one knee and not just squatting on the sand, opens the ring box to reveal a silver engagement ring with a big, beautiful, colourful opal stone – my favourite. Is there anything that feels as wonderful as when you realise a man actually listens to you when you're just babbling about things that aren't important, like what your favourite stone is?

'I've known I loved you since the second I laid eyes on you four years ago. You're the most amazing, most interesting, most beautiful woman I've ever met, and I can't believe I haven't asked this sooner. Will you marry me?'

'Yes!' I squeak instantly, without even pausing for thought.

An instant but cautious smile appears on his face. 'Are you sure?' he asks.

'Of course I'm sure,' I reply, pulling him up from the ground.

Leo slips the ring on my finger before kissing me, grabbing me in his big, strong arms and twirling me around.

Mia from four years ago might have thought marriage was stupid, but Mia now loves Leo so much. It had crossed my mind, every now and then, what I'd say if he asked, but I never really gave it too much thought. We'd mentioned marriage, but I'd never been able to imagine him pulling the trigger. But now he's popped the question and it's the easiest question I've ever had to answer.

'Your folks are going to be over the moon – that's why your mum is making a special lunch, you know, to celebrate,' he confesses.

Thank God I didn't make a scene over the fact we were being summoned for lunch today.

'That's very sweet of her,' I say. 'And confident.'

'She knew you'd say yes,' he tells me. 'So did I.'

'Is this why you were so quiet last night?' I ask, suddenly feeling a lot better about the fact he didn't want to have sex with me.

'Yeah.' He laughs awkwardly, running a hand through his hair. 'Last-minute nerves.'

I smile widely as I stare down at my ring. 'This is just . . . incredible. I've never seen anything like it.'

'It's an Ethiopian fire opal,' he tells me. 'The ring was handmade. There are real diamonds in the band, but I remember you telling me that opals were your favourite.'

'I did,' I say with a smile. I can't believe he listened *and* remembered. 'I just wish you'd given me some warning. I would have made sure I looked less . . . like this.'

'Mia, you look great. I've never seen you look anything less than gorgeous. Even when we're eighty, I'll still see you as my blonde, bikini-dropping bombshell.'

'When we're eighty, neither of us will be able to pick up dropped bikinis,' I reply.

'Good,' he replies cheekily.

As we approach the beach house back door, I let go of Leo's hand.

'Listen, I'm going to go and smarten up and repaint my nails because if any photos are taken to remember this special day, I don't want to be looking like this in them,' I say, pointing down.

'OK,' Leo replies, grabbing me for one last kiss. 'You go get changed and then we'll tell everyone the good news together.'

'OK,' I reply. 'Won't be long.'

'OK, fiancée,' he calls after me jokily.

I can't help but smile.

I reach the top of the stairs and slowly make my way towards our bedroom. Thankfully, although I didn't have time to paint my nails before we left, I did have the foresight to chuck a bottle of deep-purple varnish into my make-up bag, with the intention of hopefully painting over the chipped blue stuff at some point. This is a move I often pull, to save time. In fact, under the chipped blue polish is chipped red polish that I covered with blue. The blue will cover with this dark purple shade but after that the only colour that will save the day is black, and when that looks messy I'll have to finally make time to strip off the six months' worth of polish that has built up. LA Mia always had perfectly manicured nails but Mia now doesn't have the time or the money for that.

'Hey,' Mike calls out as he leaves his room.

'Hey,' I reply.

As I reach out to open the door, the light bounces off my beautiful ring, catching Mike's eye.

'You said yes?' he asks, sounding surprised.

I nod.

'Oh, man. I owe Leo ten pounds,' he tells me. I hope he's kidding.

'So everyone knew?' I ask him.

'Yeah,' he replies. 'But I didn't think you were the marrying kind.'

'I could say the same thing about you,' I point out.

Mike is a tall and slender guy. He's had spiked, dyed-black hair for as long as I've known him, and with the exception of his wedding suit on Belle and Dan's big day (which didn't really look quite right on him), he's always wearing scruffy clothing. He's kind of stylish with it, though, so I assume it's intentional. He has a very unkempt beard now, which makes me think he's moving with the trends, not that I think he'd ever admit it. Mike likes to act like he doesn't care about things, but I'm sure he does or he wouldn't be getting married.

'Yeah, well, we all fall eventually, right?'

Mike's use of the word 'fall' reminds me of a conversation Leo and I had before we got together. It was just before Belle's wedding, when I thought I was heading back to LA in a few days and was doing everything in my power not to fall in love with Leo, because we lived so far apart, and because it had been so long since I'd had a proper relationship, I was scared I wouldn't know how to be in one at all – least of all with someone who lived on a different continent to me. Back then I was writing romantic movies for a living – despite not being very romantically inclined myself – so, after I tried to cool things off with Leo, he countered my decision with some of my own words about love, taken from one of my films. I told him love wasn't really like walking on air, that it was like jumping off a building, and that it didn't matter how long you were falling for, it was always only a matter of time before you hit the ground and got really hurt.

After bickering for a few minutes Leo finally agreed with me, that falling in love was like jumping off a building, because it was scary and because it took your breath away, but that real love was the person on the ground, waiting to catch you. It's been four years since he said those words to me, but I recall them all the time because Leo is the person who always catches me. So, even if Mike is right, and I'm 'falling' like we all do eventually, I know there's an amazing man waiting to catch me in his big, fireman arms. I'm not falling, I'm jumping.

I just smile at him. There's no point trying to explain it.

'See you at lunch,' I tell him, disappearing into my room to try to smarten myself up. I've got an engagement to celebrate – but what do I wear?

I blast my hair with dry shampoo before applying my make-up and quickly layering on a fresh coat of nail polish over my current severely chipped coat – it's the best I can do at short notice.

I grab a few outfits from my case and try them on in front of the full-length mirror. As I examine my body, I can't help but sigh. The girl looking back at me is not the girl who looked in this mirror four years ago. I used to wear whatever I wanted, but now I tend to stop and think about what doesn't show off the things that make me feel self-conscious sometimes. I was an overweight teenager, bullied by Belle and her friends for being quiet and a bit weird, which is why I felt so empowered and confident when I moved to LA and transformed myself into someone it felt good to be. I always thought that people might treat me better, if I looked 'better' – more conventionally attractive – but if I'm being honest, people just treated me a different kind of badly. Well, it didn't endear my family to me, because they thought I'd got ideas above my station, and I might have got more attention from men, but I wouldn't say it was always the kind I wanted. I soon realised that, really, it would probably never matter what size I was, that I just needed to be happy with myself, and I am now.

Still, everyone goes on a diet before their wedding to look their best in their dress, right? I grew up on a diet (no pun intended) or size zero celebs, 'circles of shame' in magazines, and TV shows where they would essentially roast people for the way they looked before giving them a fashion make-over, a gastric band and burning off their wrinkles. If there's one thing I know about wedding prep, it's the pre-wedding diet (or attempt at one, at least). And they always say the best time to start is today. Having said that, I think I'll start tomorrow. After all, not only are we celebrating, but my mum is making a special lunch today, and my life won't be worth living if I don't eat it.

Chapter 5

I gently tap my fingers against the keys of my MacBook – not because I'm typing, because I'm stressed. I have two chapters left to write and then I can send this book to my editor, and I really can't wait to see the back of it.

When I was living in LA I was part of a team of screenwriters responsible for all the big romcom hits of our generation, but leaving LA meant leaving my job too, and back here in Kent there's not much call for big-screen romcom writers. I looked into other writing jobs, but writing romantic comedies is what I'm good at, so I transitioned from writing movies to writing novels. Working with a team of screenwriters, I was in a sunny city, in a big, fancy office, with a well-stocked table of fresh food put out every morning. I could grab a Starbucks on my way to work, do my job with ease, flirt with my boss's latest handsome assistant and plan the night's social events with whichever movie stars were hanging around the office that day.

Writing novels is not as social as writing movies. It's October, so Kent is pretty cold, and instead of being in an office I am in my living room. I'm wearing a onesie because I'm freezing. I'm all alone because, other than emailing my editor or my agent, I work entirely by myself, and I don't really eat properly, I just grab things when I can.

It's been three months since Leo proposed, which means it's been three months since I made the decision to get back to my LA diet and exercise regime, and I've snapped right back into shape. I'm happy to admit that LA Mia was maybe a bit too thin, but thanks to all my hard work I've lost that stubborn stone everyone warned me I'd put on when I got a boyfriend – although I think the weight gain was more to do with the fact that I was eating too much junk while I was working. I'm really happy with the way I look again – I've even been taking vitamins and using special conditioning treatments to try and encourage my hair to grow longer again, because now I've got my body back, I want my hair back too.

It's Saturday night and the street outside is abuzz with students. Leo is at work and I'm here alone, trying to work, but I'm getting so easily distracted.

I walk over to the living-room window to see what's going on outside. There is what I'd guess is a nineteen-year-old man, holding a traffic cone to his crotch as he chases near-naked girls of a similar age across the street, prodding them in the butt with his plastic appendage. Our house sits in the middle of a long road that leads from the university right into the centre of town, which is why there are so many students around. Our house is also situated right in the middle of the Merry Mile, a famous pub crawl that runs from the uni into the centre, in which participants dress up and have a drink in each pub along the way.

I study the students, trying to work out who they're all supposed to be. There's one guy dressed up as a Minion and another one dressed as a sanitary towel (you'd be surprised how popular that one is among men, and my inner feminist isn't sure whether it's empowering or insulting), and the girls are all random things (a cavewoman, a cat, a nurse) that don't involve much clothing, which is unfathomable to me because it's freezing out there. It suddenly occurs to me that I'm fourteen years older than these kids and I feel like such an old lady, spending my Saturday night in my pyjamas.

When I think about my life back in LA, it feels like something that happened in a dream a long time ago. I might have got myself back into a shape I'm happy with, but Mia from four years ago wouldn't have been caught dead in a onesie – least of all a tea-stained one – spending a Saturday night at home while everyone else was out having fun. I would've been out having cocktails, bumping into Margot Robbie, begging her to introduce to me Leonardo DiCaprio so I could be his latest blonde squeeze, not here, putting off doing my work by watching a Minion with a traffic cone for a dick.

I head into the still-unfinished kitchen and put the kettle on. We haven't got much done with the house over the past three months. Leo has been working a lot and I've been working on my book. Leo has been taking all the overtime he can get because it turned out the house had some major electrical problems that needed fixing before we could get on with anything. Now that's done and finally all of the rooms are painted white, ready for us to make each one our own. I am hoping and praying we start with the kitchen because it's really hard to keep up the healthy eating when it's almost impossible to cook in there. I'm sure it will feel easier to eat healthier when this book is done too, because it's too easy to just keep writing and eat an entire tube of Pringles for dinner, rather than cooking, only pausing momentarily to wonder if Pringles tubes are getting smaller or your hands are getting bigger. Well, that's what I'd have been doing this time last year, anyway. These days I have to waste time I don't really have making healthy snacks I don't really want.

Armed with my cup of tea I sit back down on the sofa, grab my laptop and try to get back on with my work. The sooner I get this book done, the sooner I can send it off and get to work on the next one. It's hard to function as an adult when you write books for a living because you have no real guaranteed income.

By the time your publishers and your agent take their cut you are left with what you're left with, and you have to survive from quarter to quarter without a top-up. You never really know how much you're going to be paid from one quarter to the next, so it's hard to make plans. Were I not lucky enough to live with Leo, and were it not for the fact he has a good job, I'm not sure I'd feel financially comfortable doing this for a living.

I am about to start typing when I hear a loud bang on the door. It's a bit late for knock-on-the-door, just-stopping-by visitors, but not so late I'm scared to see who it is.

'Hello, boys,' I say, seeing my friends Rory and Iwan on the doorstep.

'Mamma Mia,' Rory bellows after swigging from a bottle of bourbon and passing it to Iwan before giving me a hug.

'Hi,' I laugh. 'You boys seem like you've had a good night.'

'We're heading into town now,' Iwan slurs, his thick Welsh accent sounding even stronger thanks to all the alcohol. 'We thought we'd see if you and Leo fancied it?'

'Leo is working,' I tell them. 'So am I, to be honest.'

'Come on, come out with us,' Rory whines. 'Come on.'

I can't help but laugh at his drunk tantrum.

Rory and Iwan share a flat in the house next door. While the houses are aimed at students, they're also marketed to young professionals as a cheaper alternative to the swanky apartments in the more favourable parts of town. They both work together at a digital agency, Rory as a project manager and Iwan as a web developer. Iwan definitely looks as you'd expect him to, with his handsome good looks, his trendy beard and his geek-chic hipster clothing. Rory, on the other hand, seems to only take style inspiration from James Bay, with his long, messy hair always covered with a wide-brimmed hat and his stick-thin legs encased in the skinniest of skinny jeans. Leo and I have been friends with Rory and Iwan for years now. In fact, it was them who let us know about this house going up for sale.

'I really need to get this book finished,' I tell them, 'but then we'll go out to celebrate – next weekend maybe?'

'Boo,' Rory, clearly the drunker of the two, heckles me.

'You want a drink before we go?' Iwan asks.

'Just made a cuppa,' I tell him.

I close the door and plonk myself down on the sofa, sighing deeply. I would love to go out, but I need to be responsible. Just a few more chapters and then I can send this off, and finally start having some fun.

Chapter 6

Waking up, I feel Leo's heavy arm draped across my body before I open my eyes and see him lying next to me. He was working most of last night, so he can't have been asleep very long. I grab my phone from my bedside table and see that it's 11.49 – just about midday, but it is a Sunday, after all, and I was working until pretty late. Not as late as Leo, so I climb out of bed, careful not to wake him, pulling on my dressing gown before heading downstairs to make a cup of tea.

As I try to navigate the unfinished kitchen, I grab a mug and the teabags, eyeballing the jar of instant coffee as I do so. I've never liked instant coffee, having always been too much of a coffee snob, but ever since I gave up drinking coffee, even my weird fantasy of eating a spoonful of granules straight from the jar feels like something I might enjoy. I don't do it, though. I make my tea and sit on the sofa, opening my laptop once again in the hope of getting some work done.

My fingers are about to hit the keys when there's a knock at the door. Perhaps it's Rory and Iwan again, on their way home from their wild night out.

'Belle,' I blurt, unable to hide my surprise when I open the door to see my sister standing there, hugging an armful of magazines.

'Mia,' she replies. 'Can I come in? Don't worry, I know it's a mess.'

I physically bite my tongue to stop myself saying something in response to that.

'Sure, come in,' I reply. 'Tea?'

'Yes, please,' Belle replies.

I leave my little sister in the living room while I go and make her a drink. As the kettle boils I riffle through one of the bags of clothes sitting on the kitchen floor, grabbing myself a bra and a sundress (this must be the bag with the summer clothes in), hurrying them on in the kitchen so my sister doesn't get to make any remarks about me not being dressed.

'So, I bumped into Leo last night,' she calls from the living room.

'You bumped into Leo last night?' I repeat back to her. 'Were you on fire?'

'Har-har,' she calls back, as I carry her tea through and place it down on the pile of boxes we're using as a coffee table. 'My God, look at you, you've lost so much weight.'

'I haven't really,' I reply. 'It's mostly that I've toned up the bits that I'd let get a bit wobbly.'

'Don't let Gran see, she'll go berserk,' my sister warns.

Despite being younger than me, my sister dresses beyond her years – beyond my years too. When we were younger Belle was always one of the popular kids because she was slim, sporty and followed every trend going. I, on the other hand, was a bit chubby, a bit weird and painfully shy. Belle is curvier these days and she looks great; she's just a few too many steps ahead of herself, in full-blown mumsy mode with her style, and if she'd take a little of my advice, she could look amazing.

'Anyway . . .' She gets back to the task at hand, passing me a stack of wedding magazines. 'Leo mentioned that you hadn't really started planning the wedding and asked if I had any old magazines I could bring you to get you started.'

So my sister just so happened to bump into my fiancé at work, who asked if she happened to have any old wedding magazines lying around from more than four years ago, and she did, so she's just brought them over for me. I mean, if I were the cynical type, I'd think Leo messaged my sister and asked her to give me some wedding magazines in an effort to get me to start planning, because I'm yet to start, but I've been so busy with so many other things. Let's say I buy into the idea that Belle ran into Leo at the fire station, it still doesn't explain why these magazines are in perfect condition and the dates show they're the latest editions.

'And,' she starts, even more excitedly, 'there's a wedding fair in town next week.'

'Thank you,' I say brightly. 'But let's get Mike and Rosie's wedding out of the way before we start planning another one.'

'Get it out of the way?' my sister shrieks. 'Mia, you're so unromantic. It still baffles me that you write romance for a living. It baffles me even more that you're getting married when you clearly have no interest in weddings.'

'I don't have "no interest" in weddings,' I clap back. 'I'm getting married, aren't I?'

'Where?' she asks.

'I don't know yet.'

'When?' she continues.

'Next summer – I don't know yet.'

'Who will be your bridesmaids?' she persists.

Ah, now I understand what's happening here. My sister is just trying to secure her role as chief bridesmaid.

'Well, I thought about asking the cousins – Meg, Hannah and little Angel . . .' I start, teasing my sister a little by not immediately asking her.

'Well, let me stop you there,' my sister says, shuffling to the edge of her seat. 'Auntie June has already vetoed that idea.'

'Erm, Meg is seventeen and Hannah is not only nineteen years old, but she's got a three-year-old kid of her own, so I'm pretty sure they don't need Auntie June's permission.'

'Look, don't shoot the messenger, but that's what Auntie June said and they respect their mum's wishes.'

'Dare I ask why?' I start, pretty sure the answer will only make me angry.

'She's worried you'll dress them . . . like you.'

'You can tell me what she actually said,' I insist.

'Like floozies.'

Nice. Good old Auntie June.

'Well, OK, so obviously I'm going to ask you,' I continue, on a more positive note.

Belle winces.

'Surely you're not worried I'll dress you like a floozie?' I ask in disbelief.

'I just feel that, after everything that happened when you were a bridesmaid for me . . .' she starts. 'You were such a bad bridesmaid. And I don't want you thinking I'll be trying to settle the score or any business like that.'

'Belle, that never crossed my mind.'

It's crossing my mind *now*.

'Oh. Well, I just don't think it would be appropriate,' she says firmly. 'I don't see why I should help you with your wedding when you did such an awful job with mine. I mean, I'd do a great job, for sure—'

'Fine,' I cut her off. I'm not going to beg.

'Well, who else can you ask?' she persists, suddenly so clearly desperate for the honour, but not until I plead with her.

'Belle, I've told you, I'm too busy to start planning it right now,' I snap. 'I should be working right now, in fact.'

'OK, fine,' she replies. 'I'll get going then.'

'I'll see you at Mike and Rosie's wedding next weekend,' I tell her as I walk her to the door.

Once my sister is gone, I sit back down on the sofa and eyeball the pile of wedding magazines, with all the smug, happy, white-wearing brides on the cover, who probably knew exactly what they wanted from their big day, and they've probably known since they were, like, eight years old. I'm not like most girls. I haven't been planning my big day since I was a kid. While most girls were draping net curtains over their heads and playing with dolls I was outside playing football with my friends or inside watching wrestling on TV. Even now, as an adult, I have no idea what I want my wedding to be like, and I suddenly have the added problem of not having anyone willing to be my bridesmaids, because I don't have any female friends or willing family members. I've always got on better with boys. I like video games, violent movies, listening to music full of swearing – all hobbies that make my sister, and girls like my sister, look down their noses at me.

I'm just going to concentrate on finishing this book, get Mike and Rosie's wedding out of the way and then I'll see about planning my own. You never know, attending a wedding might be exactly the inspiration I need to get me going.

Chapter 7

After a long and heavily religious church service (which I definitely don't want), and a trip to a hotel outside town on an open-top bus (which was not nice in October), we finally arrived at the reception. We're pretty much done with dinner now and I already have a long list of things I absolutely don't want for my wedding.

Rosie looks beautiful, as always – she's just got this kind of easy beauty about her, whereas I have to spend hours putting make-up on to look alive – but two things I absolutely don't want for my big day include having my hair piled up on top of my head like a Mr Whippy, held in place with a tiara, and wearing a big, white dress, with loads of ruffles and shit hanging off it and bits connecting to other bits in places that will limit my movement. Yes, Rosie looks great, so long as she stands still. The second she starts moving she looks so terribly uncomfortable, I feel sorry for her. Apparently she's got some kind of contraption under her dress that she can use to help her use the loo without assistance, but unless it's a hoist, I'm not sure it's going to help her all that much.

This wedding is exactly what you'd expect a wedding to be – and it's exactly how I'd write it, if I were trying to include every wedding cliché I could think of.

All in all, I wouldn't say it was a bad day, just not my taste. The speeches were relatively painless, if a little cringeworthy, and the food was OK – I pretty much just picked at my roast dinner. Who wants to eat food doused in gravy at a wedding? I didn't want to risk spilling anything down my dress.

'You really do look amazing,' Leo tells me, holding my hand over the table.

'Thank you,' I reply. 'Kind of makes all those extra slices of pizza I've resisted recently feel almost worth it.'

Leo laughs.

'Ladies and gentlemen, if I could have your attention, please,' the DJ booms over the PA. 'The bride and groom are about to take to the floor for their first dance.'

I'm sitting at a table with my parents, my grandparents, Leo and Belle – Dan's the best man, so he's up at the top table. I think I'm doing a pretty good job of being chill, given my surroundings. As soon as my gran clapped eyes on me, she told me I was too thin, like I knew she would – my granddad told me I looked great, though, like I knew he would, the sweetheart.

My mum and Belle immediately turn their chairs to face the dance floor, excited for what's about to come. It's not that I lack confidence, but the thought of having everyone watching me as I 'perform' my first dance makes me cringe. I don't think I've ever seen a first dance that didn't make me want to punch myself in the face until it stopped. As Mike and Rosie take to the floor, I allow myself to feel a little hope that this time might be different, that this dance might impress me. But then a chimney sweep walks out onto the stage. He's wearing a wireless mic, attached to his ear, which he adjusts into a favourable position just before the music starts.

'Is that . . .?' I start, but I don't need to finish my question. It's 'Chim Chim Cher-ee' from *Mary Poppins*.

'Oh, what a beautiful waltz,' my gran coos as she watches.

I look at Leo and pull a face. He looks as confused as I am.

Mike and Rosie slow dance until the song is finished.

'Step in Time,' the chimney sweep calls out. 'Everyone, join the bride and groom on the dance floor.'

As people get up and make their way to the dance floor the chimney sweep bursts into a version of 'Step in Time' that he expects everyone to dance to. Many people oblige.

'Oh, I so want to join in but Dan is dancing with his mum,' Belle moans.

'Shall I?' Leo asks me quietly.

'Go for it,' I tell him with a laugh.

'Come on, Belle, I'll dance with you,' he says, taking her by the hand and leading her onto the dance floor before linking arms with her, ready to step in time with everyone else.

I turn to face my granddad, who is sitting at the other side of me.

'Whaaaat is happening?' I ask him.

My granddad laughs. 'It's tradition to have a chimney sweep at your wedding – it's for good luck,' my granddad explains. 'The groom shakes his hand and the bride gives him a kiss, and then they'll be together forever, supposedly.'

'That's pretty stupid,' I say.

'You're not wrong, kid,' my granddad replies.

I have so much love, adoration and respect for my granddad, Jack – he's so kind and funny. He knows exactly what the women in our family are like; in fact, he jokily refers to my mum, my gran and my Auntie June as the three witches. My granddad is absolutely hilarious, constantly cracking jokes, winding up my gran and playing little pranks on people. I like to think I've inherited my granddad's warmth and his wicked sense of humour, which is why I haven't turned out like the other women in the family.

My granddad is eighty-four years old, and until recently he never really seemed it. His arthritis is getting quite bad now, which is making it harder for him to move around and do things like he used to. He still enjoys pottering around in his shed, though, and I still love to go and sit out there with him and help out with his tomato plants or whatever he has on the go. I think he uses his shed as an escape from my gran, but even though she nags him and thinks he's a bit silly sometimes, I can still tell that they love each other.

I absolutely adore the story of how my gran and granddad met, but I'm not allowed to talk about it because my gran gets cross – I've always said I'll put it in a book one day, though. My gran was in her early twenties, working as a cashier in a bank. She was this glamorous, kind-of-snooty type, but she was model-gorgeous, so of course she was engaged. My granddad was a painter, working in the bank for a few weeks while the place had a makeover. He instantly took a shine to my gran, but she wouldn't give him the time of day because she thought he was just some scruffy, dirty painter, whose hands were always covered in too much paint, and who was far too cheeky for his own good. But even though she was never anything but cold to him, my granddad saw something he liked and persisted in asking my gran out, until one day she gave in and said yes, just to shut him up, and in little more than a fortnight she left her fiancé for him.

They actually got married for a really unromantic reason four months after they met – a tax rebate – but I guess they were meant to be, because here they are, still married more than fifty years later.

'You having this at your wedding, kid?' he asks. 'Or are you going for something a bit more modern like *Frozen*?'

'My granddad knows what *Frozen* is.' I laugh.

'Oh, little Angel makes me watch it with her twenty times a day, so I know all the words,' he says and laughs.

Angel is my cousin Hannah's little girl. I was actually there when everyone found out Hannah was pregnant because it was at Belle's wedding, and when my auntie found a pregnancy test in the bin, she assumed it must have been mine – an assumption based on nothing but my hemline. So you can just imagine my Auntie June's face when it turned out to be her fifteen-year-old daughter who was pregnant. Hannah is nineteen now, and she's taken to being a mum really well, I think. Angel seems like a sweet kid, but, like I said, I don't really spend too much time with my extended family, unless we're at family events.

'Speak of the literal devil,' I say as the Edwards family arrive for the evening do.

My granddad chuckles.

'Hello,' June says, puffing air from her cheeks. 'Sorry we're late. *Someone* was acting up.'

She turns and shoots her son, Josh, a filthy look. My fourteen-year-old cousin has no fucks to give, though.

'Have you been a naughty boy?' my gran asks him, but Josh doesn't hear her voice. I can see his wireless, in-ear headphones poking out of his ears from under his longish, messy hair, but no one else has realised he's listening to music yet.

'If you're not a video game, he's not interested,' my Uncle Steve jokes, taking the seat next to me. 'Looking good, Mia.'

'Thanks, Uncle Steve,' I reply.

'Are you starving yourself again?' my auntie enquires as she sits down.

I didn't think I was the first time. Honestly, you order sushi *one time*, at a family meal, and no one lets you forget it. In hindsight, I should have ordered chips with it, then no one would have said anything . . .

'Only when it comes to your cooking,' I joke. June isn't impressed.

'I'm off to the bar,' Josh says, wandering off, staring at his phone every step of the way.

My Auntie June doesn't like me. I know, that sounds like something a whiney teenager would say, but she doesn't. My Uncle Steve *does* like me, and so do my cousins, which I think makes my auntie dislike me all the more. She thinks I'm a bad influence, because her kids think I'm cool.

'I actually don't know what I'm going to do with him,' June says as she wrestles her cardigan off.

'What's he done now?' my mum asks.

'So . . .' my auntie starts, lowering her voice a little, but not so much that she can't be heard over the music, which has been consistently awful since the first dance finished. 'Cotton Eye Joe' by Rednex is currently playing. 'He's always got his phone in his hand; he's never off it. So, the other night, he's playing some shooty game online – oh, what's it called, Stephen? Lots of swearing and violence. They were on a pier, by a big wheel . . .'

'GTA Online,' I tell her. 'Man, that's a sweet game. I play when I'm not working, or when I'm putting off working.' I laugh.

'Mia, you're a woman in your thirties,' my auntie reminds me.

'Well, at least we know you're not losing your memory,' I tell her. She might not remember the name of the game, but she knows how old her niece is. I imagine that's what she was trying to make clear by stating my age, and not implying that I'm too old/female for video games.

'Anyway . . .' she says, getting back to her story. 'I took him some crumpets up to his room – he doesn't even say thank you, he's too busy calling someone a mother-effer through his earpiece – so I do what any responsible parent would do and take his phone downstairs to check.'

'Does she do that with yours?' I joke to my uncle, giving him a nudge with my elbow.

'Only sometimes,' he replies solemnly.

'So, I find this picture of him and he's only smoking a marijuana cigarette!' she squeaks, the disgust catching in her throat.

'Where on earth did he get that? He's only fourteen,' my mum says, horrified.

I know my auntie is dull and way too uptight with her kids, but that is actually terrible. I can't believe my baby cousin is doing drugs. I really never would've thought he'd be the type.

He might be your typical, video-game-playing, adult-ignoring, horrible teenager now, but he's always been such a sweet kid. I can't believe it.

'Oh, it wasn't real,' my auntie explains. 'It was toilet roll. I asked him why he took such a photo and he said it was "just a joke for Snapchat" – it had some kind of number code on it, maybe a hidden message.'

I swallow my cocktail the wrong way, spluttering as I laugh to myself.

'Was it 420?' I ask.

'Yes,' she says quickly. 'What does that mean?'

'It's just a joke,' I tell her. 'He's trying to be funny.'

'I don't think it's funny,' my auntie says seriously. 'I suppose you do?'

'I mean, I get the joke,' I tell her. 'He's only being a silly kid – don't worry. You can't get high rolling up an Andrex.'

My auntie shakes her head. 'Look, I hate to say this,' she starts, and I know that, if she's saying it, she's happy to say it. 'But I seem to remember a certain someone letting him watch a Quentin Tarantino movie when he was just ten years old . . .'

'Oh my God, you're never going to let that go, are you?' I say. 'So I let the kid watch *Pulp Fiction* – I don't even think anyone smokes a joint in that film. It's mostly cocaine they're doing. If he starts snorting lines of talcum powder in the bathroom, *then* you can blame me.'

No one is amused by this, apart from my granddad who chuckles subtly.

'I'm going to go and find Leo,' I announce as I push my chair back, carefully readjusting my dress to make sure I don't flash anyone. Well, that's one of the things about strapless dresses – one false move and there's nothing to hold them in place.

Tonight I'm wearing a black Alexander McQueen dress with mesh panels that I think is beautiful, but which my mum deemed inappropriate for a family wedding. I bought this dress back when

I was living in LA, when I could afford dresses like this. So, sure, it's like five years old, but it's couture and it fits, so I'm happy. I feel a little bit like the old me – just enough to make me happy.

'Mind if I borrow him?' I ask Belle, who is still dancing with Leo.

'Sure,' she replies. 'I could do with a drink anyway.'

'You cutting in?' Leo asks me.

'Erm, more like cutting you out,' I tell him. 'Let's find somewhere to sit, that isn't near anyone I'm related to, and chill out?'

'Sure,' he replies.

The dance floor is in the centre of the room, under a large disco ball, pinging off different-coloured lights in all directions. Making a ring around the dance floor are the tables we all sat at to eat; then, around the edges of the room, a few sofas are dotted. Leo and I find one away from everyone else and sit down. Leo sits back with one arm stretched out along the back edge of the sofa, so I cuddle into him, resting my head on his chest.

'So, promise me we're having a chimney sweep at our wedding,' he says.

'Oh God, wasn't that weird? My granddad says it's tradition, for luck.'

'The funniest bit about it is that, during the song, when we were all dancing, he gave Rosie a kiss – but because he had all that black stuff smeared on his face, he left her looking like she had a black goatee. They mustn't have had a dress rehearsal, because she was fuming when she realised.'

'So, we'll probably give that a miss on our big day.' I laugh.

'They make a cute couple, right? I mean, he's a dick, but he makes her happy,' Leo muses.

'Yeah. Mr and Mrs Ryan – Rosie Ryan,' I say, to see how it sounds out loud.

'Sounds like a superhero . . . or a porn star . . . or both,' he jokes.

'It does.' I giggle. 'But it works.'

'Does Mia De Luca work?' he asks.

'Erm, it sounds like something an Italian would say.' I laugh.

'Well, it's something this Italian is going to be saying for the rest of his life.'

Leo smiles, until he notices the look on my face.

'What's up?' he asks.

'Nothing,' I lie.

'Mia, I know when you're lying, your voice gets much higher.'

I bite my lip as I wonder whether now is the time or the place to tell the truth.

'Well, I've been thinking, and I'll probably just keep my name.'

'Why?'

'Because it's *my* name,' I say.

'Your real name or your fake name?' Leo asks.

I grew up Mia Harrison, but when I moved to LA and reinvented myself, I legally changed my name to Mia Valentina, because I thought it sounded more the part. Now that I'm writing novels for a living, Mia Valentina makes a great pen name too. I just feel like it's my name now. It's my identity and I've worked hard for the achievements and reputation that go along with it.

'My "fake" name is my real name – you know that,' I remind him.

'Hmm,' he says, taking his arm from around me.

'What?' I ask.

'I think it's interesting . . . it seems to me like you haven't thought about getting married at all – other than deciding you don't want to take my name.'

'Hey.' I turn my body to face Leo, placing my hand lightly on his cheeks. 'Leo, I love you so much, and I'm so hyped to marry you. And I know you think I'm not thinking about our wedding but . . . I'm going to a wedding fair next weekend.'

'Really?' he asks, looking visibly relieved.

'Yeah, Belle came over last weekend and brought me a stack of wedding magazines, and told me about the fair, so I'm going to go.'

'That's awesome,' he replies. 'I'll come with you.'

'Are you sure you want to? Aren't you working?'

'Nope,' he replies. 'And I'd love to come. I'm so relieved. For a second, I was worried you hadn't been thinking about the wedding *at all*.'

I grab Leo and kiss him to reassure him that I love him. I do love him, so much. I've just been so busy and so distracted, but I will go to this wedding fair and I'll make a start on planning the wedding, and it's all going to be great. I need to make more of an effort, to show him I'm serious.

Chapter 8

Yesterday I went to a wedding fair with Leo, so today I am browsing for jobs online, because weddings are *so* expensive and my unreliable income isn't making me feel confident about being able to get married next summer, like we planned.

Everything at the fair was so expensive and, for the most part, so stupid. I appreciate that rings, venue hire, food and drink are very expensive but unavoidable costs of getting married. But things like giant chocolate fountains, men who pose as topiary and to-scale ice sculptures that look like the happy couple are just excessive.

To say that it was only a money issue would be a lie. The truth is that working from home is so boring, and I spend so much time alone, that I think it would do me good to find a job in a place where I could make friends and see people every day. On quieter days the only person I see is Leo, and if you knew what a social butterfly I used to be, you'd know how hard I'm finding spending so much time alone these days.

So far, I'm not having much luck. I've looked at all kinds of writing jobs, from journalist jobs to copywriting gigs, but there's nothing. On the off-chance, I even looked at the film and TV section, just in case anyone was looking for a writer of any description, but the only two jobs that came up were looking for actors, one listing looking for movie extras and the other staff for an escape game – and neither of these things appeal to me.

I grab the remote and fire up Netflix with the intention of putting something on in the background, but you know how it is with Netflix – sometimes you'll spend longer trying to choose something to watch than you will actually watching it. In the end it's easier to put *Gossip Girl* on for my third rewatch, because there's no ailment that can't be cured by a little exposure to Chuck Bass.

It only takes a few minutes of observing the lavish lifestyles of the Upper East Siders before I start feeling bad about my surroundings. Our living room has looked worse, much worse, but it definitely looks better now we have flooring down and clean white walls, a blank canvas ready for us to make our own. But I'm surrounded by boxes, most of them being used as furniture, and it's been so long since we moved in I couldn't confidently tell you what was in them anymore.

I look over the job listings in the area generally, running a hand through my messy bed hair as I rule out being an army officer (just try and imagine a girly girl like me doing a job like that), a code coordinator (I have no idea what that is) or a bartender (sadly, although I have many hours of experience, they're all on the wrong side of the bar). My fingers catch in a knot in my hair, which I'm careful to untangle. I need to go and slather my locks in coconut oil because I'm fairly sure that's what's helping it grow back so quickly and so much stronger than it was. I'll probably cover myself in coconut oil, for good measure, because I don't think I know of a health or beauty problem that coconut oil hasn't been hyped as the solution for. Chuck Bass and coconut oil – that's all I need.

Once again, the listing for a 'Games Master' at Houdini's Escape Rooms comes up. I don't really know too much about escape games, but I imagine they're exactly as they sound. You lock people up and they try and escape for fun, right? The listing says its minimum wage and zero hours, but this could be exactly the kind of gig I need to fit in around my writing commitments; it could be fun, and could make me the extra wedding money I need. The application says to send in a CV with relevant experience, but I don't suppose I have any. I've always been a writer, ever since I graduated.

I glance at my watch; it's 17.35. Looking up Houdini's, I see that they're open until late, and it's only a short walk away – why don't I go scope the place out and see what I make of it?

After washing my hair and applying my make-up, I open up my wardrobes (cardboard boxes) and see what I can find. An oversized black jumper dress and a pair of black over-the-knee boots seem like the right kind of thing, given how cold it is outside. I grab my leather jacket, pile on the rose-gold accessories (and my engagement ring, of course) and I'm good to go.

I am about to walk out of the door when my mobile starts ringing. It's my agent, Lindsey.

'Hello,' I say, answering quickly, terrified there's a problem with the manuscript I stressed myself out to finish on time.

'Hello, Mia, how are you?' she asks brightly.

'Great, ta. How are you?'

'I'm doing well, thank you. I just wanted to let you know that Tamara is reading your manuscript and she's really enjoying it, and I've already finished it and I think it's great – maybe your best yet.'

I let out a huge sigh of relief. I'm pretty sure Lindsey tells me every book I write is my best work yet, but I do feel like she believes in me, and it's always good news to hear that Tamara, my editor, is enjoying it too. Having a strong team around you, rooting for you and doing everything they can to make your books a success, is just as important as the writing itself – what does it matter if you've written an amazing book if no one reads it?

'That's great news, thank you,' I tell her.

'So, what are you going to do now?' she asks. 'Take a little time off?'

'I wish,' I reply. 'I've got a wedding to pay for – I'm actually job hunting.'

'What?' Lindsey squeaks. 'Mia, you're an amazing writer, so early in your career as a novelist. The money gets better.'

'In time for my wedding or my next cripplingly expensive trip to IKEA?' I laugh awkwardly. 'It's not just that; I get so bored between books. Everyone is at work and there's no one to have any fun with . . .'

'Listen, Mia, I'm putting forward a few of my clients for a job – it's nonfiction, but I feel like you could be great for it. Shall I put you forward?'

'What is it?' I ask.

'It's a ghostwriting job,' she tells me. 'It will pay very well – two authors have dropped out already, so it won't be easy. Let's leave it at that – I don't want to get your hopes up.'

I can't help but pull a face. There's no way a romcom writer like me is going to get a nonfiction gig that two other authors have already dropped out of, and even if I could, why would I want to work with someone who sounds so difficult? It would have to pay *really* well.

I finish my call and head for the door. Obviously I'd much rather have a writing job but I've got a wedding to pay for – and maybe the way to do this is by locking people up.

Chapter 9

It turns out that Houdini's has always been under my nose, but – funnily enough – has always escaped my attention. It's right in the town centre, above a sports bar I've been in a couple of times. You can't really tell too much about it from the outside so I've popped inside to have a look, but the room I've walked into looks like a dentist's waiting room.

'Hello?' I call out. 'Hello . . .'

A young girl pops out from around a corner, causing me to jump out of my skin.

'Welcome to Houdini's my name is Jezebel how can I help you?' she sings, without pausing to take a breath.

'Er, hi,' I start, unsure what to say.

'Do you have a game booked?' she asks.

Jezebel is an interesting character. She's rocking a scene-queen look I haven't seen since 2005, with her big, black hair complete with side-swept fringe, punky, ripped clothing and multiple facial piercings.

She has her septum pierced and I can't stop staring at it. It must get in the way, surely? It works with her look, though. I'm not sure I could pull it off. When I was younger I was desperate for a nose ring but my mum wouldn't let me have one. That's why, the second I turned sixteen, I went to the local piercing place with my best friend so we could get matching nose rings done. It was all going so well until I watched my friend get hers done and passed out. I soon changed my mind.

'I popped in to have a look. I saw the listing for the Games Master job online and I . . .'

'Oh, sweet,' she says. 'I'm the manager, at the mo. The previous guy had to leave. We had to get the police involved – major drama in the office. So I'm kind of winging it, but we're short-staffed and looking for cool new peeps. Do you live nearby?'

'Yeah, just up on Prince Street,' I tell her.

'No way, me too,' she squeaks, giving my arm a playful punch. 'What you studying?'

'Erm, I've already graduated,' I tell her honestly.

'Ahh, right. This summer just gone? I'm only a second-year. Wouldn't have pegged you as much older than I am.'

If Jezebel is a second-year, that makes her twenty years old, maybe? I know I look young for my age, but if I'm passing for fourteen years younger than I am, I'm onto a winner.

'How about I introduce you to the others in the office and then show you around, see if you dig the place?'

'Erm, OK, sure,' I reply. I've only ever had writing jobs where I had to submit my portfolio or a pitch beforehand, but is this how job hunting goes in the real world? You just show up at a place and they start you off, no questions asked. She hasn't even asked me my name yet . . .

'Follow me, doll,' she says, taking me by the hand as she leads me into the office.

Inside the office is a long, banana-shaped desk with five people sitting at five computers, all wearing headsets. Some are engrossed in the games they are spectating; others are chatting and messing around.

'That guy down the end, that's Rich. He's a music student – don't worry, you don't have to pay as much attention to the games as he is. Oi, Rich.'

A skinny, dark-haired guy with thick, black-rimmed glasses looks up to wave at me before instantly getting back to his game.

'Hi,' I say, but he's way too busy to give me too much attention.

'These two in the middle, practically smashing at the desk, are Bully and Hayley. Guys, this is . . . Did you tell me your name?' she asks me.

'Sorry, it's Mia,' I say, bemused by it all. I really didn't expect to waltz in here and be given a job.

To say that Bully and Hayley were smashing would be classed as an exaggeration. Hayley has her chair to one side, with her legs draped over Bully's. He keeps running his hand up her leg, from her ankle all the way to her inner thigh, but that's as close to smashing as it gets.

'This beautiful lady here is Lea. She's a student too – we're all students. Well, except for you, Mia.'

'What did you study?' Lea asks me, effortlessly multitasking chatting to me, texting and running a game.

'English literature,' I tell her.

'I nearly picked that,' she tells me. 'I went for film in the end. I just prefer movies to books, y'know?'

'Yeah, me too,' I reply.

'Why'd you choose lit then?' She smiles.

I laugh it off, rather than explain that I mean I prefer writing movies to writing books.

Lea has her long brown hair wound up in a bun on top of her head. She's definitely dressed casually; in fact, I think it would be fair to say that she's wearing her pyjama pants to work today.

'And last but not least, this is Sam. He's a first-year, studying PE, which – is that even a real subject? I don't think so.'

Sam gets up from his seat to shake my hand. He's tall and skinny with messy blond hair. He's wearing shorts, even though it's November, but he's had the good sense to pair them with a jumper, just in case he gets cold.

'Hello, beautiful,' he says as he shakes my hand.

'Hi,' I reply, stifling a laugh. I'd be old enough to be his mum, if I'd been more interested in boys than getting good GCSEs when I was fifteen.

'Are you the new girl?' he asks. 'It's about time we got some talent. No offence, ladies.'

'None taken, you little creep.' Jezebel laughs. She grabs me by the hand again, leading me out of the room. 'You're so far out of his league, it's hilarious.'

She plonks herself down on one of the sofas in the waiting room, pulling me down with her.

'So, we've got five rooms here: Zombie Apocalypse, Houdini, Illuminati, The Hole and Candy Land. There's something for everyone really. So we greet customers, shove them in a room, lock the door and then we watch them on the computers and send them hints if they need them. Have you played before?'

'I haven't,' I admit, suddenly very curious about how it all works.

'So, the rooms are full of locks – padlocks, key locks, number locks – on doors, cupboards, drawers and boxes. There are all kinds of different puzzles and riddles. People just figure shit out and it unlocks a thing, and then that gives them more clues for another thing, and next thing you know they're out here and we take their picture and send them on their way.'

'Does it take a long time to learn the games?' I ask.

'Nah,' she replies casually with a bat of her hand. 'It's an easy gig. The owners never bother with the place. Your girl Jezebel is running the show now. You interested?'

'Erm . . .'

Now that I'm here, I'm not sure what to do. The place seems very relaxed – a little too relaxed, though. It's being run by a bunch of students, only a couple of years off being actual children. They do all seem really happy here, though, so maybe I could be too. Maybe working here would be fun, a great daytime distraction and a bit of extra money for this wedding I haven't started planning yet.

'Tell you what, why don't you let me show you the ropes, and then a few of us are going to the bar downstairs after, so come for a drink with us and get to know the others too.'

'OK, sure,' I say. 'That'd be great.'

'Awesome-o,' she replies. 'Think about which game you wanna run first and we'll train you up on that one. I'm going to grab my phone, tell the others we've got one more for Beer Pong tonight.'

Jezebel runs off excitedly.

Well, Leo is working until late, so I might as well go out, rather than sit at home alone, waiting for him to come back. I feel like I never see him anymore, but I know it's only temporary. Before we know it the house will be done and then we'll be married and we can spend more nights curled up on the sofa together.

I'm not going to get ahead of myself here; I'm just going to see how tonight goes. I just feel like getting a real job, of some description, will be good for my mental health. It's not good for a girl to be at home all the time, making up fake worlds full of fake people, all having fake conversations and fake feelings.

I could do this for a bit, even if it's just until it's time to start work on my next book. And I can still plan my wedding while I'm working here. How hard can planning a wedding be?

Chapter 10

Staggering out of the bar with my new potential colleagues, I don't have any idea what time it is, but I know I should probably head home. The good news is that everyone who works at Houdini's is a student, so we all walk home the same way. It's like I've found my perfect friends and colleagues in one neat little package. It's funny that they're, like, ten years younger than me – at least – but we seem to be on the same wavelength. Plus, they think I'm their age, which is a huge boost to my thirty-three-year-old ego.

Jezebel hooks her arms around my neck with the familiarity of someone who has known me all my life. In fact, the entire Houdini team seem to have fallen in love with me.

It's been a great night. I've really enjoyed hanging out with new people, making them laugh, playing Beer Pong with them – even if I am terrible and I hate the taste of beer.

'I don't wanna call it a night,' Jezebel whines, her breath smelling so strongly of beer I hold my own, so I don't have to endure her second-hand beer fumes.

'Let's go upstairs,' Sam suggests. 'Ring of Fire!'

'Yeaaaah, Ring of Fire,' Jezebel replies. 'You're coming up, right, Mia?'

'Erm . . .'

I suppose I could hang around for a bit . . . well, it saves me making my own way home, especially seeing as I'm a little tipsy. Plus, I'm enjoying bonding with my new teammates.

'Come on,' Sam insists.

'OK, sure,' I reply.

'Let's do this,' Sam yells meaningfully as Jezebel removes the office keys from her bag and unlocks the door.

'So, you guys are allowed to hang out here after work?' I ask cautiously.

'Not really,' Jezebel replies. 'But no one will ever know.'

Once we're inside Houdini's, everyone works together to clear a space in the centre of the room, just like they did when they were showing me how to reset the game rooms earlier. Bully disappears inside the Houdini room and re-emerges with a deck of cards. He spreads them out in a circular shape in the middle of the room while Jezebel places an empty cup in the middle. As we all take our places in a circle around the game set-up, Hayley and Lea walk out of the offices with two bottles of various spirits each.

'Ring of Fire!' Sam screeches excitedly.

'I don't know how to play this one,' I admit. I thought about pretending I did, but I don't want to embarrass myself in front of my new friends. There are eight of us sitting on the floor, ready to play – Jezebel, Sam, Hayley, Bully and Lea from earlier, along with two guys whose names I don't remember.

Everyone in the room cries out in shock.

'What? You don't know how to play Ring of Fire? And you went to uni?' Sam says in disbelief.

I don't even know if this game existed when I was their age, but even if it did, I had other things on my mind back then. Even though I went to university, I never really did the student-life thing. You know, living on a diet of nothing but noodles and cheap booze, doing minimal studying on minimal sleep – that sort of thing. Studying always came before socialising for me.

'Sorry.' I laugh.

'It's OK, she'll pick it up as she goes along,' Jezebel insists. 'Let's just play.'

'Basically, we all have a drink in our hands, and we take turns at picking up a card, and what everyone does depends on what card is pulled out. You go first, Mia.'

This sounds like a very confusing game for drunk people to play. Too much to remember.

'OK,' I say confidently. I reach out and carefully select a card, turning it over to show the room what it is. 'Four of hearts.'

'Fours are whores, so all the women have to drink,' Sam tells me.

Wow, really? I know already that it must have been a man who invented this game. No one here bats an eye, they're obviously all used to playing it.

I laugh in disbelief as I sip from my plastic cup. Oh wow, it's neat, cheap vodka. I've already had a few tonight, and I don't think I'm the seasoned drinker I used to be.

Sam goes next.

'Eight,' he announces as he flips a card over. 'Eight is mate, so Mia, I choose you. Every time I drink, you have to as well.'

'OK.' I laugh.

A few other people take a turn, with a variety of consequences. If someone gets a two, two is you, so they pick a person to have a drink. Three is me, which means the player drinks. Seven is Heaven, which means the last person with their hands in the air has to drink – which is me, every time, because I keep forgetting what all the numbers mean. The worst one of all is when a king is drawn – each time someone has turned over a king, they've poured a little bit of their drink into the cup in the middle of the ring, making one nasty-looking cocktail.

I take my turn, turning my card over to reveal the fourth and final king from the deck. I go to pour some of my drink in the cup, but Sam stops me.

'That's the fourth king, Mia – that means you've gotta drink the king's cup.'

'I've gotta drink *that*?' I squeak in shock, because it looks disgusting. But put it down to how much I've had to drink already, put it down to the fact everyone is chanting my name, put it down to peer pressure, put it down to whatever you want, but I grab the cup and chug the contents, draining every last drop to a room full of cheering and applause. As I finish, Sam launches himself across the floor, throwing himself at me for a celebratory hug. I quickly wriggle free from his grasp and fix my dress so I'm not flashing my underwear.

As Sam sets up the next game, I can't help but notice that Jezebel is looking upset. I scoot over to her, talking quietly so only she can hear.

'Do you like Sam?' I ask her.

'I hate him; he's such a sleaze,' she replies quickly.

'Yeah, but do you *like him* like him?' I ask.

'Is it that obvious?' she replies. 'He's not interested in me. I'm ploughing my way through Matcher at the moment. Not having much luck there either.'

Ergh. Matcher is a dating app I researched for a book not too long ago. I feel so lucky I've never had to put up with the crap women get on those things.

'So you need to be very critical of potential matches,' I advise. 'Don't just look at their photos and read their bios, look in the background of their photos and read between the lines of their bios. Keen to seem like more than your average beardy, buff, banterous Matcher boy, blokes will use euphemisms – sometimes without even realising it. Like, if they say that they "live for the weekend" then they're probably boring on the other five days of the week. Those who are "brutally honest" are probably just rude. People who "tell it how it is" generally have no filter.'

As Jezebel starts laughing, I realise I'm babbling.

'Sorry.'

'No, tell me more,' she insists. 'You're so much wiser than

all of us.'

That's because I'm old.

'If they insist their mates made them sign up for the app, they're too proud. Worst of all, if they say they're looking for an "open-minded girl" then run a mile because what that really means is that they're looking for fifty shades of *wehey!* – like, they're the kind of guy with a very particular set of skills . . . no . . . wait . . . that's from *Taken* . . . Unconventional desires, that's *Fifty Shades*, right? I haven't read the book, or watched the movie, but I know the meme.'

'You're so funny,' Jezebel insists. 'I really hope you take the job.'

'I'm really thinking about it,' I tell her, hiccupping loudly at the end of my sentence. It's been so long since I drank this much.

'So, if we can get Hayley and Bully to stop getting off with each other for, like, ten minutes,' Sam yells for the benefit of the happy couple in the room, 'we can play Spin the Bottle: Truth or Dare.'

Oh God. I'm an engaged lady. I can't play Truth or Dare with a bunch of kids.

Before I know it the game is underway. I just need to hope and pray it doesn't land on me.

It's amazing how many rounds I get through unscathed, while other members of the group reveal a series of embarrassing facts, take off random items of clothing and swap saliva with whomever they are told to.

Sam spins the bottle, which, thankfully, flies past me, landing on Bully, who is sitting opposite me.

'Truth,' he says.

'OK,' Sam starts, a cheeky glimmer in his eyes. 'If you and Hayley had to have a threesome with one of us, who would it be?'

'Mia,' he replies. His answer takes me aback, causing me to spit my drink out.

'Huh?' I say, wiping vodka from my chin with the sleeve of my dress.

'We both think you're really fit,' Bully tells me. 'We'd love to get together with you sometime.'

'I'm flattered.' I laugh, unable to hide my awkwardness. I don't care if I have to drunkenly make my own way home, this is definitely when I leave.

'Mia, I dare you to bang Bully and Hayley in The Hole,' Sam says.

My eyebrows shoot up at his words, until I remember The Hole is a room here.

'It's not my turn,' I say, laughing it off.

'Come on,' he insists. 'We can all watch in the office.'

'I'm engaged,' I insist, waving my left hand around like a dancer from a Beyoncé music video so they can see my ring.

'Of course you are.' He laughs. 'You all just need a little encouragement.'

Sam ushers Bully and Haley into The Hole before picking me up, throwing me over his shoulder, plonking me down on the floor next to them and running out, locking the door behind him.

'I'm not having sex with you,' I tell them, very matter-of-factly, just in case they thought I might. 'Do you guys come up here and play games often?'

'Yeah,' Hayley replies. 'Ever since the old manager got the sack.'

Wow. These guys are like teenagers with a free house while their parents are away for the weekend. They just get drunk and get off with each other – I've heard of close friends, but this is ridiculous.

'Let me out, please,' I shout, waving my arms at the CCTV camera. I wait thirty seconds, but no one comes. 'I said let me out, you little cu—'

Jezebel opens the door. 'Come on, Mia,' she insists. 'You don't have to if you don't want to.'

How very kind of her.

'Come on,' she says, ushering me out. 'Have another drink with me.'

'No, thanks,' I tell her, refocusing my eyes, trying to determine if I'm sober enough to walk home. I grab my phone from my bag to see a couple of missed calls from Leo, and the fact that it's 3.02 a.m. Shit. I'd better get an Uber and get myself home to my fiancé.

Chapter 11

At first, it's the drum, banging inside my head. Then it's the deathly bright light, melting its way through my eyelids, stabbing into my brain. Finally, my nose catches a whiff of something familiar, something that usually appeals, but not today. Today it's making me feel . . .

'Oh God, I'm gonna throw up,' I announce, jumping up, making a run for the bathroom.

'I'd come after you but it will put me off my bacon sandwich,' Leo calls after me.

I'm sick a little, but not enough to feel better. Glancing down at my body, I see that I'm in my underwear, which means my wonderful fiancé must've undressed me and put me to bed, because I'm not one hundred on what really happened last night.

I wash my face, brush my teeth and take a long, hard look at myself in the mirror.

I make my way back to bed, walking in a slow, controlled and careful way, so as not to aggravate the angry drummer practising on my brain.

I lie down on the bed carefully next to Leo, who is drinking a coffee. He looks like he's been up for a while – he's probably been for a run too.

'Good night was it?' he asks.

I place my pillow over my face. 'No,' I mumble.

'It was coming up to 4 a.m. when you got in,' he tells me. 'Where were you?'

Leo doesn't sound angry, but I'm sure he's wondering where the hell I was until 4 a.m. while he was working for most of the night, when he thought I was at home in bed.

'I went to get a job,' I tell him honestly.

'A job?' he replies. 'When you came in you told me you'd been partying with students. Well, I think you got the job.'

'What do you mean?' I ask, uncovering my face so I can see his.

'You got in, I put you to bed and you fell straight asleep. But then your phone started ringing – just some number, someone you didn't have in your contacts. After the fifth missed call I figured it must be important, so I answered it. It was a girl called Jezebel, who asked if I was your dad and then told me to say that everyone was very sorry about locking you in a room so that you could have a threesome.'

I visibly cringe.

'She seems like a sweet kid,' he says sarcastically.

'So, I really did go for a job,' I begin to explain. 'I saw this listing for a Games Master at Houdini's in town – it's an escape game.'

'Yeah, I've been,' he tells me. 'Team-building thing with work. Absolute shit-show there.'

'I know that now.' I laugh, carefully, because my head is still banging. 'They said they'd show me the ropes, then they invited me out, then we went back to the office to play Circle of Hell or something and next thing I know they're locking me up for a threesome. I told them I was engaged . . . they didn't believe me. I think they thought I was their age.'

'So, are you going to take the job?' Leo asks.

I look at him in disbelief.

'I'm kidding.' He laughs. 'Come here.'

My lovely fiancé gently scoops me up effortlessly and holds

me close.

'Is everything OK?' he asks.

'Of course,' I reply. 'Why do you ask?'

I stroke his chest affectionately as we chat.

'It's just, going out with students . . . it's not some kind of statement or cry for help is it? Like, if the house and the wedding are too much for you . . .'

'It's not a cry for help, I promise.'

'What made you think you wanted a job?' he asks.

'I don't know,' I reply. 'I was thinking, the house is expensive, the wedding will be expensive, I'm so bored at home alone between books . . .'

'You don't need to worry about money,' he assures me. 'And I'll start dialling down the overtime a little. I know it feels like we hardly see each other at the moment. Let's go out tonight,' he suggests. 'Spend some time together, figure out what you can do with all this free time now your book is finished.'

'I'd like that a lot,' I reply, smiling widely.

I miss Leo when he's working, of course I do, but I think the thing that bothers me the most about all this overtime is just how scared I am while he's at work. Everyone knows being a fireman is a dangerous job, but that danger feels all the more real with Leo.

Leonardo, Leo's dad, was a fireman too. One day, back when Leo was eight years old, his mum and dad took him to the park. It was the perfect hot, sunny day – Leo told me how vividly he remembers eating ice cream, and playing football with his dad, just like it was yesterday. On their walk home, as they approached the convenience shop at the end of their street, Leo told me his dad stopped dead, like he knew something was up – then they smelled the smoke. Leo's dad wasn't on duty, but if there's one thing Leonardo believed (and that Leo has learned from him) it's that firemen are *always* on duty.

There was a woman screaming that her little boy was in the flat upstairs, so while everyone else was running out of the shop,

Leonardo ran inside. By the time the fire engines arrived, it was too late. Leonardo was a true hero, though, saving the little boy's life. Once the boy was well enough, he and his mum went to visit Maria, Leo's mum, and Leo to tell them what a hero his dad was. Part of the building collapsed, and the little boy would have died if Leonardo hadn't pushed him out of the way, but saving the little boy cost him his life. That's a true hero, and we're lucky to have people like that in the world, but Leo is just like his dad, and I know that, if it came down to it, he'd give his life for a stranger too, and that petrifies me. I don't ever want to lose him. I don't ever want to get that call to say he's not coming home.

'What are you thinking about?' he asks me. 'You look intense.'

'It's my headache,' I reply. If he knew how much I worried about him, he'd probably feel bad.

'I know a cure for that,' he says, walking his fingers from my thigh, up to my collarbone. Laying me back on the bed, Leo gently climbs on top of me, very respectful of my hangover. As he kisses me I lock my legs around his waist, only for our moment of passion to be interrupted by my ringtone.

'Ouch,' I cry as each beat of the shrill chime chips away at my brain. 'If this is the sexual deviants at Houdini's again . . .'

Leo leans over to grab my phone, to stop it ringing.

'It's your agent,' he tells me, quickly passing me my phone. 'I'll leave you to it.'

I sigh. So close . . .

'Hello, Lindsey,' I say brightly. 'How are you?'

'Very well, Mia. You?'

'Can't complain,' I lie. I can complain, about so many things, but I won't, because when people ask how you are, they don't actually want to know, do they?

'Well, I have some good news . . . you got the job.'

'Which job?' I ask.

'The ghostwriting job. I put your name forward for it and it's yours . . . if you want it.'

'No way! That's amazing. You said it was nonfiction, though?'

'Yeah, so . . . have you heard of Dylan King?' she asks.

Have I heard of Dylan King? Who hasn't! Dylan used to be in this huge band called The Burnouts, along with his brother Mikey. But then they had this huge argument, the band broke up and they haven't spoken since. Dylan is a huge solo star now, whereas Mikey has just kind of dropped off the face of the earth. It's fair to say Mikey was the talented guitarist and Dylan was the hot frontman, but women adore him and men want to be him, so he's just gone from strength to strength since going it alone musically.

'I have,' I reply, waiting with bated breath to find out what this job is and how it involves Dylan King.

'So, the job is ghostwriting his autobiography,' she tells me.

'What? That's awesome,' I squeal. 'But how did you swing that? I have no experience . . .'

'Erm, well, it's important to remember that two authors with lots of experience have already pulled out of this project, so perhaps a different approach is what it needs. But, erm, well, Dylan asked for your Instagram handle, looked you up and then said he wanted you for the job.'

Back when I was living in LA, I was vaguely Instagram famous. I'd post lots of poser-ish selfies and pictures of all the fabulous places I'd go. I don't post nearly as much these days, but all my followers are still there.

'That's . . . unusual?'

'It is,' she replies. 'But you have a job and . . . check your emails.'

I quickly load up my inbox and read the project brief Lindsey just set me.

'It pays *how much*?' I squeal, my eyes widening so much my headache kicks up a notch.

'I know, right?' She laughs.

'Why am I wasting my time writing novels?' I ask, semi-seriously.

'Two people have already quit,' she reminds me. 'I don't think it's easy money. Still, congratulations.'

'Thank you,' I squeak, hurrying off the phone to tell Leo.

I find him downstairs in the kitchen, measuring where the cupboards are going to be.

'You know, I think I can get this finished in no time at all – especially if we get Dan and Belle over. Dan can help,' he says, looking around at everything that's still to do.

'Maybe just Dan,' I say, quickly moving on. 'Anyway, forget kitchens for today, I have some good news . . . I have a new job and it pays *this much* . . .'

I show Leo the email.

'Wow . . . that's like . . . you definitely don't need the threesome job.'

I laugh. 'Nope. I'd need to sell a lot of novels to make this kind of money,' I tell him. 'Thing is, it sounds like it might be tricky. I'll be ghostwriting an autobiography for a musician, and apparently two people have quit already . . .'

'You can wrangle celebrities. I've heard your stories from before we met.' He laughs. 'Which musician?'

'Dylan King.'

'Oh shit. He's a real celebrity . . . and a dick, if everything you read in the news is true.'

'I guess we'll find out,' I say.

'Right,' Leo says, clapping his hands. 'Put that phone on silent and get back up those stairs. We'll make it a full day of celebrating.'

My sexy fiancé chases me halfway up the stairs before grabbing me and throwing me over his shoulder, carrying me the rest of the way, dumping me down on the bed.

Leo is the sexiest man I have ever laid eyes on – and Henry Cavill once asked me to help him practise his lines, so you know my boy is gorgeous. It comes with the territory, being a fireman, but for as long as I've known him, I don't think I've seen him with more than fifteen per cent body fat. He's strong – so strong,

I think his muscles have muscles and sometimes I just stare at them because they're so perfect, they look sculpted.

I watch him, standing over me, as he removes his vest, messing up his dark hair that's usually perfectly blown back. He gives me that cheeky smile that emphasises his delicious dimples and I see that glimmer of mischief in his green eyes that I love so much, the one I saw the day we met. When Leo looks at me, I see something light up inside his eyes, and it makes me feel amazing.

He climbs on top of me, scooping my body up from the bed with one arm, just enough so that he can unhook my bra before laying me back down. Then he takes hold of both my wrists and holds them firmly above my head.

'My God, I love you,' he blurts out. 'Look at you. Look at that face.'

As he gazes into my eyes, I swear I can see just how happy he is.

'I love you too,' I say.

I don't think I could be happier right now if I tried.

Chapter 12

'Italian restaurants always make me think of our last holiday to Italy,' Leo says, swigging his beer.

'That was a great holiday,' I reply. 'The sun, the sea . . . all the sex.'

'Those things were great.' He laughs. 'I think the bit that meant the most to me – and I know I've never told you this, and I probably should have – was that last night at my nonna's apartment when we were all sitting out on the balcony, drinking ice-cold drinks and eating taralli, and she turned to me and she said: "This one is a keeper." I knew then that I needed to ask you to marry me.'

'That was a year ago.' I laugh, sipping my cocktail.

'Well, it took me a little time to build up the courage,' he says.

'That was a great holiday,' I reply. 'The pizzas at that place on the beach – my God. Best thing about that trip, though . . . none of my family was there.'

'Your lot aren't that bad,' Leo says with a smile.

'Erm, they've invited themselves on our date tonight,' I point out. 'That's too much.'

I was so hyped to go on a romantic date with my wonderful fiancé that when my mum called and demanded we go over for dinner, I told her we had dinner reservations we couldn't cancel so late in the day, at which point she called the restaurant, amended my booking to accommodate four more people, and then called me back to let me know it was all sorted. So, here we are, sitting at a table for six, waiting for my parents, Belle and Dan to arrive.

'Look at it this way, you can share your news with everyone now, and they'll all think you're amazing and talented . . .'

'You've known them for over four years, Leo. Even you can't believe what you're saying,' I point out with a laugh.

Tonight we're dining at Carlo's, an Italian restaurant in town. After Belle's wedding I went straight back to LA to sort things out there before moving back to England, but when I did finally get back, this restaurant was where Leo and I had our first official date. It's just your typical Italian restaurant. There's nothing overly special about it (unless you count the courgette fries; they're too good), but it's special to me.

'Hello, hello,' my mum mumbles as the Harrison-Ryan rabble arrive and take their seats. 'You're here before us, Mia. It's a miracle.'

'I mean, it's my date . . .' I start before giving up.

I give the waiter a chance to take the newcomers' drinks orders before getting down to business.

'So, seeing as you're all here, I have some news,' I start, pausing until I'm sure I have my parents', Belle's and Dan's full attention. 'I've landed a new writing job, ghostwriting Dylan King's autobiography.'

'Whose?' my dad asks.

'Ghostwriting?' my mum echoes back. 'So, you mean doing the hard work and not getting the credit?'

'Well, yes, that's what ghostwriting is, Mum. It pays really well, though. It pays for house stuff and wedding stuff – and more.'

'Speaking of the wedding, have you started making arrangements?' my mum asks. 'Belle says you're refusing.'

Leo looks at me.

'I didn't say she was refusing. I said she wasn't bothering,' Belle adds, talking about me, not to me.

'I'll get more done now I know I can afford it,' I reassure everyone.

'So, will you get to meet Dylan?' my sister asks.

'Yeah, I have to shadow him for a while,' I explain. 'I need to find out all about him, listen to his stories, observe his lifestyle and turn it into a book about his life. I'm so excited.'

'Wow,' Belle says, seeming genuinely impressed. 'That's pretty big news. I'm not sure anyone could top that . . . except . . .'

Oh God, is she really going to try and upstage me?

'We're pregnant,' she squeaks at the top of her voice. Diners and staff all around the restaurant hear her news and applaud.

'Both of you? What a funny coincidence,' I reply.

'Well, just me, silly,' Belle says. 'It's still early, so we were going to wait, but seeing as how we're sharing news . . .'

'Oh my goodness, Belle, that's fantastic,' my mum cries, not only showing an emotion, but projecting it at a person too. If I didn't know better, I'd think she'd had therapy.

I cannot believe my sister. She just couldn't stand me having good news to share. She had to go and upstage me, and she's certainly found a great way to do that – even my dad is crying!

As if it wasn't supposedly bad enough, having my little sister get married before me, now I'm getting married and she's one-upped me with baby news. It doesn't matter how many steps I take, my sister is always ahead of me.

'Let's keep this between us for now,' my sister says. 'Early days.'

'Well, congratulations to you both,' I say. I'm pleased for them, I really am. I'm just annoyed at her timing, but I'm sure she wasn't trying to upstage me.

'This is wonderful, just wonderful. We have so much to look forward to,' my mum says. 'Presumably the wedding will still happen before the baby? Still planning it for the summer?'

'We can race.' Belle giggles.

'We might just get in there first,' Dan says, suddenly interested because now there's something he can win.

'I'm getting round to it,' I tell them. Again. Not that it's anything to do with them; all they have to do is attend.

'Are you letting Leo be involved in the planning?' my mum asks.

'Am I letting him?' I repeat back to her. 'Hey, Dan, which bits of your wedding did you plan?'

'Well . . .'

'Your suits, presumably – at least,' my mum chimes in, jogging his memory.

'No, well, Belle picked those to match the dresses, which I wasn't allowed to look at . . .'

'What about you, Dad, what did you bring to the table for your wedding?' I ask.

My dad pulls a face. 'I don't know. It was years ago, Mia,' he replies. Solid input from my dad there. Now he's in his sixties, he's quieter and duller than ever. He's basically furniture at this stage, the amount he socialises with people.

'See, men don't give a shit,' I say.

'Language,' my mum says. I may be thirty-three years old, but ticking me off for swearing is a reflex I don't think she'll ever shake.

I'm not wrong, though. Men very rarely give a shit about the finer details of the wedding – I hardly give a shit myself.

'I'd actually like to be involved,' Leo says.

My mum and Belle look on, smugly. I try to give my fiancé a subtle kick under the table, as though to say: *shh, you're not helping*, but I miss and end up kicking the table leg, causing a loud bang.

'Oops,' I say, trying to cover it up. 'Clumsy me.'

'Do you remember Mrs Turner?' my mum asks me.

'Erm . . .' I rack my brains.

'Old Mrs Turner,' my mum adds. 'Purple rinse.'

Still nothing.

'Her husband, Malcolm, got an award from the council for going around all the parks, picking up the dog mess during the school holidays so the kiddies didn't paddle in it.'

'I'd definitely remember that guy, I'm sure.' I laugh.

'They lived two houses up from your gran and granddad, until they moved – they used to let you play on their tree swing when you were a kid, long before Belle was born,' my mum continues. 'Remember?'

'I don't think so . . .'

'You must,' my mum insists.

'OK, sure,' I lie. 'I remember.'

'Well, Mrs Turner has a daughter called Deborah. She's a wedding planner. I could ask her to give you a hand,' my mum says.

Wow. I had to get lost down memory lane just so my mum could tell me she knows a wedding planner. I'm pretty sure she could've told me without my recalling some old lady's house where I played on a swing when I was three.

'I don't need a wedding planner; I'm going to do it,' I reply. 'But thank you for the offer,' I add, not wanting to throw kindness in her face – y'know, just in case that was kindness.

Why is everyone so concerned about my wedding? I'm going to plan it, I really am, but what's the rush? We're aiming for next summer. If places book up, we'll just do it when the place we want is free – we don't even know where we want yet.

I know there's so much to do. I know there's the venue, the food, the dress, the suit, the cake, the photographer, all the dumb extra shit you're supposed to have, and the small but very real issue regarding the bridesmaids, and how I don't have any because I don't really have any close female friends, and my female family members all said no . . . I'll panic about all this later, though, because right now I have a job to think about. I'll get around to wedding stuff eventually.

Chapter 13

'Are you pregnant?'

I blink at Rita, my new hairstylist, in the mirror.

'Hmm?' I say.

'Are you pregnant?' she asks again.

'No. Why, do I look it?' I ask defensively.

'No, no,' she replies quickly. 'It's just, your blonde has come out quite brassy in a couple of places . . .'

Oh God, this has happened to me before, except it was my entire head of hair that went orange. Why is it so hard to find a hairdresser you can trust? Since my chemical cut, courtesy of a local hairdresser, I'm finding it harder and harder to trust people with my locks.

'Don't look so worried – it's fixable,' she assures me. 'But are you sure you're not pregnant?'

'I'm sure,' I tell her with an awkward laugh.

I mean, I'm not trying to get pregnant, and Leo and I are always careful, so it's very unlikely, isn't it? As a person who has always suffered with bouts of anxiety, rather than spend my time being constantly petrified of getting pregnant, I googled the heck out of all things period and pregnancy, so I knew exactly what I was up against. These days I use an app that keeps tabs on my period for me – one quick glance while my hairdresser is off mixing more colour confirms exactly when my next one is due.

Leo calls me Web MD, because I'm forever googling health matters and symptoms online, but I like to know what I'm dealing with. I've always worried about stuff like this, and it seems crazy to me that there are people who don't actively worry about their health. I seem to worry more when I'm stressed about other things, but sometimes life feels like a series of close shaves before I finally encounter the thing that's going to be serious. So I'm either not worrying about anything at all, or I'll just be in the bathroom, looking in the mirror, and I'll feel a sharp pain somewhere and think: 'This is it, then' – because it's absolutely appendicitis, and not just trapped wind. Of course, it never has been appendicitis – my appendix is still in there – but it's one more thing to worry about, right?

Today I have my first meeting with Dylan at his London home. Now I know there's going to be more money coming in, and because I'm about to be rubbing shoulders with the rich and famous, I thought it would be a good idea to fully channel LA Mia, and splash out on my hair. To fully return to my glory days I need to go longer and blonder, so I've been here since the crack of dawn having my hair transformed by a barrage of peroxide and head full of extensions. Then I'll need to find some toilets, get changed, plaster on some make-up and then hop on another train to Dylan's house. It's just an informal first meeting so I'm not too worried, although it has been a while since I hung out with a celebrity.

'I'd probably take a test if I were you,' the stylist persists.

'Thanks,' I reply.

Wow, the service here is exceptional – a hairdresser and gynaecologist rolled into one. I won't just be leaving here with long, blonde locks. I imagine my pelvic examination is next.

There's no way I could be pregnant, surely . . . I'll probably hold off from texting Leo and my parents for now. Can you imagine Belle's face, though, if I was? She'd think I'd done it on purpose to upstage her. But there's no way I'm pregnant – what would I do if I was? I'm not ready for a baby. The last baby I held was Belle, so I was probably only five or six years old. People just look at me and decide I'm not the kind of person who should be allowed to handle their kids. *But* I'm not pregnant, so none of this matters – I can only deal with one problem at a time.

Chapter 14

As I make my way along the pathway to Dylan's front door, I am taken aback by how beautiful his house is.

I'm standing outside a massive, double-fronted detached house, cloaked in privacy, with high walls, tall trees and large electronic gates, somewhere between Primrose Hill and Regent's Park. The front of the house is floodlit, and light is pouring out of the large, curved window that sits above the front door. I hate these dark winter evenings; it must be amazing to have such a big, light house where you don't feel the darkness outside. Through the window I can see the spiral staircase that leads upstairs. It's simply amazing. It certainly puts my little house to shame.

Before I knock on the door I touch up my lip gloss, straighten my outfit and smile brightly. It's show time.

'Hello,' a forty-something man says, opening the door. He's very tall, well over six foot, and skinny too – with the bright hallway backlighting him, he looks a little like Slender Man, which creeps me out for a split second.

'Hi, I think we just spoke on the gate intercom. I'm Mia Valentina. I'm here to see Dylan.'

'Hello, Mia,' he says, offering me a hand to shake. 'I'm Mitch, Dylan's manager.'

I shake his hand. I've read all about Adrian 'Mitch' Mitchell, Dylan King's manager. He used to be The Burnouts' manager, until Dylan and his brother Mikey had their huge fallout. They actually had a legal battle over who got to keep him as their manager – can you imagine? A custody battle over a grown man.

'Nice to meet you.'

'So, what I was trying to tell you over the intercom . . . Unfortunately, something has come up,' Mitch explains. 'Dylan is going to need to reschedule.'

'Oh,' I start, unsure what else to say.

'He said to pass on his apologies, but . . .' Mitch's voice tapers off as a noise echoes through the house. Is that . . .? 'Erm, yes, so . . .'

The sound of a woman groaning fills the hallway.

I purse my lips and widen my eyes as I look at Mitch, waiting for some kind of explanation. He doesn't offer one.

'So, I can call you to reschedule,' he says, raising his voice, trying to drown the sex noises out.

'Is he here?' I ask, already well aware of the answer.

'He's working,' Mitch replies.

'Oh yeah? On who?' I ask.

Right on cue, a skinny blonde in her underwear peers over the banister.

'Dylan says can we have more champagne,' she yells down.

'That his wife?' I ask sarcastically.

'No, Dylan isn't . . . Oh, that's a joke, right?'

I nod.

The groaning continues before the blonde disappears, so, of course, he's got two of them in there. Well, at least now I know his reputation isn't just hype. He really is a womaniser.

'Well, I'll go then, I guess. All the way back to Kent, after travelling all the way here. For nothing,' I tell Mitch, laying it on thick.

'It's out of my hands, unfortunately,' he tells me, showing me to the door, and just like that the first day of my new job is over in under five minutes. I wouldn't mind, but I'm being paid a flat rate for the project and not by the hour.

As I walk back down the driveway, I call Leo.

'Hey, how's it going?' he asks, sounding a little frazzled.

'Dylan stood me up – for two chicks,' I add.

'You can't blame him for that.' Leo laughs.

'So, I'm on my way home – are you OK? You sound stressed.'

'No, I'm fine, it's all good. I'm glad you're coming home, though. I could do with a hand.

'What's up?'

'Hannah has a date and her babysitter cancelled, so she's dropped Angel off for us to look after.'

'I'll be there as soon as I can,' I tell him, ending the call.

Great, just what I need. I was supposed to be hanging out with a rock star tonight and instead I'm babysitting a three-year-old. Then again, it sounds like Angel is much more mature than Dylan. I'm a professional – who does he think he is, standing me up like this? I'll bet he's used to people kissing his arse all day long . . . but not me. I'll be having words with Mr King.

Chapter 15

As I approach my own house, I can't help but notice that it doesn't pack the same punch as Dylan's. His big, beautiful house was on a nice, clean, quiet street. Unlike my house, on a street almost always abuzz with drunk people. Dylan had a Range Rover in his garden. I have a condom in mine that I cannot bring myself to move – I don't think it's used because the first time I noticed it, it was inflated to the size of a large marrow. Still, I'm not in a hurry to touch it.

Another significant contrast between mine and Dylan's life is the company. The two people Dylan arrived home to entertain are very different to the two I'm about to walk in on . . .

'Hello,' I call out, closing the door behind me. I slip my coat off and hang it up on the coat rack (read: put it down on top of a pile of boxes).

'Oh my God, look at you,' Leo greets me. 'Your hair is all long and blonde . . . You look just like we did when we first met . . .'

My fiancé's jaw is practically on the floor and it makes me wish I'd got back to my old self much sooner. Still, it was a gradual process of not looking like myself – the same goes for not feeling like myself – but hopefully now I'm getting out to work and hanging out with interesting people (in theory, if it ever happens) that will change too.

'Thank you,' I reply, all smiles, but then I notice Leo's face fall. 'It's OK, isn't it?'

'It's gorgeous,' he replies. 'It's just a little weird, to see the old you again. You look *exactly* like the old you . . .'

'You fell in love with the old me,' I remind him.

'I did,' he replies. 'But she was hard work . . . You're happy with how things are now, right?'

'Of course I am,' I insist. 'Now, never mind how I look, why aren't we talking about the fact that you look like that chimney sweep from the wedding. Why are your hands all black?'

'OK, don't freak out,' Leo starts gently.

'Already freaking out,' I tell him.

I follow Leo upstairs into our bedroom, only to find our newly painted white walls covered in black smears. Sitting on the floor, all smiles, brandishing a black YSL eyeliner, is my first cousin once removed, three-year-old Angel Edwards. I don't know which has more black on it, the wall or her face, and I don't know which will be more expensive to replace, the white paint or the eyeliner (it's *definitely* the latter).

'What happened here?' I ask her gently, as though as three-year-old might be able to give me a reasonable explanation.

'I helped,' she mumbles, in that cute way three-year-olds talk.

'You helped?' I ask.

'I helped to do the house.'

Oh shit, that is an almost reasonable explanation.

'Thank you,' I say. 'But you're not supposed to use make-up; that's for your face . . . which, I guess you also did. But we'd better get you cleaned up.'

'I like to look pretty like my mummy and like you. But not like my gran – she looks old,' Angel babbles.

Those harsh words against my Auntie June almost make this worthwhile.

'Your gran does look old, doesn't she?' I reply. 'Like a baddie from a Disney film. OK, let's get you in the bathroom.'

I usher Angel towards the bathroom.

'Hey,' Leo calls after me.

'Two secs,' I tell Angel. 'Yeah?'

'I thought you were going to hit the roof,' he says. 'I didn't realise you were so good with kids.'

'I'm not going to scream at a three-year-old,' I say. 'I'm going to scream at you later, for not keeping an eye on her.'

Leo laughs.

'We'd make a good team, if we had kids, right?' he says.

'Oh God, don't . . . I've already had one pregnancy scare today.' I laugh.

'What?'

'Nothing, nothing. My hairdresser thought I might be pregnant . . .'

Leo's eyebrows shoot up.

'I'm not,' I insist quickly. 'She just took the stuff off my hair a little prematurely.'

'Wouldn't have been the worst news,' he says with a smile.

'Are you kidding me?' I ask. 'With the wedding coming up and my new job and the house being like it is?'

'OK, fine, one excuse would have been enough, sorry I mentioned it,' he says stroppily. 'Sorry the idea bothers you so much.'

Leo and I have had several discussions about what we want for the future over the course of our relationship. I might have been a commitment-phobe before we met, but the deeper in love I fell with Leo, the faster that scared feeling faded. When he proposed to me, sure, it was a surprise, but we had talked about the idea of marriage and we both knew where we stood and that we were both happy to do it. But when it comes to kids, well . . . I'm not sure. I don't *not* want kids, I'm just never sure that I do. I'm not sure I'd make a very good mum – or that any of the mums in my family have turned out to be good mums, so why would I be any different? I just need a bit more time with this one.

'It's not the time,' I tell him.

'OK, but it's a time-sensitive thing, right?'

I tilt my head inquisitively.

'Like, women only have so much time to do these things, right?' he continues.

I puff air out of my cheeks. 'Can we talk about my ticking biological clock some other time, please? I need to wash Angel before her mum sees her, Instagrams it, and my auntie accuses me of trying to make her grandchild go viral or something equally ridiculous.'

Leo scratches his head. 'Sure.'

'Mia, Mia, come look how pretty I am,' Angel calls from the bathroom.

As I walk in I catch Angel just in time to see her putting the finishing touches on her fringe (or what used to be her fringe) with a pair of scissors.

'I look *so* pretty,' she sings. 'I look like a princess.'

Angel dances for herself in the mirror, singing some song I imagine is from some Disney film I haven't seen – probably the modern kind with feminist female leads, where the princesses don't have to rely on Prince Charming to save them from evil witches or the passage of time rendering their old ovaries useless.

'Ohhh shit,' I can't help but say.

'Swear,' Angel ticks me off. 'I'll tell Mummy.'

'That's the least of my worries,' I say to myself.

Leo hurries into the room to see Angel holding a pair of scissors, blonde locks on the floor all around her and a big empty space where her fringe used to be.

'Still want kids?' I ask him.

'Not so much right now,' he says, grimacing.

'OK, Angel, let's get you in the bath,' I say calmly. 'It's all fine, it's all going to be fine.'

'I'll, erm . . .' Leo stares at me blankly.

'Clean the wall, I guess?' I suggest.

'OK,' he replies. 'Got it.'

I run a bath but I'm terrified that three-year-olds aren't allowed Lush bath bombs or water that is too hot. I lift Angel into the tepid, plain water and sit on the floor next to her.

'Mummy gives me *Frozen* bubbles,' she tells me.

'I don't have any, sorry,' I reply.

'It's OK. Do you like my hair?'

I reach out to examine her hair, moving what is left of her fringe, trying to brush it forwards, but it's not exactly helping. What did I think – that she was one of those dolls with retractable hair like I had when I was a kid?

'I want a horse for Christmas,' she tells me, splashing the water.

'A hat might be a better idea, chick,' I tell her, but she's not listening.

'A big horse that's a girl,' she continues.

'Leo,' I call out.

'Yeah?' he says, appearing in the doorway.

'We've got two choices. We do nothing, and leave this issue for Hannah to sort out – although it will be very much our fault and we'll be in lots of trouble . . . or maybe it will only be my fault, because isn't it always?'

'Or?'

'Maybe your mum could help?'

Maria De Luca is a hairdresser and an all-round-lovely lady. When we were away for Belle's wedding and a hairdresser made my hair look awful, Maria was happy to help me out. Maybe there's something – anything – she can do, to make this look not quite so awful.

'Good thinking,' he says. 'I'll give her a call.'

'Hey, Angel, how would you like to look even prettier?' I ask her.

'Like a princess?' she asks.

'Exactly like a princess,' I tell her.

'Yes!' she says, punching the air, splashing water everywhere.

'My mum says she'll try and help,' Leo says. 'I'll go pick her up.'

'OK, thank you so much,' I call after him.

'Do you think Mummy will be mad I cut my hair?' Angel asks.

'Not with you, sweetheart,' I tell her honestly.

Half an hour later Angel is clean and I've blow-dried her hair, just in time for Leo getting back with Maria.

Maria claps eyes on Angel and laughs gently.

'Oh, love,' she says as she examines my little cousin's new 'do.

'Are you gonna make me look like a princess?' Angel asks Maria.

'I am, sweetheart. I am.'

Maria takes out her hairdressing kit, laying it flat on top of some cardboard boxes. Leo lifts Angel up and sits her down on a sturdy box that is just about the right height.

'So . . .' Maria starts. 'I mean . . . it's not ideal . . . but I could cut her a thicker fringe and hopefully the hair on the top will disguise the underneath while it grows?'

'Oh, could you do that, please,' I reply.

'Will her mum be OK with that?' Maria asks.

I pull a face. 'More so than this.'

Maria looks at Angel again, her cheeky little face smiling widely, still looking adorable even though her hair looks awful.

My heart is in my mouth as Maria snips away, but I trust she knows what she's going.

'Leo tells me you have a new job, Mia,' she says.

'Yeah, ghostwriting an autobiography for a singer,' I say. 'Although I turned up for my first day today and he was . . . indisposed.'

'I suppose you're used to that, having worked in the movie business,' she replies.

She's not wrong. I've worked with celebrities, made friends with some of them and even dated one or two. I only have one ex, if we can really call him that, who everyone has heard of and that's actor Jimmy Menzel. I met Jimmy when we were shooting a movie I'd written on location in New York. The director was an absolute nightmare, constantly demanding changes, so in the end I flew to New York for the duration of filming, and enjoyed a fleeting romance with Jimmy. I suppose, given that he couldn't even remember his assistant's name, the fact he made a point of remembering mine is quite a big deal, but he was selfish, childish, impatient – and possibly a drug addict, I realised towards the end of our time together. So I suppose, when it comes to Dylan, I'll expect that, and if he's a better person than Jimmy, then I'll only be pleasantly surprised.

'Yeah, I'll soon get him under control.' I laugh.

'And the wedding planning . . . how's that going?' she asks.

'Yeah, good,' I lie. I look over at Leo who has his eyebrows raised. 'Well, I mean, I'll be starting soon. Just as soon as I get this job started. We both want to plan it together and we're having a bit of trouble coordinating at the moment.'

'OK,' Maria replies. God, I wish I could tell what she's thinking right now. She's got this look on her face, like she's thinking *something* . . .

'I'm bored,' Angel whines.

'Your mummy will be here for you any minute,' Leo tells her. 'Don't you want to look your best for her?'

'OK, fiiiine,' she replies.

A few more snips and Maria is done.

'There. What do we think?'

'I want to see, I want to see,' Angel begs.

Maria takes a mirror from her bag and hands it to Angel.

'Wow, I look so cool,' Angel chirps.

'You do. And normal,' I add, breathing a huge sigh of relief. 'Maria, thank you so much.'

'What's family for?' she asks.

Right on time, there's a knock at the door.

'That will be Hannah,' Leo says, hurrying for the door.

Hannah is only through the door thirty seconds when she notices Maria.

'Did you have to call in the cavalry?' She laughs. 'Oh, wow, Angel, look at you . . . Why does my daughter have a Zooey Deschanel fringe?'

'OK, don't freak out,' I start, ushering Hannah to one side. 'But Angel sort of found some scissors and cut her fringe quite short . . .'

'Oh sh . . . ugar,' Hannah replies. 'You know, one of my mum's friends made her this beautiful ragdoll, and she cut its hair. She's obsessed with making everyone and everything look like a princess, but for some reason, in her head, princesses look like they've got their head stuck in a blender.'

I laugh. 'So you're not mad at me?' I ask.

'It was gonna happen sooner or later,' Hannah says with a shrug of her shoulders. 'I think she looks cute.'

'Ah, thank God. I thought you were going to kill me – or your mum was, at least.'

'We don't have to mention it to her,' Hannah says. 'Don't worry about it.'

I grab my cousin for a hug.

'You're my favourite.'

'You too.' She laughs. 'Don't tell Belle.'

It's late now, and everyone has gone home. Leo and I are sitting at the edge of our bed, admiring Angel's handiwork.

'Who knew eyeliner was so hard to get off?' Leo says.

'Me. Every night,' I joke. 'I'm guessing we're going to have to repaint in here?'

'Let's not worry about it tonight, let's just go to sleep,' he says, squeezing my hand.

'You want that conversation about having kids now?' I laugh.

'Maybe in a few years, when I've forgotten about this,' he replies. 'You too tired for a dress rehearsal?'

Leo wiggles his eyebrows.

'Never too tired for that,' I reply.

Chapter 16

Have you ever been so cold that your teeth started chattering? That's me right now, hanging around outside the London Studios, waiting for one of Dylan's people to come out and let me in.

It's November, so of course it's cold, but the audience members queuing up to get into the studio all came tooled up with coats, hats and scarves. I, on the other hand, thought it more important I turn up looking as glamorous as possible, which I think I've achieved with my meticulously curled, newly lengthened locks and my black lace and velvet dress. I'd look great, had my skin not turned purple.

Dylan is here to record a TV appearance, performing his new single at the end of a chat show. At the moment he's chilling in his dressing room, so we're going to have our first meeting there. It's just a quick chat to get to know each other. Apparently his schedule is so hectic that the person working with him has to shadow him and get as much information as they can in between his commitments. I spoke to Lindsey about where the other writers had struggled and apparently it was down to Dylan being a combination of unaccommodating and unforthcoming.

'Mia,' Mitch calls out, gesturing the direction he wants me to walk in with his head. 'Christ, girl, don't you have a proper coat?'

'The jacket looked better than a coat,' I tell him honestly.

'Did someone tell you Dylan has a soft spot for pretty blondes?' he asks. 'That why you got the job?'

I raise my eyebrows as I follow him. 'Erm, no, I got it because I can string sentences together,' I reply. 'Were my predecessors male or female?'

'We had a fella first of all, then a woman – older than you, though. Dylan didn't like her. She didn't like him either, or me for that matter. She complained I "mansplained" things to her – some BS invented by feminists. It's where men supposedly explain things to women that don't need explaining.'

I laugh, until I realise he isn't joking. He's mansplaining mansplaining to me.

'Anyway, through here,' he says, before knocking on the dressing-room door. 'Courtesy knock.'

Oh God, what am I about to walk in on?

'Come in,' a voice calls back.

'In you pop,' Mitch tells me. 'I've got to go and see about some business.'

Mitch darts off, leaving me alone. I take one final deep breath before walking into Dylan's dressing room, mentally preparing myself for what I might be about to clap eyes on . . .

The dressing room is exactly as I imagined it. There's a large dressing table, with lights around the mirror. There are fresh flowers on every surface. There's a platter of food out that looks so good I just wanna plough my face into it. The walls are white and everything is spotless. The room might be what I expected, but Dylan isn't. He's sitting at the dressing table – in here all alone – all dressed up and ready for his performance.

'Hello,' he says, standing up. 'Mia, is it?'

'Mia Valentina,' I reply, offering him my hand cautiously.

Dylan shakes my hand before pulling me close, embracing me as he kisses both my cheeks in that showbiz way all industry people do. I'd forgotten about that.

'Dylan King,' he says, as though he needed an introduction. 'Wow, your hands are freezing. Can I get you a tea or a coffee?'

I blink several times. 'Erm . . . a tea would be wonderful, thank you.'

'Milk and sugar?' he asks, heading for the door.

'Just milk, please.'

'Sweet enough?' he jokes. 'Be right back.'

Alone in Dylan's dressing room, I wonder if I just imagined that. I was expecting a diva – the Dylan you read about in the news, the kind who would blow off a work meeting for a threesome.

Soon enough he's back, placing the mug down in front of me before sitting on the sofa next to me.

'Hi,' he says with a big smile.

'Hi,' I reply.

Dylan King is undeniably sexy. He isn't buff, or classically handsome . . . but there's just something about him. He's got that rough-and-ready bad-boy look about him. His relaxed demeanour and his dad bod make him look like he doesn't give a shit, and something about that is seriously sexy. Like, this is him, take it or leave it.

He's taller than me, but not that tall, 5'11" maybe. He's got dark-brown hair, very short on the sides but long and tousled on top, and he's rocking designer stubble – although maybe that's just because he's neglected to shave. He's wearing black, skinny-fit trousers, a black waistcoat and a white shirt with sleeves rolled up, showcasing all the tattoos on his arms. I noticed a flat cap on the dressing table but I'm not sure if he'll be wearing it onstage. His look is sort of styled, but in an unstyled way. Everything about him seems effortless, like he doesn't have a care in the world. That must be nice.

'How are you?' he asks.

'I'm good . . . you?'

'I'm doing great,' he replies.

I frown.

'What's up?' he asks. 'Oh, sorry about yesterday, something came up.'

'Yeah, I think I heard,' I reply.

'What do you mean?'

'I mean I was at your house and I could literally hear what "came up",' I tell him.

He laughs. 'Sorry, yeah. Letting off steam. But I'm here now, and I'm ready to work.'

I raise an eyebrow in disbelief.

'What?' He laughs again. 'I am. Look, I've been the perfect gentleman since you got here. I got you a cup of tea – I don't get anyone anything, not even myself.'

I glance at the mug in his hands.

'Mitch just gave me this. It's a vodka on the rocks.' He chuckles. 'Look, I'm sorry about yesterday. Let's start fresh today, yeah?'

'OK, sure,' I reply. I'm willing to give him the benefit of the doubt because I'm a reasonable person, but also because it's kind of difficult to resist his charm.

'You look like your pictures,' he tells me.

'Erm, thank you, I think.'

'You're welcome. Not too many girls look like their pictures these days, with airbrushing and angles – and even just filters, you know? You can work wonders with a filter.'

'Looks matter to you?' I ask.

'Looks matter to everyone, right? You put all that make-up on; you bought that dress. And before you get mad at me and say you're not doing it for anyone but yourself, OK, sure, but that still means looks matter to you.'

He's got an excellent point.

'So—'

'You got a boyfriend?' he interrupts me.

'A fiancé,' I tell him, holding up my left hand.

Dylan immediately takes my hand and examines my ring. 'Hmm,' he says.

'What?' I ask curiously.

'Well, either you've bought yourself this ring to play hard to get – which is working, by the way – or you've got a fiancé who doesn't value you. This can't be worth much.'

Dylan caresses my hand as he speaks. I quickly snatch it from him.

'You know not everyone is a millionaire, right?'

'I like you,' he tells me confidently. 'You're not taking my shit. Most people just take it. Since I made it, there's only been two people willing to call me out: my brother and my best friend.'

'Well, that's good,' I reply.

'Yeah, except I don't see either of them anymore,' he replies, chewing his lip thoughtfully. 'But I've got you now. What do you think of this hat?'

Dylan jumps up and grabs his flat cap, tossing it to me to examine.

'I don't like it,' I tell him honestly.

'Then I won't wear it,' he tells me, all smiles. 'I've got a good feeling about you. What does your fiancé do?'

'For work?'

'Yeah.'

'He's a fireman,' I reply.

Dylan pulls a face to show his indifference. 'Anyway . . .' he continues. 'The other two didn't really get very far, so we're starting from scratch with the book. You're OK to follow me around for a bit?'

'I am,' I tell him. 'I just need to get enough information from you and then you can leave me to it.'

'Sweet,' he replies. 'Well, I think I'm on in ten, so maybe we'll start another day? But stay here, watch the show on the TV, eat something.'

'Thank you,' I reply.

'I can't believe you're engaged,' Dylan says with a laugh. 'You know that's probably just going to make me try harder, right?'

I shrug. 'It's not going to make a difference,' I say with a confident smile.

'Game on,' he tells me. 'Game on.'

Mitch comes back in and takes Dylan off, leaving me here to drink my tea and pick at his food.

I'm sure Dylan is joking, about trying harder to woo me, but I'd be lying if I said that it didn't make me feel giddy, being around celebrities again, commanding their attention. And this is Dylan King – *the* Dylan King. Still, I'm a happily engaged lady, and I'm here to do a job. No amount of him flirting for sport is going to derail that.

I've got a good feeling about this job. I think it's going to be fun and just the right amount of challenging. I'm not sure how I feel about Dylan yet, though . . . Why do I get the feeling he's going to be trouble?

Chapter 17

I slip off my dress and climb into bed as quietly as possible. It's not enough, though. Leo wakes up.

'Hey, go back to sleep,' I tell him, kissing his cheek. 'You're up early tomorrow.'

'It's OK. How was it?'

'It was . . . OK,' I reply. 'Good.'

'You sure?' He laughs.

Leo rolls over onto his back, lifting his arm so I can cuddle into his chest.

'Yeah, just . . . I don't know what to make of Dylan. He wasn't what I expected, but he was . . . but he wasn't, y'know?'

'Not really,' he says. 'You seeing him again tomorrow?'

'Yes.' I yawn dramatically. London might not be far, but all this back and forth is exhausting for someone who is used to working from the comfort of her own sofa.

I lift my head to give Leo a kiss.

'Ergh, you stink of beer,' I tell him. 'Have you been out tonight?'

'Just a couple of drinks with a few of the guys from work. I got some serious work done on the secret room this evening before I left,' Leo tells me sleepily. I look up at him to see that his eyes are closed, but he's smiling.

'I can't wait to see,' I tell him. 'Goodnight.'

No reply. When he falls asleep, he falls asleep all at once, not like me, who just lies in bed thinking about all the things – what I've done that day, what I'll be doing the next day, what I need to worry about, that stupid thing I said back in 2008, et cetera.

There's one room in our house that I'm not allowed to set foot in. Leo calls it the secret room, and it's a surprise for me, apparently. He's so excited about it and working so hard on it that I'm not even tempted to peep. The fact he's doing something like this for me is so amazing, and just one of the reasons I love him so much.

Leo may be asleep, but I just feel so much better when I'm in his arms. It's my happy place, locked away in his bicep where no one can get me. He's surprisingly comfortable for someone with such a hard body.

I'm cold, so I snuggle closer. There's no way I'm going to want to get up in the morning, but I've got to travel to London – again – to see Dylan. Tomorrow we're having our first proper session and I'm nervous. I've never done anything like this before. My plan is to try and get him talking and record our conversations. That way, when I listen back, I can get a feel for his tone of voice and try to retell his stories in a book-worthy way.

I reach out to hold Leo's hand, like I often do while he's sleeping, but something doesn't feel right. I sit up, careful not to wake him, to look at his hand. He's got a white plaster covering the back of his hand – he must have hurt himself at work. I love that Leo has a job he enjoys, that he's good at, that makes a difference to the world, but it's so dangerous. I'm sure there's nothing seriously wrong with his hand but that's just this time. He's got years of work ahead of him and it's a dangerous job every day.

I cuddle back up to him, holding him that little bit tighter this time. I love him so much. If anything were to happen to him, I don't know what I'd do.

Chapter 18

When I met Dylan yesterday the only thing I knew for sure was that he wasn't what I expected. The Dylan I'm dealing with today, however, is exactly the Dylan I expected – an arsehole.

'Because he's shit, Mitch,' Dylan yells at his manager.

Maybe it's since I saw his semi-chauvinistic side, but I can't help but notice how weaselly Mitch's features are today. He might look like a weasel but his mannerisms are those of a snake, slinking around Dylan all the time, doing whatever he asks, even if he disagrees with it.

'OK,' Mitch replies. 'I'll tell the label.'

I have no idea what they're talking about. Sitting here, in Dylan's living room, I tuned out during their entire conversation. Instead of listening in, I took a moment to truly examine the room. It's kind of stylish, in a bachelor-pad kind of way, which makes me think he probably had a designer in to deck the place out for him – that's what we need for our house, a team of experts to come in and just make it look like a house that can be lived in, and not the plain-walled box museum it currently appears to be.

'I can't be fucked today,' Dylan whines, sighing loudly in an entirely put-on way.

How charming. I don't know if he's knows he's being rude or if he just doesn't care.

'What's that face for?' he asks me.

I didn't realise I was making a face.

'Fucking hell, your fella must have his hands full with you,' Dylan scoffs, his south London accent the strongest I've heard it yet.

'How so?' I ask, a little bit offended.

'Do you pull a face like that at him every time he displeases you?' he asks.

'He doesn't drink in the a.m.,' I say to myself under my breath.

'What was that?' Dylan asks, sitting up, shuffling to the edge of his seat.

For a moment we hold eye contact, until Dylan picks up his drink – a vodka on the rocks – and knocks it back.

Then it hits me. The Dylan I met last night was sober because he was about to go on TV. The Dylan I'm sitting here with now has obviously had a few.

'How long have you been with your fella?'

'Four years,' I reply.

'You said you're engaged? When are you getting married?'

'Next year.'

'When next year?'

'Summer maybe,' I reply. 'I thought I was supposed to be asking you questions?'

Dylan laughs. 'He better-looking than me?'

'Probably,' I say with a smile.

'I like you.' Dylan cackles. 'Man, I like you. You're not kissing my arse.'

I shrug. Part of me thinks I should probably be sucking up to him and pandering to him like everyone else does, but he seems to respond well to the honesty.

'Go on, ask me some questions,' he says, lying back on the sofa.

'Tell me about your childhood,' I prompt him, pressing record on my Dictaphone.

'Well . . . fucking hell, look at me lying here, you there taking notes. It's like therapy. This isn't an intervention is it?'

I laugh. 'Nope.'

'I've had a bit of therapy. Did a stint in rehab a couple of years ago,' he confesses.

I already knew this. It was all over the news at the time.

'How was that?' I ask. 'By the way, anything you don't want in the book, just say.'

'Off the record then,' he starts, drumming on his stomach with his hands as he chats. 'Just between us. Had a bit of shit in my personal life so they checked me in to clear my head. I'd been hitting the coke a little hard, if we're being honest. I cleaned up, but it was a load of old bollocks. They had us sitting outside in a circle, listening to some prat in a dress telling us to imagine the wind blowing around us, chimes jingling in our ears and shit. I told him he was making a mug of me, that hearing bells in my ears is what was happening when I was on drugs, not off them.'

'Yeah, that sounds like an interesting technique.' I laugh.

'So, Dr Valentina, my childhood . . . Well, I was born, and I was fine, but then my little brother, Michael, was born. Special, precious little Mikey. You know how you hear of couples getting a dog, but then they have a baby and the dog is out? I was the King family dog. Everything was all about Mikey, the perfect son. We all had to fit our shit around all his lame extracurriculars. So my parents would always be off with him, spectating or cheering or whatever, and I'd be home alone, cooking my own dinner.'

Wow, this is sounding awfully familiar. Dylan is the Mia in his family; Mikey is the Belle.

'So, I would act up at school, just to get a bit of attention probably – if we're psychoanalysing it. I was always in detention. I got excluded a few times.'

'It doesn't sound like you and your brother spent much time together as kids,' I say.

'No, we weren't buddies,' he replies.

'So, how did you wind up in a band together?'

'So, Mikey started classical guitar lessons when he was, like, six or some shit. Only he gets more impressive as he gets older and our parents are super into it – whatever it takes to nurture his talents. So, skip a few years, I'm sixteen years old, just about done with year 11 and ready to get the fuck out of school. We go out for my auntie's birthday one night, just the family and her close friends gathered at her local. I'm bored out of my nut. There are no fit birds there. People talk to my parents. They wanna talk about Mikey – but I'm used to that. The DJ starts taking karaoke requests, right, so why not? It'll kill a few minutes – maybe I can make the barmaid laugh, even though I'm way too young for her to look twice at. So I look over the songbook and there's all these Elton John tracks – who doesn't love Elton John? It's the Nineties, so I do "Can You Feel the Love Tonight". I get on the little stage – it's not even really a stage – and grab the mic. The intro plays and no one gives a shit, but then I start singing . . .'

Dylan stops his story for a few seconds and stares at the ceiling. I don't prompt him; I just leave him with his thoughts.

'No one, er . . . no one knew I could sing,' he confesses, little hints of emotion peppering his sentences. 'I swear, I thought my old man was gonna burst into tears. I had the room, man, every single person, all eyes on me. I liked it – the way it felt, entertaining everyone, everyone watching me, mesmerised by my voice. I think my parents pushed my brother and me together,' he recalls. 'So we started a band, found the other members, and the rest is history.'

'Wow,' I reply.

Dylan laughs. 'Yeah, woe is me, my parents love my brother more, et cetera,' he jokes.

'Oh no, I totally get it,' I tell him. 'My little sister is definitely the favourite child in my family. I grew up in her shadow – even now, she's front and centre and she had the dream wedding and now she's pregnant and I, her *older* sister, am in her dust, struggling to find my arse with both hands – sorry.'

I realise I'm ranting. It's a sore spot for me.

'Two things,' Dylan says, sitting up. 'First up, seems like we have more in common than we realised.'

'I guess we do.' I smile, happy to have found some common ground with him – it's just a shame it's this.

'Second thing – I can help you find your arse.' Dylan wiggles his eyebrows at me.

I laugh. There's nothing like a joke to lighten the mood.

'Come to my show tonight,' he says. 'See me in action. You really should, if you're writing about me.'

'I would, but the last train—'

'Fuck the last train,' Dylan says. 'I'm staying in a hotel. I'll have Mitch book you a room. Come on, Mia. You need to see me doing my job.'

I think for a second. 'Yeah, you're probably right. Just need to make a call.' I stand up and head for the hallway.

'Yeah, make sure your fiancé doesn't mind me stealing you,' he calls after me.

99

Chapter 19

It's been a long time since I attended a gig. It's not that I don't love music. I was always too busy when I was in LA, and since I moved back home, I don't know, it's just never really been a priority. I didn't really feel like live music was missing from my life . . . until tonight.

After Dylan and his brother fell out – and disbanded – Dylan went solo, and in a Robbie Williams/Justin Timberlake/Zayn Malik kind of way, he somehow managed to become an even bigger, even more successful star than he was before. Tonight he performed at a charity concern, to an audience of five thousand people – at the Royal Albert Hall, no less. The event, set up to raise money for the Magical Star Foundation (a kids charity Dylan has always supported), was completely sold out, but Dylan told me I could watch his set from the wings and . . . I can't think of a better way to put it . . . he took my breath away. Sure, I've heard his songs on the radio, and I've seen his music videos, and I've read all about him in the news . . . but we live in a time of autotune, where the production can make or break a song. But Dylan's voice speaks for itself. It's amazing and unmistakable and, whether he was thrusting his hips to his more lively songs or belting out his ballads, he left me with goosebumps.

After his set, Dylan went off to do a few interviews before heading back to his dressing room. He told me to enjoy the show and meet him there, so after I'd watched a couple more acts, I headed backstage, with the hope of getting back to business. The sooner I get everything I need, the sooner I can write this book, the sooner I can get paid and get on with planning my wedding.

I could hear Dylan in the shower so I made myself at home, relaxing in the comfortable chair, eating his strawberries and sipping his champagne – this is the life. After five minutes Dylan emerged from the bathroom in nothing but a towel. There's just something about him, and it doesn't matter that he isn't buff or classically handsome – it's just the Dylan King package that makes him so attractive to seemingly all women.

'You want me to drop the towel so you can get a better look?' He laughed.

'I was looking at your tattoos,' I told him. 'How many do you have?'

'Fuck knows,' he said, examining his chest and arms. 'I got some individual ones, got my sleeve, a few of them merged, had a few covered with better shit when I was sober. They all tell a story; I just don't always remember them.' He laughed, running a hand through his wet hair.

I climbed out of my chair to get a closer look. On the left side of his chest, creeping over his shoulder, his ink makes it look like his skin has been torn from his body, slashed open as though a lion has clawed him. Through the gaps of seemingly torn flesh, a page of fancy writing peeps through.

'Song lyrics,' he told me. 'My own, obviously.'

I'm not really a fan of tattoos, but I have to admit this one is truly a work of art. As I admired his work, Dylan raised a hand to gently push a piece of my hair behind my ear.

'Hey, what are all those numbers on the backs of your hands?' I asked, suddenly noticing them.

Dylan held his hands out in front of him to reveal a series

of three- and four-digit numbers inked on in a variety of styles and shades.

'I, er, I stay in a lot of hotels, and I'd forget my room number a lot, so drunk Dylan would get them tattooed on – it's a good system.'

'But there's so many now,' I pointed out. 'How would drunk Dylan know which one was the right one?'

'I said it was a good system; I didn't say it was a great one.' He laughed.

Dylan's body is a canvas that tells a multitude of stories. There are his tattoos – painstakingly detailed, beautiful, expensive-looking ones that clearly took a lot of planning and skill, and then some that aren't as detailed or as high quality that he had done on random drunken nights. He also has a few scars, like the little patch that's missing from the outside edge of his left eyebrow that I'd always thought was a fashion choice, but it turns out it's from fighting when he was at school. And then there's the one on his arm that he simply and casually explained came from the time he tried to climb out of a hotel window to get away from a girl he didn't want to sleep with, which makes me wonder what on earth he could have found wrong with this girl to make him not want to sleep with her, because so far I've seen him flirt with girls indiscriminately.

After Dylan got dressed we headed to the afterparty. I've been to some swanky parties in my time but – and maybe it's just because I haven't been to one in years – tonight is something else. We're in an enormous function room in a hotel, the one I'm staying in tonight. I did have second thoughts about staying in London. It's not that Leo minded – he's working nights anyway and I think he's just so happy I'm enjoying my job – but I realised I didn't have any of my stuff with me. I told Dylan this and he simply told me he'd take care of it. When I checked into my room I found everything I could possibly need waiting there for me – a toothbrush, a hairbrush, a bag of make-up and toiletries, an iPhone charger and an oversized Burnouts T-shirt (that's Dylan's old band).

At the party I met all kinds of amazing people, from celebrities to people who work for the charity. I had a chat with a guy called Mark, who is head of PR for the Magical Star Foundation, who was there with his pregnant wife – they seemed like such a happy couple and being around them made me miss Leo more than I had expected to, seeing as how I'm only away for one night. Mark told me that Dylan is such a huge part of the charity – a constant driving force; that's what he called him. He told me not to let Dylan's reputation precede him, and that those who knew him knew he was actually a good guy. Amid the drinking and the constant swearing and the stories of rehab and shagging endless girls, I do see glimmers of normal-human Dylan, rather than rock-star Dylan, and it's nice. I'm sure he'll want his autobiography to be page after page of sexual conquest and nights he doesn't quite remember, but I really want to show his human side.

Earlier, when he was talking about his family – that was real and relatable. To see something genuine in him endeared him to me, and to realise that even rock stars have to deal with family shit that is entirely out of their control made me feel better about my own family.

At the party tonight Dylan was unmistakably drunk, but a sort of weirdly manageable level that he seems to constantly maintain. He didn't seem overly drunk, not really, he just seemed like the charismatic life of the party. He's truly a joy to be around. Everyone within a twenty-foot radius of him at the party had the time of their lives, but I do wonder if it's a coping mechanism for him. Still, I've had an amazing time, and a fair bit to drink myself. Dylan introduced me to everyone, made sure I always had a drink in my hand and we even hit the dance floor together.

Now I'm back in my room – my big, luxurious hotel room, all alone in a bed that could comfortably sleep four of me. There's a great big bath that I'm going to spend some serious time in when I wake up and a TV the size of my bedroom window. I've been living in an unfinished house for so long, I forgot just how amazing it is to be truly comfortable, surrounded by nice things – things that don't smell like paint.

From the lovely, sweet-smelling, soft bed sheets to the room service I just polished off (a cup of tea and a chocolate brownie), I am in heaven. But as I swipe a hand over the large, empty space on the bed next to me, I think of Leo and wish he were here to enjoy the perks of the job with me.

My phone vibrates, snapping me from my thoughts.

'Speak of the devil,' I say, answering the phone to my amazing fiancé. 'I was just thinking about you.'

'Yeah?'

'Yeah, I'm just at the hotel. I'm in bed . . .'

'Oh really, you dirty girl.' He laughs.

'Not like that,' I reply. 'Although . . . where are you?'

'I'm at work,' he tells me. 'On a break. Thought I'd check in, make sure you weren't bored and alone in a hotel.'

Truth be told, I've only been here about thirty minutes. There's no point bragging to Leo about what an awesome night I've had, though – especially when I'm sure he must be missing me as much as I'm missing him.

'I'm fine – don't worry about me,' I assure him. 'That reminds me, what's wrong with your hand?'

'What?'

'Your hand,' I repeat. 'You had a plaster on it last night. I felt it while you were sleeping.'

Leo laughs again. 'Have you been holding my hand while I'm asleep again, Mia?'

'Don't change the subject,' I joke awkwardly.

'I grazed it at work; it's not a big deal. And for the record, I think it's cute that you hold my hand while I'm asleep. Anyway . . .' Leo's tone suddenly changes, which makes me think real manly fireman types have just entered the room, so he needs to keep a lid on the cuteness. 'I'll let you get some sleep in your no doubt big, comfortable bed.'

'And I'll let you get back to work,' I tease. 'Don't hurt yourself again.'

'I'll do my best.' He says before lowering his voice a little. 'Love you.'

'Love you too,' I reply.

I hang up the phone and make myself comfortable in bed. I hate sleeping without Leo. I love having him to cuddle up to and keep me warm at night. Still, this is only temporary and, you never know, if I can get more high-profile ghostwriting jobs and keep making money like this, he could retire sooner rather than later, which will mean less worrying for me and more nights in the same bed. Either way, I get to spend the rest of my life with him and I can't wait.

Chapter 20

'Oh God, I'm in brunch heaven,' I squeak.

Dylan laughs at me. 'I've never seen anyone look at a latte like that before.'

'Well, I gave coffee up a little while ago,' I confess. 'But I've given up giving up now.'

Dylan stabs a sausage with his fork and takes a bite. 'The best time to plant a tree was twenty years ago. The second best time is right now,' he says through a mouthful of food.

'What?'

'If you're not recovering, you're relapsing,' he continues. 'I don't know, they used to say shit like this to us at rehab.'

'It's a cup of coffee, not a crack pipe.' I laugh. 'Are you going to take it off me?'

'Oh, Mia, I wouldn't dare,' he replies, pretending to quiver with fear. 'Plus, I can't say anything, can I?'

I pick up the latte glass and take a theatrical sip. As the hot, sweet vanilla latte warms its way from my lips to my stomach, and that first buzz of caffeine hits my system, I feel alive.

'Oh, such a bad girl,' Dylan teases.

'Buddy, you don't know the half of it,' I reply.

'So, tell me,' he insists, suddenly very interested.

I take another bite of my pancakes with strawberries, banana and maple syrup before responding. My God, this is good. I'd forgotten how much I loved staying in hotels, having expensive meals – especially ones paid for by work.

'All I'm saying is, you might think I'm this boring, engaged writer, but four years ago things were very different. I was living in LA, writing screenplays, hanging out with movie stars, refusing to settle down . . . So, there's hope for you yet,' I tell him.

'Or there's hope for you yet,' he replies. 'Maybe you are a bad girl.'

'*Was.*' I laugh. 'Definitely was. If you'd told me four years ago that this would be my life now, I probably would've thrown myself in the sea. When you meet someone you love, you actually want to change. I mean, you were married once, right?'

'Yeah, we're not talking about that,' he says curtly.

'Dylan, we're writing your autobiography – the story of your life. Your wife and kids are a huge part of it.'

'Leave it, Mia,' he snaps.

Dylan is a womaniser and has been ever since he found fame. He's one of those celebrities who is always romantically linked to someone, but never has a girlfriend. He is every inch the rockstar cliché, so everyone was surprised to learn he was not only getting married, but that his fiancée had twins on the way. This was maybe five years ago, but I remember reading about it at the time because they decided to get divorced almost immediately, adding his name to the list of shortest celebrity marriages. He didn't do as badly as Britney Spears' fifty-five hours, and he even beat Kim Kardashian's seventy-two-day marriage, but they can't have stayed together for more than a few months. Dylan has never publicly opened up about it and, weirdly, neither has his ex, which is just unheard of in these situations, because the media will pay big money for these secrets spilling.

We're sitting in silence. Actual, complete silence now that I think about it. I glance around the dining room to see that we're the only people here.

'It's dead in here,' I say, changing the subject. 'Kind of strange, for such a big hotel.'

'I hired this room for breakfast,' he tells me casually. 'I don't like to be disturbed. Don't look at me like that, like I'm some kind of arsehole, but I can't get through a meal in public without having to take a photo with everyone in the room and sign a million autographs, and I love my fans, but I need to eat.'

'I completely understand that,' I tell him, reaching out to squeeze his hand. I can see the frustration building up inside him. Sometimes, when I look into his eyes, his head looks like a truly dark place to be. I know being famous has its perks, but it must be horrible sometimes.

'Are you coming to the studio with me today?' he asks. 'We can talk on the way and between takes.'

'I can't today, unfortunately. I've got to go and see my mum.'

'How old are you?' he teases, suddenly a little more like his charming, easy-going self. 'So, a day off work, eh?'

'It won't be a day off, trust me,' I tell him. 'My mum is hard work.'

'So take me with you,' he says, straight-faced.

'Some other time.' I laugh, unsure if that was a joke or not.

Dylan grabs his napkin and wipes his mouth. 'OK, well, come over to mine tomorrow.'

'OK,' I reply. 'Thank you for last night – and for breakfast.'

'Never heard a woman say that to me before,' he jokes. 'They don't usually get breakfast.'

I laugh again as I stand up. 'See you tomorrow.'

I slip on my coat, grab my bag and head for the door. I've got an afternoon tea date with my mum, back in Canterbury, so I'd better get a move on. My mum and I don't really have the kind of relationship where we socialise, which makes me think she has summoned me for a talking-to about something or other. Usually when she calls upon me she has a list of things we need to address. But after that I get to go home and spend an evening with my wonderful fiancé, and I can't wait.

Chapter 21

I am one of those people who is almost always late. I try my hardest, I really do, but I'll probably always be the kind of girl yanking up a stocking as she hops down the stairs, slapping on her lippy in the car as she reaches into the deepest depths of her brain for an excuse that will be more believable than the last.

I'm late to meet my mum today – hopefully, if I tell her I've been working, that will be a good enough explanation, but she's always had a real bee in her bonnet about my lateness. If I am here for a ticking-off, I can't think of anything worse than being late.

Dashing in through the doors of Sally's Tearoom, one of my mother's favourite haunts, I scan the room for her angry face. But instead of seeing my mother sitting there, tapping her watch, I am greeted by three moody faces: my mum, my auntie and my gran – the three witches. Legend has it that if they summon you, and you stand before all three of them at the same time, you will be forever cursed.

When I said I couldn't think of anything worse than being late for my mum today, I was wrong. Being late for my mum, my gran and my auntie is the worst thing.

'Hello,' I say breathlessly as I approach the table. 'How goes it?'

'You're late,' the three of them snap, in perfect harmony.

'Fifteen minutes,' I point out. 'You know what trains are like. Actually, you don't. I forget you're all middle-class housewives who have your husbands drive you around.'

Oops, that one didn't go down well. It's true, though. They're currently all full-time homemakers and very much of the opinion that a woman's place is at home, taking care of her husband and kids. It makes me wonder if my sister will do the same when she has her baby.

'We've ordered afternoon tea,' my mum informs me. 'And I just have a few things to go over with you.'

My mum pulls out a piece of paper from her handbag. Oh wow, when I guessed she'd have a list for me, I didn't realise it was going to be a literal list.

We make small talk in the cute little café until the food arrives, my mum obviously figuring she should wait until I've got something sweet to help all the crap she's about to give me go down. The food, which does look delicious, is served on a variety of different plates, in different shapes and sizes, with different patterns.

It takes the waitress several trips to lay out finger sandwiches, scones, cakes and pots of tea.

My mum, auntie and gran load up their dainty little tea plates with sandwiches. I'm still pretty full from brunch, though, and even if I weren't, I didn't exactly have a healthy breakfast this morning – or a healthy evening last night, what with all the free food and alcohol.

'Eat, Mia, eat,' my gran insists.

I smile, pouring myself a cup of tea, but my gran keeps her eyes on me.

'I'm so full from brunch,' I tell her. 'I ate so much.'

My gran purses her lips. 'You're looking very thin, Mia,' she says.

'Thanks,' I reply, even though I know it wasn't intended as a compliment.

'Do you have a problem again?' my auntie asks.

'Did I have a problem *before*?' I laugh.

As far as I know, the only problem I had before, that I still have, is this lot being on my case.

'Ladies, I am perfectly healthy. I don't have a problem. If you want me to eat a cake for the sake of it, I will eat a damn cake,' I say, half amused, half irritated.

I take a fruit tart from the centre of the table and stab a strawberry from the top.

'Mmm,' I moan theatrically. 'Delicious.'

My mum glares at me as she stirs her tea. I must be showing her up again.

'OK, Mia, first order of business: Christmas,' my mum starts.

Oh God, I know we're days away from December, but I think I'd blocked out all thoughts of Christmas. I loved my Christmas Days in LA, because I didn't really realise it was Christmas. It was just like having a really chilled day off work. Now I'm back home, Christmas is a family affair again. With most of Leo's family living in Italy, he and his mum have celebrated with us the last few years, so I don't even have an escape there.

'So, first of all, the family Christmas party—'

'Oh God,' I moan, sounding more like a teenager than a thirty-something. 'I might be working this year.'

'If you loved me, you'd make sure you could be there,' she replies.

'Well . . .' I say, implying I could take or leave her, just like I could take or leave the party. My mum isn't amused. 'I'm kidding, I'm kidding. I'll be there.'

Every year we have a big Christmas party for all our family and friends. It's a nice idea, I suppose, but not really my sort of thing. I hate these forced-fun family events my lot throw because they think they're supposed to.

'Next,' I say, as I continue to pick at my tart. It's delicious, so it's not exactly a hardship.

'Christmas Day,' my mum continues, as instructed. 'We're

thinking a big family Christmas dinner, with everyone there. I'll keep you posted on the details as I assume you'll be attending.'

'Consider this miserable look on my face my RSVP,' I joke.

'Next,' my mum carries on, ignoring my hilarious comment.

'Next?' I ask. 'We're not pencilling in Easter already, are we?'

'Next, your wedding,' my mum continues.

'That's after Easter,' I point out, suddenly uncomfortable and lacking in witty remarks.

'Is it?' my mum asks. 'Because you haven't made a single arrangement. Are you even trying?'

'I *am* trying,' I insist.

'How do you think this is making Leo feel?' my gran asks.

'He knows I'm busy,' I tell them, not that it's any of their business.

'So this is all because you don't have the time?' my mum asks.

'Yes!' I squeak. 'I love Leo, and I said yes, didn't I?'

'OK,' my mum says softly. 'But you forget that we remember the old Mia, the one who told us she'd never get married. The one who insisted we spend your wedding fund on Belle's wedding because you'd never need it.'

That definitely didn't happen – me insisting, I mean. They definitely spent my half of the wedding fund on Belle's wedding.

'But if you really are just too busy, I have a solution for you. And a present,' my mum says brightly.

'Oh?'

Why don't I like the sound of this?

'Do you remember Mrs Turner?' my mum asks. Oh God, it's like Groundhog Day.

'Yes,' I say, getting the answer right this time. 'Purple hair, lived near Gran and Grandad, her husband used to go around picking up literal shit from the ground.'

That's about as much as I remember.

My mother winces at my language. 'Well her daughter, Deborah . . .' Oh God, yes, I remember now. Deborah the wedding planner.

'She's a wedding planner, so I've hired her to help you sort this wedding business out.'

'Honestly, I don't need a wedding planner,' I insist.

'Well, I've already paid her and given her your number, so she'll be in touch. Don't throw kindness in my face, Mia.'

I'd much rather throw this jug of milk, the way I'm feeling right now.

I exhale and recompose myself.

'You're quiet today,' I say to Auntie June. 'Silent, in fact.'

My auntie pushes her plate away from her in some kind of strop. Why do I get the feeling I've upset her without realising it?

'I can't even look at you, Mia. Not after what you've done,' she says.

I mean, I could have done any number of things to make her this angry. This could be because I said shit three minutes ago, or because I keep taking the Lord's name in vain, or it could just be because I'm breathing.

'Fine, I'll bite. What have I done?' I ask.

'Last night we had a family dinner,' she starts.

'Oh, what did you make?' my gran asks.

'Chicken chasseur, in the slow cooker,' she replies. 'And an apple tart for dessert – Steve loves a tart.'

I open my mouth to make the obvious joke but my mum stops me.

'Mia,' she snaps.

'We had a lovely dinner and after we all gathered in the family room to watch a film. I sat my sweet little Angel on my lap and stroked her hair as we watched. Hannah had taken her for an interesting haircut the day before. She'd got this big fringe that just looked out of place on a child, and Hannah couldn't for the life of her remember where she'd taken her for it.'

Crap. I know where this is going.

'So I brushed it from her eyes, so she could see, and underneath I found the remnants of her previous fringe – chopped off. And do you know where little Angel says she got this new haircut? Mia's house.'

'What?' my mum says as my gran gasps dramatically. It's so like June, to drop a story like this in front of everyone for maximum effect.

'She found some scissors, she cut her hair, I helped fix it. No harm done,' I reason.

'Mia, you shouldn't have scissors lying around when you're babysitting,' my mum points out.

'I'm sorry, I thought they were on a higher shelf, with my bong,' I joke. 'And it was kind of a last-minute thing, so Hannah could go . . . out.'

I don't mention that she had a date, just in case she hasn't told her mum.

'And I think she looks adorable with her fringe,' I insist. She does – she looks cute as hell.

'God help the children you have,' my auntie says. 'Assuming you can.'

Not quite sure what she's getting at there – whether she's suggesting I might not be able to bring myself to do it or assuming I won't be able to get my organs to work after years of loose nights out or something else offensive. I'd roll my eyes if the ladies weren't all staring at me.

'Well, my hairdresser thought I was pregnant the other day, so she has faith in me.' I laugh.

'What?' my mum asks.

'Nothing,' I reply. 'It's a joke.'

'Don't make any of your weird jokes to Deborah, please,' my mum insists. 'And no mention of her dad picking up dog mess.'

'It was literally at the top of my list of things to discuss with her,' I say sarcastically. 'But all right. Am I OK to get going now?'

'Certainly,' my mum replies. 'Are you spending the night with your fiancé tonight?'

'Yes,' I reply, and I can't wait. Get me out of here.

Chapter 22

I'm never really sure at which point in our relationship I moved in with Leo. I'd be tempted to say it happened gradually, but on the other hand, it sort of happened all at once.

I think my family were excited when I told them I was moving back to the UK, but I think they thought that, along with coming back, I'd be going back to how life was before I left home, with me silently going with the flow, happily invisible. So they found me a flat – a small one above a chippy – and committed me to six months' rent. In LA I rented a place in the Hollywood Hills – a bachelor pad, previously rented by a movie star. Inside, it was amazing, but the view outside was even better. It was so modern, so stylish and so hi-tech.

On the day I moved into my tiny flat, Leo came to help me get set up and the look on his face when he stepped inside is one I will never forget. This was a man who hadn't seen where I lived previously, and even he thought the new place was awful. It turned out that one of my dad's friends was looking to rent the place out while he was away, and by telling him I'd take it, my dad thought he was doing us both a favour. He had described the place to my dad as 'Tardis-like' – a euphemism I wasn't quite nerdy enough to understand. My dad assured me that his friend said the place had 'star quality' – what he didn't mention was that it was one-star quality. Its 'star quality' appeared to have exploded, leaving me living in a black hole.

I know I was used to the finer things in life. It wasn't vital that I lived somewhere I could match the lighting to my mood . . . but at least somewhere a little bit more modern, with a little bit more space – then maybe I would have had a chance at being happy there. My flat wasn't like a Tardis, it was like a weird little time machine that gave me a glimpse of what life was like forty years ago every time I stepped inside. The rooms were all furnished with garishly patterned Seventies artefacts and had an unidentifiable (but most definitely unpleasant) smell that no amount of air freshener or burning scented candles could mask. The only time I'd get any relief (for lack of a better term) from the weird pong came each evening, when the smell of greasy chips would drift in through the tiny windows, making my furniture, my clothes and my hair smell like fried food. Every time I returned to the flat after going out, I could feel myself becoming more accepting of the smell. It's not that it was getting any less strong, just that I was adapting to it, and it made me die a little inside whenever I realised this.

I could tell, on that first day I moved in, that Leo didn't want to leave me there, but this was four years ago, when the idea of a committed relationship was a new one to me, and I think he knew better than to suggest I stay with him instead. So we started dating, just casually, seeing how things went, and when things were clearly going well I started staying over at his every now and then. We'd go out on a date or stay in his flat and watch a movie. I'd sleep over and then the next day I'd leave at the same time as Leo left for work.

I remember waking up one morning to see him getting ready for work. It was cold and dark and I could hear the rain battering the ground outside – the last thing I wanted was to get up and go back to my own cold, tiny flat. I went to get up but Leo stopped me, tucking me back into his bed with a kiss on the forehead.

'Don't get up,' he told me. 'Stay for as long as you like.'

I never left.

Tonight I'm cuddled up on the sofa with Leo, watching a movie. It's nice to spend time with him because, between our jobs, it's getting harder and harder to make time for each other. Things were certainly easier when we planned our lives around his job. Still, as soon as I'm done with Dylan, I'll just be writing at home again and we can go back to how things were. It will be easy for our day-to-day life, but I've got to admit, I'll miss having something that gets me out of the house.

'I've missed you,' I tell him.

Leo gives me a squeeze. 'I've missed you too,' he replies. 'Oh, I was thinking about the wedding today.'

'Oh yeah?' I ask.

'Yeah. Amy at work is getting married in a few months and she was talking about how much trouble she's having finding dahlias for a January wedding.'

'Oh really?' I reply.

'Yeah. Dahlias are flowers,' he tells me, realising I have no idea what a dahlia is. 'They're her favourite flower but they're out of season at that time. Anyway, I realised I don't know what your favourite flower is . . .'

'Hmm,' I reply.

'Are you mad at me?' he asks, unsure how to take my response.

'No, of course not,' I tell him. 'I just didn't realise I was supposed to have a favourite flower.'

'You're not *supposed* to.' He laughs. 'What did you have in mind for the wedding flowers?'

Flowers hadn't really crossed my mind. They seem like kind of a waste of money – what, £500? £1,000? On something that will be dead in a day or two. I could happily give the flowers a miss – are you allowed to do that?

'I'm not sure yet,' I tell him. 'But we're meeting Deborah

tomorrow, so we can see what she thinks is good for the time of year.'

'That was nice of your mum, to hire you a wedding planner,' he says.

Maybe it was nice of her, or maybe it was just her way of making sure I cracked on with the planning. Everyone seems to think I'm incapable of doing it.

'Yeah,' I say in agreement.

Leo laughs. 'Mia, I've told you a million times, I can tell when you're lying. Your voice goes much higher.'

'No, it is nice of her,' I agree. Whatever her motivation, she's just trying to make sure the wedding goes well and I appreciate that.

'Are you excited yet? Or is it too soon?' he asks.

'I'm excited to be your wife,' I reply.

'I'm excited for that as well,' he replies, giving me a squeeze. 'Man, I'm tired. Shall we get in bed?'

'Sure,' I reply. 'You head up; I'll just move these cups.'

'Love you,' he sings as he heads up the stairs.

'Love you too,' I call after him.

I lie back on the sofa and stare at the ceiling. Something has just hit me: I am not excited about this wedding at all.

Chapter 23

This morning I met Debbie Turner, daughter of Mrs Turner with the purple hair and Mr Turner who picks up dog shit, wedding planner extraordinaire.

Supposedly Debbie and I have met before, and she claims she remembers me, but I don't remember her. She's a tall, slim woman with wild hair – dark-brown, crispy-looking curls that I wouldn't like to try and run a brush through.

We started off having a catch-up, with Debbie telling us all about her kids, how well they're doing at private school and a comprehensive list of all their sporting achievements to date. Most impressive. But then, as she ran us through the list of things we'll need to consider for our big day, she asked a question I didn't have an answer for: what was our wedding budget? The truth is that we haven't really talked about that yet. Sure, we have more spare money since I took this job, but it's not like I'm getting a regular salary. This is a one-time payment, and when the money from this job runs out, I don't know for sure that I'll have another to replenish the money with.

Even though I made good money writing movies, between my extortionate rent and my lavish lifestyle, my outgoings were high. It was fine at the time, because I'd finish one movie and get to work on another, so the money was always coming in, but when I lost my job and moved back here, without an income, I began blazing through my savings quite quickly. If I'd thought there was even the slightest chance I could've lost that job, I would've been more careful. It just goes to show, you should never feel truly safe and secure anywhere. Always have a backup plan.

The biggest shock of the morning came when Debbie told us how much the average couple spends on their wedding. She reckons £30,000 on average, including the honeymoon. Thirty-fucking-thousand pounds. On one event. That's, like, a year's salary for some people – *who are doing well*. I've spent lots of money on things in the past, but I've only really spent money on big things that hold their value.

'It will be the most stupendous day of your life, though,' Debbie explained to me, in an attempt to retrieve my jaw from the floor.

Leo whistled at the price in disbelief, but quickly added that, no matter how much it was going to cost, it would be worth it. Very sweet of him to say so, but we could do so much with £30k – think of the things we could do to the house with that money.

Debbie had arrived to meet us all sickly sweet, but then, as soon as she realised I wasn't your typical blushing bride, I could see her enthusiasm draining by the second. I think I put the final nail in our relationship coffin when we were saying goodbye and she asked if we had any questions.

'Why do they call the meal a wedding breakfast when it's almost always in the afternoon?' I asked. It turns out she meant did we have any questions relating to our wedding plans, and not did I have any childish curiosities. Debbie said she would make some appointments for me to attend to try to work out what I wanted, and we left it at that.

Now I'm back in London, back at Dylan's house, back to my wedding-free safe space.

'You look stressed,' Dylan points out.

'You look . . . drunk,' I reply.

'Very perceptive.' He laughs.

I know I don't know him very well, and that I'm just here to work for him, but if we were friends, I'd ask him about his drinking. I know he's a rock star, but he's drunk way too often.

'I met with a wedding planner today,' I tell him. 'She was one of the most annoying people I've ever met. Everything is "stupendous" and her enthusiasm for wedding stationery was, frankly, troubling to me. How could someone get so excited about embossed lettering on invitations?'

Dylan laughs again.

'Did you have anything to do with planning your wedding?' I ask. It's a cheap technique, and I'm relying on the booze to open him up a little, but I need to get him talking about his marriage at some point.

'I ain't talking about it,' he says, grabbing a beer from the fridge before heading back to the living room. I grab my Dictaphone and follow him.

'Tell me a random tour story,' I insist. 'Let's get things flowing.'

'Just need to figure out one that I remember,' Dylan jokes, plonking himself down on the sofa. He makes himself comfortable for a second before sitting back up and patting the sofa next to him. 'Sit here.'

I take a seat next to him, placing the Dictaphone down on the coffee table in front of us.

'I don't like that thing, man. It makes me think I'm talking to a journalist. Journalists don't treat me like a human, I'm nothing but a source of money to them. If they can trick me into saying something stupid they win the lottery. Sometimes I just want to feel normal. Like, Mitch and my publicist are next door in my office having a meeting about me at the moment. I'm never alone.'

'OK, so we'll ditch the Dictaphone,' I say, in an attempt to make him feel more comfortable. 'We'll just talk and I can write things down later. That'll be much more relaxing, right?'

Dylan nods. 'OK, so this is a story no one knows,' he starts, swigging his beer. 'In fact, maybe don't put this one in the book. We're just chatting.'

'OK, sure,' I reply. I kick off my shoes and pull my feet up onto the sofa, like a child ready for story time.

'So this is a long time ago, man. We're on the tour bus, on the way back from Glasgow, I think, and there's me, Mikey, Taz, our drummer and Kelly, who used to be our bassist. Well, his name was Jamie, but we called him Kelly because he looked like Kelly Osbourne did in 2002, with his black and pink spiky hair. Then we had Mitch, our driver, dunno his name, and my buddy Nicole who used to tour with us sometimes. So it's late, it's winter – I dunno what year it was, but it was when we had those crazy snowstorms, remember?'

I nod. I don't remember at all, though. I was probably sunning myself in LA at the time.

'So we break down in the middle of nowhere. It's the middle of the night, the bus is fucked, there's no heating or nothing. Driver tells us we passed a sign for a town. Lundsgill, or something like that. So, I drop a post on the socials like "All right, we're stranded in Lundsgill. Anyone wanna help us out?" and my phone blows up like it always does. But as I'm scanning the replies, there's this one girl who goes: "I live here, you can come stay with me." So, great, we're in there; *I'm* in there, and it's all going to be fine. So she DMs me where she lives and we turn up there, and she lives on some farm with her family, and she looks nothing like her profile picture, not even close, man. But her parents are friendly and they've got all these spare rooms so we decide it's best to stay there – the whole country is at a standstill pretty much, so it's here or the freezing-cold tour bus that's broken down in the middle of a long, lonely road.'

'Shit,' I blurt, hugging my legs. 'What happened next?'

'So this fan, she's, like, in love with me, but she's young and she's not my type . . .' Nice priorities, Dylan. 'So I ask my buddy Nicole to pretend to be my girlfriend, thinking she can share a room with me and this chick will leave me alone, but her parents are old-fashioned and poor Nic has to room-share with this fan – she said there were pictures of me all over the walls, one with a lipstick kiss on. Like, it's funny until you're snowed in there, right?'

I nod, completely captivated.

'Next morning the dad wakes us up early, gives us all farm duties. Says we've gotta pay our way; it's only fair – weird as shit, man. So later in the day, the wife cooks. We're all eating when we realise Kelly has vanished. And I'm thinking, we're staying on this farm where they make meat, but you don't see no animals, and I've taken a little something to take the edge off, so I'm tripping big time and I figure they've killed Kelly and we're eating him . . .'

My jaw drops so hard, I hear a pop in my ears. 'You thought you were eating your bassist?'

'Well, he was the biggest, so if you were gonna eat one of us . . .' He laughs. 'So I tell everyone and they think I'm just off my face, but they don't wanna risk it, so we wait until it gets dark and we sneak out – we were badass, sneaking out of this farm unnoticed, but I'm motivated by fear for my life. I've never been so fucking scared. So we make it to the bus, get on and there's Kelly, asleep under a pile of clothes. Lazy git just didn't want to do any work. The weather was much better by morning, and I guess someone from the label sent 4x4s for us to get us home safe. Weird twenty-four hours, though.'

I blink a few times. My God, why did I agree to turn my Dictaphone off?!

'That's . . . I don't even know what that is,' I reply.

'It feels good to tell someone,' he replies. 'What else do you wanna know?'

Chapter 24

The past week or so has been a bit of a blur, what with me dashing back and forth between Canterbury and London, trying to spend as much time with Leo as possible in between meetings with Dylan and long planning sessions to get this book finished ASAP. Then, of course, there's all the time I'm spending avoiding Debbie, the wedding planner from hell. The woman has no chill whatsoever. Worse still, she doesn't respect my wishes or my taste at all. She's constantly trying to force things she thinks we should have, like an extortionately priced, handcrafted white chocolate unicorn sculpture. In August. Is she high? You don't need to be a scientist to figure out what's going to happen there.

Not only is working with Dylan a great way for me to hide from Debbie, but it's giving me a taste of a life I never thought I'd get to live again. I've been following him to gigs, TV appearances, parties – all of which are full of fabulous people and free food and drink.

Today is a break from writing and from working on the house, and we're gathering at my gran and granddad's house for Sunday dinner. Leo and I are the first to arrive, which will hopefully score me some brownie points with my gran – unless we're too early.

Leo is making small talk with my gran, so I sneak out into

the back garden to see my granddad, who is hiding in his shed.

'Now then, kid,' he says as I walk in.

I squeeze him and give him a kiss on the top of the head before sitting down next to him.

'Look at all these plants,' I say sarcastically.

'It's winter, kid. And I'm only out here to listen to the radio in peace.'

'Your secret is safe with me,' I tell him. 'How are you?'

'Not too bad,' he replies. 'The legs aren't so good today; I just can't make them go.'

I rub his shoulder. 'I'm not enduring Sunday dinner without you, even if I have to carry you in,' I joke.

He laughs. 'How's the new job going?'

'Ah, it's great,' I reply.

'Glad to hear it,' he replies. 'Kind of makes it OK that we've hardly seen you.'

'We need to get you a phone,' I say, taking my iPhone from my pocket. 'There's this thing called Facebook – I'll show you – we could call and chat.'

I can't be showing as online for more than a few seconds before a call starts coming through.

'Oh shit,' I blurt. 'It's my old boss.'

'Oh?'

'I'd better answer,' I say. 'Hello?'

'Mia Valentina, long time no speak,' Skinner says cheerfully.

Skinner was my boss at Pink Inc., the screenwriting team I was a part of back when I worked in LA.

'I know,' I reply. 'We haven't spoken since you fired me because I wouldn't leave my sister's wedding to work.'

I hear my granddad snigger quietly.

'Possibly,' Skinner replies casually. 'How have you been? I hear you write books now?'

'Yeah, great, and I do. It's all going well, thanks, really enjoying it, getting lots of good reviews.'

'I don't doubt you're good,' Skinner replies. 'But you were awesome at writing movies.'

I was, which is why it's such a shame that *he fired me*.

'Listen, I've been trying to get in touch with you for days and this was all I had. Do you know what time it is here? But I figured I wanna catch you online; I gotta think like I'm in a different time zone.'

'Right,' I reply. 'So, what's up?'

'Remember *The Unhappy Couple*?' he asks.

'Remember it? I won an award for it,' I remind him.

'A well-deserved award,' he says. 'The powers that be want a sequel – *The Unhappy Marriage* – and, well, they want the same writers to do the screenplay, and Molly got married, then pregnant, then quit – who saw that one coming? And Savannah is being real choosey about who she'll work with, but she's too stressed to do it alone . . . Bottom line, we want you back.'

'You want me back?' I repeat. 'Like, you want to give me my old job back?'

'Yeah,' he replies. 'I'm not happy about the way we ended things and, of course, you would be coming back to a better package than you had before.'

I don't think Skinner feels bad for sacking me at all, but I think he needs me now and that puts me in a very powerful position. Not only would getting my old job back mean more money, more fabulous parties and more time in sunny LA, but I'd be doing a job I loved, that I was really fucking good at. It always has been and always will be my dream job. I can't believe I'm getting a second chance.

But then I remember Leo and our house and our life here. There's no way he'd want to leave his family – even if he said he would – and I wouldn't want to go without him, even if it was for just one project. We sure could use the money, though, and I could do the right things with it this time.

I know I'm still writing, but there's no way I could ever be as successful writing books as I was writing movies. I'm just not sure writing movies fits in with my new life. Money and success, or love? Surely it's a no-brainer.

'I'll give you some time to think about it,' he offers.

'OK,' I reply. 'Thank you.'

'I just got offered my old job back,' I tell my granddad after the call ends.

'Kid, that's brilliant. Congratulations. Are you going to accept?'

'I'd be lying if I said I didn't miss it, and that I didn't need the money . . . but Leo wouldn't want to move, and whether he agreed to, even though he didn't want to, or whether he suggested I go alone for a few months . . . it just wouldn't be fair.'

'That's very considerate of you, kid. I'm proud of you. I guess it would throw the wedding off too, hey?'

'Yeah,' I reply. I hadn't thought of that.

'I hear your gran on the phone to your mum, talking about the wedding,' he starts. 'I think they're worried you're not actually going to get married.'

'It's because I haven't made any real plans yet,' I tell him. 'I'm going to; I'm just so busy.'

'You sure?' he asks me.

My granddad, as always, can tell when something isn't right.

'I . . . I don't know what's wrong with me,' I admit. 'But I meet with Debbie and I look at all the different options and I don't want any of it. It just fills me with this feeling of . . .'

'Nothing is worth you getting anxious again, kid.'

When I was a teen I was anxious almost all the time and, at one point, it really got on top of me. I was bullied at school for being bigger – amazing, isn't it, that the biggest crime you can commit as far as your peers are concerned is to be 'not thin'. Living your life as a bigger teenage girl is one of the hardest things you can do – I know it may seem like a very first-world problem, but you can't even imagine what it's like. The thing that always amazed me was just how many people would tell me I was fat, as though I didn't realise. Kids at school would tell me, people would shout it from passing cars – even my PE teacher would yell it at me as I failed my sixteenth attempt at the high jump. Ah, the high jump, the highest of academic achievements.

Your weight should have no bearing on your worth as a person whatsoever, but it does, and so back then, no one gave me the time of day. It got me down and soon enough my low mood turned into anxiety – *about everything*. It was a really awful time where I struggled from one panic attack to the next, and although I got through it, you never really get past it. It still rears its ugly head every now and then, if I'm especially stressed, and that's what my granddad is worried about.

'I'm OK,' I promise. 'I'm sure I'll get into the swing of it soon – it's my first wedding.' I laugh.

'And hopefully your last.' My granddad smiles.

'In the spirit of that sentiment, let's not mention this job offer to Leo,' I suggest. 'I don't want to put him in a difficult position.'

'Sure,' my granddad replies. 'Pass me my stick, will you?'

I hand my granddad his walking stick and watch helplessly as he struggles to pull himself to his feet.

'I just can't make my legs go,' he tells me, shaking his head. 'Few Yorkshire puddings will see me right.'

I smile. It's so like my granddad to be so positive when he's feeling so bad. I offer him my arm to help him back into the house where hopefully dinner is ready.

The thing I love about my grandparents' house is that – even though I'm sure it has – I don't feel like it has changed a bit over the course of my life. I used to spend a lot of time here when I was a kid, and all the things that make me think of back then are still present today. My gran still has a bowl of ornamental soaps in her bathroom, shaped like a variety of things, from fruits to seashells. I used to love playing with them when I was a kid, although I learned from a very early age that we didn't use these soaps to wash hands. I'm not sure if the ones there today are the same ones, or just similar.

However, it was the large glass cabinet in the dining room, full of crystal figurines, that I always so desperately wanted to play with, but was never allowed to touch. Perfect, sparkling little swans, rabbits, cats and all sorts of animals made of perfectly clear crystal that beamed a rainbow of colours when the sunlight shone through the dining-room window of an evening. Even today, as we sit and eat dinner, despite being a grown woman, those little figurines will tease me, their bright little colours catching my eye, still making me want to touch them, just once . . .

'How are the plants coming along?' my gran ask. As she fills a pan with water, the pipes in the kitchen make a weird noise. It's like a sort of clunking, gurgling sound.

'Pardon me,' my granddad jokes.

My gran rolls her eyes at his toilet humour. 'Your plants, Jack, how are they coming along?'

'Coming along nicely,' my granddad replies, giving Leo and me a sneaky wink.

I wonder if this will be Leo, in fifty years' time, telling little white lies to get a break from me. Breaks are all we seem to be getting from each other at the moment, and even when we are together, we're summoned to things like this.

I feel guilty, not telling Leo about my job offer, but what would be the point? It would put him in an unwinnable situation and I wouldn't want to do that to him. I'll just wait for Skinner to call back and tell him I don't want the job. It will be hard, because I don't just miss the job and the money. *The Unhappy Couple* was my baby and, since he mentioned the idea of a sequel, my head has been buzzing with exciting ideas. Things have changed, though. I have a different life now, with different responsibilities. I know Leo would never hold me back, and maybe he'd be willing to move to LA with me – he suggested this once before, before we even properly got together – but I know family is his life, and even if he were willing to do it, he'd be making a huge sacrifice.

Sometimes I worry that we want different things from life, like I take my happiness from my career but Leo takes his from his family and friends – then again, he doesn't have a family like mine. The bottom line is that I love him and, when I moved here to make us both happy, I never mentioned the possibility of moving back to LA one day.

I can't just take off to LA for a few months to write a movie . . . not without creating an unhappy couple all of my own.

Chapter 25

As I approach the children's ward, I cancel Debbie's fifth call today and turn my phone off – well, you have to turn your phone off in hospitals, don't you? She's trying to pin me down for some appointments but I'm trying to put wedding planning off until after Christmas. The plan is to finish up with Dylan before Christmas, then start writing the book in the New Year and get that finished ASAP too. Life would be so much easier now if I didn't have wedding planning to try and squash into the mix as well.

I'm currently being ushered through the children's ward by Mark Wright, head of PR for the Magical Star Foundation. Dylan is already in there visiting the kids and Mark has very kindly agreed to let me join him.

Mark is a handsome fellow. He's got these kind eyes that focus on you when he talks to you, making you feel important, like you have his full attention. It isn't just the way he listens to every word you say attentively, but the passion he throws into his own words . . . You can tell he really cares about his job, and you can tell that he really appreciates everything Dylan does here.

'You seem like you have a good relationship with Dylan,' Mark says, holding a door open for me. 'That's good, you know, for writing the book.'

'I think we do,' I reply. I'm never sure. It's all or nothing with Dylan. He's either completely human or a complete arsehole. Sometimes I feel sorry for him, and sometimes I want to slap him.

'He doesn't let many people in,' Mark explains. 'I worked with him for years before he considered me a friend. He seems to like you a lot, which is good for the book. No one ever writes warmly about him. Everyone focuses on the negative things. Look at all the work he does here, and yet the likes of the *Daily Scoop* would rather report on his sexploits than the life-changing work he does.'

It means a lot to me that Dylan likes me and trusts me. I imagine being so famous means he constantly has people sucking up to him, so that must be why he appreciates absolute honestly and people around him who won't pander to him.

'I'm doing my best.' I smile.

Mark ushers me into the relatives' room, where Mitch and another man are sitting.

'Hello, Mia,' Mitch says cheerily. 'Have you met Charles yet?'

'I haven't,' I say, offering him my hand to shake. 'Mia Valentina.'

'Charles Pace,' he replies. 'I'm Dylan's publicist.'

'Oh, I'm sorry,' I reply sympathetically.

Charles laughs. 'It's a tough job, but someone has to do it. I hear you're writing his autobiography?'

I nod.

'Then you have my condolences too,' Charles jokes.

Charles isn't especially tall, but he has broad, masculine shoulders. He's wearing a smart, blue suit that doesn't look like it came off the rack and his short blond hair appears effortlessly messy, although I suspect it took an expensive haircut and a lot of product to achieve that look.

'So, today, Dylan is just having a chat with the kids. We've got Santa out there too, handing out presents. Someone will be along to take pictures soon,' Mitch explains. 'You're welcome to go and join him for a bit, get a feel for his charity work.'

'Thanks,' I reply.

'This way,' Marks says. 'I'll show you to the day room.'

The day room looks like a paradise for kids, with the brightly coloured walls, a big TV, toys everywhere and Dylan and Santa in the middle, surrounded by happy kids who probably don't know which one of them is the bigger deal. But then you look closer and you see how unwell some of the kids look. You see the wheelchairs and the oxygen tubes. You see the hair loss and the scars. You see almost everything that is awful about the world inflicted on those who are most helpless, and yet somehow they are able to smile and laugh at Dylan pulling faces behind Santa's back. I have been in this room less than a minute and I already feel humbled. It's easy to think that we have problems, that our lives are a mess, that we have it tougher than others . . . but we don't have this to contend with. I can't even imagine being a kid and trying to deal with something like this, nor could I imagine, if I had my own children, watching them suffer.

My mind suddenly jolts back to my conversation with Leo about having kids. How could someone like me be responsible for a small human? And if something like this were to happen, and they really needed me, could I ever be strong enough to help them through it? I can't even help myself through the day sometimes.

'Mia,' Dylan calls out.

'Hello,' I say, approaching Dylan. 'Who's your friend?'

Dylan is sitting with the cutest little girl. She's got bright eyes and the cheekiest little smile that she's hiding shyly behind a teddy bear. It's heartbreaking, to see such a happy little girl looking so weak.

'This is Lily,' Dylan tells me, holding her hand. 'She's only six, but she wants me to be her boyfriend. I keep telling her that she's too good for me.'

'Hello, Lily.' I smile. 'Dylan is right. You're way too young and pretty for an old man like him.'

Dylan frowns at me for calling him an old man. He seems very sensitive about his age for someone in his thirties.

'We're best friends, though, aren't we, Lily?' Dylan says.

Lily nods, still hiding behind her teddy. You can tell she adores Dylan by the way she's staring at him, and you can tell he really cares about her too.

'Listen, Lily, I'm going to introduce Mia to some of your friends. Is that OK? And when I come back, I'll see if Santa has another present for you.'

Lily nods excitedly.

'So, how are you?' Dylan asks me, ushering me across the room.

I cock my head. He seems different today.

'I'm good, thanks. How are you?'

'Yeah, not bad,' he replies. 'Santa just told me I'm on his nice list this year, so I have that to look forward to.'

I laugh.

'This is my main man, Naoki,' Dylan says, offering out his hand for a fist bump. Naoki obliges. 'Naoki, this is Mia. She's writing a book about me.'

'Hi, Mia,' Naoki says, offering me a fist to bump too. Why do I get the feeling Dylan taught him this?

'So, Naoki has problems with his . . .' Dylan pauses for a second. 'It's no good, I'm too thick to remember.'

Naoki laughs. 'My heart,' Naoki, who can't be more than eight, replies with a giggle.

'Man, I thought it was your feet – it's a good job I'm not a doctor. They do let me wear this white coat, though, so I can impress girls. Tell Mia what we think about your heart problem.'

'Is sucks, man,' he replies, sounding like a mini Dylan.

'Yeah, man, it sucks,' Dylan repeats back to him, holding Naoki in the most delicate of headlocks. 'Naoki thinks he's cooler than I am because he has a girlfriend and I don't.'

'You could be his girlfriend,' Naoki tells me.

I open my mouth to speak, but no words come out.

'Naah,' Dylan starts. 'Mia is getting married – to a fireman.'

'Cool,' Naoki gushes.

'I reckon I could take him in a fight, though,' Dylan assures his friend.

'Dylan, the photographer is here,' Mitch says, interrupting.

'I'll go wait in the relatives' room,' I say.

'OK, I'll be with you soon,' Dylan replies.

I walk back into the room just as Santa is putting his beard back on, ready to go back out there.

'Oh my God, you're not real?' I gasp.

'I work for the real one,' the man pretending to be Santa assures me as he walks past me, giving me a cheeky wink. 'The real guy can't be everywhere at once.'

'Phew,' I reply theatrically, taking a seat on the sofa.

Everyone else is busy, so I'm just sitting here on my own.

Dylan is simply amazing with these children. The way he has a special friendship with each kid, the way he makes them forget about their problems when he's in the room – you can tell he really, really cares.

I don't know much about Dylan's own kids. I know that, during his very short marriage, his wife had twins, but after they split up – and I only have the press reports to go on – Dylan stopped having anything to do with his ex-wife *and* his kids. It amazes me, that someone who clearly loves kids so much could be so uninvolved with the lives of his own flesh and blood. His twin daughters must be five years old now, a similar age to some of the kids here. He must think about them, but he refuses to talk about them. I know he finds it hard, talking about his family, but no publisher in the world is going to pay him – or me – to write an autobiography that glosses over the tough stuff that people actually want to read about. No one cares how many birds he shagged in one night. People want to read about the real human behind the music, and about this Dylan, who I've met today. I didn't realise he was doing so much for good causes with his status and his money. I thought he was just another rock star, drinking too much and sleeping with anything that moved.

It's heartbreaking, to see what these kids are going through first-hand, but it's amazing to see the hospital, their families, the charity and Dylan all doing everything they can to make their lives better, to make sure these kids are as happy as possible. I know it must be scary, to have kids, knowing you're going to have to protect them from so much, but I'm starting to understand why people do it, and with support like this around, surely anyone can get through anything? Seeing Dylan with these kids, it kind of makes me think that maybe I do want my own someday, so I can give this unique kind of love to something so precious. That wouldn't be so bad, would it?

I don't have to sit for long before Dylan walks in, carrying two cups of coffee.

'Here you go,' he says, placing a mug down on the table in front of me.

Dylan takes a seat next to me, exhaling deeply, like he's been holding it in for hours. He picks up a wooden abacus from the toy box on the floor and fidgets with it as we chat.

'You OK?' he asks.

'Yes,' I reply.

'Good,' he says. 'I know it's tough out there.'

'It's heartbreaking,' I correct him. 'I don't know how you do it, keeping so bright, making those kids so happy.'

'Naoki, the little badass, has had three heart attacks. *Three*, Mia. And look at him, still going strong, still loving his life. This hospital is amazing, man, the things they do for these kids and their families, and so much of it thanks to Magical Star.'

'It's amazing what they do, but it's amazing what you do too. Lily is clearly in love with you.'

'Yeah.' Dylan coughs in an attempt to clear his throat. 'Lily is amazing. I'm giving her family some money, to take her to Disney World if she's well enough. Off the record, no one needs to know it's from me.'

'Dill, that's amazing.' I beam. 'I'm sure that will mean so much to her.'

'She's such a sweet little thing,' he says. 'She's shy, but she talks to me. She tells me about what she wants to be when she grows up and . . .'

I wrap an arm around Dylan to comfort him. I can tell he's upset, even though he's doing his best to hide it.

'It's OK,' I assure him.

'The truth is, she isn't going to grow up. She's too sick and there's nothing anyone can do. I can't get my head around it.'

Dylan – a mixture of upset, angry and frustrated – quickly changes the subject.

'You called me Dill,' he says.

'Oh, sorry,' I reply. 'Don't you like that?'

'No, I do,' he tells me. 'Someone I used to care about very much used to call me Dill.'

I smile and suddenly I realise something. I know what's different about Dylan today: he's sober. I mean, he's visiting children in hospital, so you would hope so, right? But even so . . . it's nice to meet sober Dylan.

'Can I just say something?'

Dylan nods, looking at me with his sad, dark eyes.

'I know you're a bit of a dick sometimes,' I start, raising my hand to halt his almost immediate interruption in protest of my character analysis of him. '*But* I know you're a good person, deep down, underneath the bravado and the bullshit.'

'Well, thanks, I suppose.' He laughs. 'You're not so bad yourself. I really hope we stay in touch after the book is done.'

'Me too,' I reply.

Chapter 26

Sitting alone in my living room, I glare at my phone, hoping both the courage and the words I need will find me so that I can dial.

Nope, I'm not ready yet.

Perhaps I could move some of these boxes, so that we can decorate the living room this weekend – move them to where, I'm not sure. It's frustrating, because sometimes it feels like we're getting nowhere with the house. Although this does prove just how busy we both are, and shows that it's not just wedding planning we don't have time for, it's everything.

I pick up my phone, again, and instantly put it back down – again.

Having decided that there's no way I can take my old job back, I now need to call Skinner and give him the bad news. I'm not stalling because I don't want to give my old boss bad news – he did fire me, after all – but because I don't want to turn down such an amazing opportunity. Not only an opportunity to get my old job back, but to get my old life back too. Well, almost my old life, but this time I would have Leo to share it all with, and that would be even more amazing.

My old job might benefit mine and Leo's lives in the long run, but in the short-term it would be so difficult. I don't know when I'd need to be away, or for how long. I don't know if Leo would come with me or not, but I know that, either way, neither of us would be happy with how things were, and even if we did agree to live in different countries while I worked on this project, what about the wedding? It's just too messy and I have too many commitments now, and the only thing I do know for sure is that Leo will do anything to make me happy, even if that means sacrificing his own happiness, and I don't want to put him in that position, where he makes himself unhappy just so I can take this job. It's one of the reasons I love him, but it's also the reason I need to say no – without mentioning it to Leo. It's the selfless thing to do.

I decide, instead of calling Skinner, to send him an email – that will be much easier.

Dear Mr Skinner, I type. *Thank you for your generous job offer. However, due to personal circumstances I will have to decline. Thanks for thinking of me. Mia.*

That will do it, right? A no is a no. I don't need to justify myself.

I hit send, before I can change my mind.

I lie back on the sofa, teetering on the edge of feeling sorry for myself, when I hear the front door open.

'Hello?' I call out.

'Hello,' Leo calls back.

He walks into the living room to find me lying on the sofa with my legs hooked over the backrest. Leo laughs at me.

'I'm having a bad day,' I say, by way of an explanation for essentially sitting upside down on the sofa. 'What are you doing here?'

'I finished early, stopped to get some supplies to make you dinner on the way home,' he tells me, raising his shopping bags so I can see them.

'You're amazing,' I tell him.

'I know,' he replies jokily.

'You still upset about yesterday?' he asks.

I get up and follow him into the kitchen, pausing for a second as all the blood drains from my head.

'Yeah and a few other things,' I reply honestly. 'What's for dinner?'

After visiting the hospital with Dylan yesterday, I went for food with him, his manager, Mark and Charles. We went to a Chinese restaurant, where they'd set up a private room, just for us. They laid out the enormous table with all kinds of different dishes and sides that smelled just too good to resist. After yesterday's blowout I need to be sensible today, but whatever Leo is making, I will happily eat. It's so amazing of him to do this.

'Calabrese-stuffed chicken breasts,' he tells me. 'And salad. I know you're being healthy at the moment.'

'My God, you're amazing,' I reply. 'I spent my entire life believing that men who listened were an urban legend, but you pay attention to every little thing I say.'

'Because I love you.' He laughs. 'It's not unreasonable for you to expect me to listen when you talk.'

Don't think I don't know how lucky I am to be marrying Leo, because I do know it, and not for one second since we started dating has it even crossed my mind that he wasn't worth giving up my life in LA and moving back home for.

'Can I help?' I ask.

'Sure, want to make the salad?'

I nod.

'I'm sorry what you saw yesterday has left you so upset,' he tells me. 'But you wouldn't be you if it didn't. You're such a sweet, caring person.'

I give him a half-smile before turning my attention back to chopping tomatoes.

'I just . . . I can't believe kids have to go through that, and parents have to watch their kids go through that,' I reply. 'I couldn't imagine watching my kids go through that.'

'Hey, Mia . . .' Leo stops what he's doing and comes up behind me, wrapping his arms around my waist. 'You know that if we had kids, the chances of something being seriously wrong with them would be small, right? And even if something was wrong, there are amazing hospitals, charities and people like Dylan to make everything OK, you know?'

'I know,' I reply, placing my hand over his.

'But, hey, does this mean you've decided you do want kids?' he says.

'I do,' I reply. 'Whether these kids were sick or not, seeing how happy Dylan made them, I want to make my own kids happy like that. And you'd be too much of an amazing dad to not have kids.'

Leo turns me around, picks me up and spins me around.

'Oh my God, Mia Valentina, you don't know how happy you've just made me,' he says excitedly. 'I feel like the final piece of the puzzle has finally fallen into place.'

I laugh joyfully as he twirls me.

I know Leo wants to be a dad more than almost anything else. I might not have been sure before, but who am I to stand in his way? And why should I sit around telling myself I'd make a terrible mother – I'll make an amazing mother. I certainly won't be cold with my kids, or favour one over the other, and if anything did happen to one of them . . . Leo is right. I'd be there for them, and there's so much support available. You can't not do things in life just because you're scared they're not going to turn out the way you wanted them to.

'I mean, we don't even have to think about this stuff until after the wedding,' he replies. 'But you've made me so happy.'

I can tell he means it. He looks almost as happy as he did the day he proposed, after I said yes.

'If you think I have time to wait,' I tease.

'What?'

'Last time we spoke about kids, you reminded me women only have so long—'

'Mia, you're only thirty-three,' he interrupts me. 'I didn't mean you were running out of time.'

'I know, I know, I'm just kidding,' I reply. 'Now get back to making my chicken, I'm starving.'

Leo laughs as he stuffs chicken breasts with mozzarella, tomato and fresh basil. The kitchen smells amazing already and he hasn't even started cooking anything yet. I cannot recommend marrying an Italian highly enough.

'Before I forget, I told Debbie we'd go look at a wedding venue with her tomorrow,' he says.

I suddenly feel my happy buzz drain from my body. 'You've been talking to Debbie?' I ask.

'Yeah, well, she was having trouble getting in touch with you, so she called me.'

That will be all those calls I rejected.

'It seems like a cool place and we can have the ceremony there too,' he says. 'So, don't worry, you're not going to need to go to church and convince anyone you should be allowed to marry me. I told my mum we didn't want to get married in a church, and she was fine with it.'

'Your mum is cool,' I tell him.

While my sister, Belle, may not have got married in a church, she still had a vicar conduct the ceremony, so her wedding was a religious affair. I'm sure my family expect nothing other than a secular ceremony as far as I'm concerned, much to their disappointment. I come from a very churchy family – you know the type, besties with the local vicar, church every Sunday, et cetera. I don't discuss my beliefs with my family, nor do I chat God with my Catholic, soon-to-be mother-in-law, because what do a person's beliefs matter to another person? It's an entirely personal thing. If we were to have a religious ceremony, would we go for my family's Anglican vicar or Leo's mum's Catholic priest? Religion has already caused enough wars so, rather than cause a rift between our two families trying to please people, we've decided that it's best for us to have a non-religious ceremony, because it has no bearing on our relationship, our wedding, or if we will or won't uphold our vows.

'Do I need to be up early?' I ask.

'Not especially,' he replies. 'You tired?'

'Kind of,' I reply. 'But I wanted to get up and go for a run first.'

'I fancy a run too. I could wake you up early, come with you?'

'That would be great,' I reply.

'I also bought breakfast, so I'll cook you something while you're in the shower and then we can get straight off.'

'Did I mention you were amazing?' I ask him.

'Once or twice.' He laughs. 'I love you.'

'I love you too,' I reply.

'Oh, by the way, I've got a stag do tomorrow night,' Leo says. 'Completely slipped my mind.'

'Oh,' I say. 'People from work?'

'Yeah, shouldn't be a late one, though.'

My phone buzzes with an email. I grab it at the speed of light to see what it says.

It's from Skinner. It says: *Sorry you feel that way, Mia. Please send your home address so I can send release forms. Regards, D.*

Skinner, whose first name is Donnie, always signs off his messages with a 'D'. I think he likes to think he's too busy to write his full name. He's the kind of guy who feels self-important enough to have a stamp made of his signature, to save him time signing things. At least he respectfully accepted my rejection without a fuss.

Well, that's that then. But, do you know what? I know I've made the right decision. And I'll be reminded it was the right choice every time I look over at Leo, the most amazing man I've ever met, a man who will always be worth more than any amount of money, or any job.

Chapter 27

Beech Tree Hall is a Grade I-listed building, sitting at the top of a long, leafy driveway, in eight acres of stunning grounds. Based on this information alone, I can safely say that Beech Tree Hall is too expensive for my wedding.

Also, the suite we're currently viewing – the Orchid Suite – can accommodate two hundred daytime guests and two hundred and fifty evening guests. Meanwhile, I can't even think of one person I can ask to be a bridesmaid for me.

Even their smallest suite – the Daffodil Suite – accommodates eighty for the wedding breakfast and one hundred and twenty for the evening do. I haven't even attempted to make a list of people we'll be inviting, but I can assure you, it won't be that many.

I whispered this to Leo as Debbie let the events coordinator know we were here. He suggested we politely view the place, even though it will likely be out of our price range.

'And we have one hundred rooms that your guests can stay in, if they choose,' Camille, the events coordinator, tells us. If they take out second mortgages, I assume.

'Lovely,' I reply.

'Well, I'll leave you to look around the room and talk among yourselves,' Camille says.

'You could be more enthusiastic, Mia,' Debbie ticks me off.

'You could be more in tune with our price range, Debbie,' I reply. 'No way can we afford this.'

'Between us – and so you start taking this more seriously – I think your parents are going to offer to pay,' Debbie tells us.

'That's way too generous,' Leo replies. 'Incredible, but way too generous.'

'She paid for your sister's wedding, didn't she?' Debbie says.

'Yeah, but that's not the point,' I reply.

My dad enjoyed a long and successful career as a private dentist before retiring with a *very* good pension. Money isn't a problem for my parents but that doesn't mean I'd happily accept their help.

'We weren't going to invite too many people,' I continue.

'But your parents plan to,' she points out. 'Your big day isn't just about you two, you know.'

I bite my lip anxiously. This wedding feels so out of my control. What I want doesn't seem to matter. It seems to be more important we please everyone else.

'We can talk to them – don't worry,' Leo assures me, squeezing my hand.

'Can you give us a moment alone, please?' I ask Debbie.

She frowns, but obliges, leaving us standing in the centre of the dance floor, in the middle of the huge room. The walls are adorned with white fabric, with tiny LED lights that twinkle like the night sky, and the tables and chairs are all covered with white material, with a golden sash wrapped around each chair. It really, really is a truly stunning venue, but (even if it were in my price range) it's not me.

'This is all too much, right?' I say to Leo, once we're alone.

'I know your parents want to invite all their friends, but we can talk to them, tell them this is just too much,' Leo assures me. 'Don't worry, OK?'

'OK,' I reply.

'I'm sure we can figure something out that makes everyone

happy.'

Sometimes it really is like he doesn't know my parents *at all*.

'Shall I call Debbie back in?' I ask.

'Give it a few minutes,' Leo says, pulling me close. 'Can you imagine us having our first dance in a place like this?'

He holds me close, slow dancing with me – well, attempting to. My lack of rhythm and my four-inch heels make it tricky.

The truth is, I can't imagine having a first dance with Leo at all. Not because I can't dance – although that is a pretty good reason – but because the thought of everyone's eyes on me fills me with dread. Most people have dance lessons now, at least, and then there's people who learn an embarrassingly cringey choreographed routine, which means everyone is expected to be good. Everyone will be watching us, judging us . . .

As Debbie walks back into the room I pull the neck of my dress from my body a couple of times to let some air in. It's so warm in here, with the windows covered and the door closed.

'Ready to see some more of the hotel?' Debbie asks hopefully.

'I'm just going to step outside and make a quick call,' I lie, my chest tightening by the second.

'Can't it wait?' she asks.

'No, I'll be right back,' I say.

'Want me to come?' Leo asks, sensing something might be wrong.

'No, no, you stay here – I won't be long,' I call back as I dash out of the room.

Once I'm outside I clutch my chest and gasp for breath. As the cold air fills my lungs and cools my cheeks, breathing slowly starts getting easier again.

It's been so long since I had a panic attack, I'd forgotten how awful they felt. It never fails to terrify me, that the symptoms of panic can so easily mimic the symptoms of something much more serious. If I didn't know what panic attacks were like, I would've thought I was dying.

Is this normal? Should I be getting so upset while planning my wedding? Am I just suffering with cold feet or is it something more? Do I actually *want* to get married? People keep calling it the happiest day of my life but, with all this stress, I don't see how it can be.

Chapter 28

'Mamma Mia,' Rory, my next-door neighbour, calls out as I walk down the street.

I've had another day hanging out at Dylan's house, asking him questions, taking notes. I have a lot of stuff to work with now, but there are still particular things I need from him – the things he doesn't like talking about. Amazing, that you can get him to talk openly about the time he kissed a drag queen (not realising they were a drag queen), but you can't get him to talk about his feelings.

This evening Leo and I are putting our Christmas tree up – our first time doing it in our new home. He was at a stag do last night and I don't know what time he got in, but it was late, and I was up and out before he woke up – hopefully his hangover has passed now because I'm so excited for this evening. This morning, before I set off, I cleared out the living room so we could make the room perfect for the festive period. Well, as close to perfect as possible. We were going to decorate the living room this weekend but now, to take the pressure off, we're going to wait until after Christmas. So I've moved all the boxes and filled the room with the furniture we'll need, as well as a few decorative items. I've left a space for the Christmas tree in the corner. The room might be white, but it's going to look amazing once the decorations are up. I'm not one of those girls who goes crazy for Christmas, but this year I'm excited about our tree.

Rory and Iwan are walking along the opposite side of the street, obviously on their way home from work too.

'Hello, boys,' I call over to them.

They make a move to cross the road so I wait for them. We might as well walk the last five minutes together.

'How's it going, Mia?' Iwan asks. 'We never see you these days.'

'I know, sorry,' I reply. 'I've been so busy with work, and Leo has been doing so much overtime.'

Iwan shrugs. 'Don't worry about it,' he assures me. 'Just come out with us this weekend – Leo too.'

'I think I might be working this weekend.'

The boys boo me.

'You got your wedding business sorted now?' Rory asks.

'Not quite,' I reply.

'I've gotta tell you, Mia, I can't see you in a white dress,' Iwan chimes in.

I stop in my tracks. 'Erm, because you don't think it's my style or because I'm not virginal?' I ask, semi-offended.

'Well, both.' He laughs.

He's not wrong.

As we approach our houses, I notice a large white van parked outside.

'Does that look like a TV licence van to you?' Rory asks me, eyeballing it cautiously, but as we get closer we see the driver get out and knock on my door.

'Hello,' I call out to him. 'Sorry, I've just got back from work.'

'Don't worry, darling,' the driver says. 'Mia Valentina?'

'Yes.'

'Got a delivery for you. Sign here.'

The driver hands me a small electronic device, which I sign my name on.

I hover on my doorstep, rubbing my hands together to fight off the cold as I wait for my delivery.

The driver emerges from the back of his van with a large bunch of flowers, all tied together with Christmassy colours, sparkly ribbons and a dusting of glitter.

'Wow, they're beautiful,' I say.

'Mate, you're engaged now. Doesn't Leo know he doesn't have to bother with flowers anymore?' Rory laughs.

Leo never actually buys me flowers.

Just when I think the driver is leaving, he pulls out another bouquet of flowers, even more beautiful than the last.

'Oh, I know what this is,' I tell the boys. 'I told him I didn't have a favourite flower a few days ago. This is probably just his cute way of helping me realise which one is my favourite, so I can have them at my wedding.'

'Soft lad,' Rory teases. 'You've got yourself a keeper there.'

I'm about to agree and say goodbye to my friends when I notice the driver dragging a large wicker basket up my garden path.

'More?' I ask.

'A few more,' the driver replies, plonking the chest down in front of me.

Another two baskets, one box and a four-feet-tall cuddly toy later, the driver seems just about done.

'Is that it?' I ask.

'Oops, don't forget the balloons,' he says, grabbing a bunch of balloons with a small envelope attached to them. 'Here you go.'

'Tell Leo men like us don't stand a chance, competing with stunts like that,' Iwan jokes.

I smile, although I'm a little confused. It's a lovely gesture. I just don't understand why.

I pull the little card from the balloons, careful not to let go of them, which would send them floating off into the dark sky.

I'm just about to read the card when I notice my handsome fiancé arriving home from work.

'Hey, you,' I say brightly. 'What's all this?'

'I was just about to ask you.' He laughs. 'Figured you'd been Christmas shopping.'

'So this stuff isn't from you?' Rory asks.

'Erm, no,' Leo replies, suddenly sounding a little suspicious.

Crap.

'Awkwaaaard,' Iwan says, doing some kind of gesture with his hands that I'm probably not nerdy enough to understand.

I take the card from the envelope and read the message.

Please reconsider. I need you. D.

Leo sidles up next to me and reads over my shoulder.

'Is this stuff from Dylan? What does he mean he needs you?' Leo asks, little pricks of anger peppering his words.

I look over at Rory and Iwan, who are staring at us from their doorstep, probably wishing they had some popcorn and a blanket right about now.

'No,' I start. 'Look, help me get this stuff inside, then we'll talk.'

Leo obliges, carrying the wicker baskets and the box while I stick to the balloons and flowers. We place everything down on the living-room floor.

'Are you not going to open them?' Leo asks, as though I might be keeping the contents from him.

I pop the tops off everything before standing back to take stock: balloons, two large bouquets of flowers, a box full of expensive beauty products and three wicker baskets full of delicious-looking things to eat and drink.

'So . . .' Leo starts, more than ready for his explanation.

'So, they're not from Dylan, they're from Donnie Skinner, my old boss in LA.'

'Didn't he sack you? Why would he be sending you such an elaborate Christmas gift?'

'Because he wants me to work for him again. That's what he means when he says "I need you" – he needs me to write a movie.'

'Oh,' Leo says. 'The note asked you to reconsider – does that mean you turned it down?'

'Of course,' I reply.

'Why?' he asks.

I'm confused. I thought turning down the job would be the thing that would make him happiest, but he seems upset.

'Well, because my life is here now,' I tell him. 'We've got the house and the wedding coming up.'

'Well, the house isn't going anywhere, and as for the wedding – nothing is booked.'

'What are you saying?' I ask him.

'I'm saying that nothing is set in stone. Just because we're together and we have this house doesn't mean you *have* to reject the job offer. Why didn't you tell me about it?'

I slip off my coat and pull off my hat before sitting down on the sofa. Leo takes a seat next to me, ready to hear me out.

'I didn't want to put you in that position,' I tell him. 'Even if I just went to do this one project, I could be there for months, and what if they wanted me to stay for longer? What if *I* wanted to stay for longer? What would that mean for us?'

Leo takes my hands in his. 'Mia, I love you. I want to make you happy – whatever it takes. But you don't talk to me. You never tell me what's on your mind. You bottle it up and stress yourself out and then we end up having a conversation like this. You should have told me.'

'I know, I'm sorry,' I say. 'I just didn't want to cause any problems.'

'So, are you going to reconsider the offer?'

'No,' I tell him. 'I don't want to go to LA; I want to stay here with you.'

'Shall we at least talk it out?' Leo asks.

'No,' I reply. 'I've made my mind up. I don't want to go. I want to stay here with you.'

'I don't want you turning down a job I know you used to love, just because of me,' he says with real sadness, like he feels he's holding me back.

'I loved the job but I love you more,' I tell him honestly.

Leo grabs me and hugs me, squeezing me tightly.

'I love you, Mia. And I can tell when something is on your mind – I could tell yesterday at the wedding venue.'

I'm not sure I give Leo enough credit for his attentiveness and his perception sometimes. Of course the person who loves me, who knows me better than anyone else, can tell when I'm not right.

'Is that all that's on your mind?' he asks.

I pause for a second. There's a voice in my head urging me to tell Leo the truth, about how I'm feeling about the wedding – but if he thinks I'm saying that I don't want to marry him, it might break his heart. It would break mine to see him think that for even a second.

'That's all,' I lie.

'I'll never hold you back, Mia,' he says, finally releasing me.

'I know,' I reply.

I know he won't because he's amazing. I'm so lucky to have him and I'm terrified that one day he'll wake up and realise how much better he can do than me.

'I thought it through, I really did. But this is my life now and I'm happier with it. Even if it might have been good financially, Dylan's publishers are paying well and this might open the door to more books.'

'I trust you,' he assures me. 'Just be more open and honest with me.'

'OK,' I agree, even though I'm keeping some pretty big doubts from him.

Leo takes off his shoes and turns out his pockets, unbuttoning his jeans as he heads upstairs. He's only been up there a minute or so when I see his phone spring to life with a message. I can't help but eyeball it as I walk past, noticing he has a message from someone called Amy. I can only see the preview, but it says: *I still have your jacket from last night. Thanks f . . .* The urge to open it is overwhelming. What was a girl doing on a stag do and why does she have my fiancé's jacket?

'Are we still putting the tree up tonight?' he calls from upstairs.

'Erm, maybe another night,' I reply. 'I'm not feeling very festive right now.'

Chapter 29

Sitting in Dylan's massive living room, waiting for him to get out of bed, I can't help but notice that – while this room is stunning and beautifully decorated – there's not much personality to it. It just looks like every other perfect celebrity living room you saw on *Cribs* – gorgeous, but soulless, like no one has ever really lived in it. I've only seen a few rooms of his massive house, but I get those vibes everywhere. He's clearly spent a lot of money here, but not a lot of time.

'Morning, Mia,' he says as he makes his entrance.

Dylan walks into the living room meaningfully chugging a cup of coffee. He's wearing a black silk robe that's . . . oh God.

'Erm, Dylan,' I say, averting my eyes, staring at the ceiling instead.

'What?' he asks.

'Erm, your robe is open.'

And he's entirely naked underneath it.

'Sorry.' He laughs.

I give him a few seconds to close it before switching my attention from his ceiling back to his person.

'Hey, don't be embarrassed,' he insists, which probably means I'm blushing. 'Do you know how many people would do anything to see Little Dylan?'

'Yes, I imagine I'm part of a very small club of about six thousand women now,' I reply sarcastically.

Dylan chuckles, sitting down on the sofa, carefully making sure he doesn't flash me again.

'Yeah, but I call very few of them back,' he tells me with a wink, swinging the belt of his robe in faux seduction.

I don't struggle to understand what women see in Dylan. He's gorgeous, charming and so sexy. If he were a poster on my wall, I'd definitely have a crush on him. Maybe he'd even be my relationship 'free pass', who knows? But now that I know him, and can see the kind of person he is, I don't fancy him. Instead, I feel like we're friends, and that means so much more. To sleep with a person like Dylan would be easy, but to befriend him feels like something to be proud of. I have to admit, though, I do feel a rush of something when he flirts with me, even though I know he's just joking. It feels nice to be desired, after months of feeling like I'd slipped back into unremarkable territory. I feel like LA Mia again, who once shared a tipsy nightclub kiss with arguably the second most attractive professional male dancer from *Dancing with the Stars*.

'So, what's happening?' he asks.

'I was just admiring your house,' I tell him. 'Well, what I've seen of it. Nice décor.'

'Oh shit, is it showing again?' he jokes, placing a hand between his legs. 'Oh, *décor*. Got you. Thanks.'

'Did you have much involvement in it?'

'Zero.' He laughs. 'You want a tour?'

'Of your house?'

'No, of my body. Yes, of course of my house. Come on . . .' he insists, jumping to his feet. 'So you've seen the living room, the kitchen, the office, the hallway. Want to come upstairs?'

'I'm not sure if you're asking out of some sort of muscle memory because I'm female, or if it's part of the tour,' I joke as we linger at the bottom of the massive staircase.

Dylan's hallway is huge. Looking up from the bottom of the wooden staircase, you can see all the way to the ceiling. The stairs lead up to the mezzanine, which boasts views of both the hallway and the front garden, which can be admired through the massive window above the front door.

'You could have one hell of a Christmas tree in here,' I tell him.

'Who would see it?'

'You. Me. Mitch – you could even have a Christmas party.'

Dylan ponders my words for a moment. 'A Christmas party could be pretty cool,' he says thoughtfully. 'Maybe over the next couple of days?'

'You can organise a big party in a couple of days? Oh, of course, you're Dylan King; you'll have your minions do it.'

Dylan laughs again. 'I'll think about it. On with the tour.'

I follow Dylan upstairs and admire the different rooms of his house one at a time, from his luxurious bathroom to his games room, which not only has a pool table and large cinema screen, but also boasts pretty much every games console from the past twenty-five years.

The tour doesn't last long and I can't help but notice he's skipped a few rooms.

'And that concludes our tour,' Dylan says with a loud clap of his hands, which echoes around the upstairs hallway.

'So, I notice you didn't show me your bedroom,' I point out first of all.

'Well, I could, but there's a girl in there, and you've already seen one person naked today.' Dylan chuckles.

I wonder if he's joking or not.

'Fair enough,' I reply quickly. I definitely don't want to see any more naked people. 'I also noticed you were very quick to steer me away from that room over there.'

I nod in the direction of another door that remained closed through the tour.

'Yeah, I mean no, I mean . . . there's nothing in there. Just junk.'

I raise my eyebrows in disbelief.

'Suuure,' I reply.

'Come on, let's go back downstairs,' he insists.

I'm about to persist when my phone rings.

'Ergh, it's my wedding planner,' I whine, like I'm a teenager whose mum is calling to tell her she has to be home by nine because it's a school night.

'Don't answer,' he advises.

'I don't,' I reply. 'She just keeps calling.'

'Give it to me,' Dylan says, swiping my phone from my hand.

'Dylan, no,' I protest, but it's too late.

'Hello,' he answers. 'Ahh, Debbie, hello . . . today? . . . Unfortunately we're in London today . . . Oh, I see . . . Well, we can't argue with that, can we? . . . OK, see you then . . . Bye.'

'See you then?' I repeat back to him once he hangs up.

'I think she thought I was your fella.' He laughs.

'You sound nothing like each other,' I tell him. They really couldn't sound more different. Leo is Orlando Bloom and Dylan is Danny Dyer – *that* different.

'Anyway, she wants us to go taste some cakes. I told her we were in London but she's got your number. Said she knew you'd be here, so she's organised a cake tasting in London.'

'She doesn't want *us* to go taste cakes, Dylan – she wants Leo and me. But he's working today. I'll have to call her to cancel.'

'Ahh, I could go for some cake, though, babe. I'll go with you, save your fella a job.'

'That's weird,' I tell him. 'You can't come to my cake tasting because you fancy some cake.'

Dylan thinks for a second. 'OK, I'll make a deal with you . . .' he starts – he must really want some cake. 'If you let me come with you today, I'll have a big Christmas party tomorrow night.'

I remain expressionless. He's going to have to do better than that.

'You drive a hard bargain, Valentina. OK, fine. After the party we can talk about the shit I don't wanna talk about, that you keep nagging me to talk about. We got a deal or what?'

'Deal,' I reply, offering my hand for him to shake. He does, so hopefully that's binding.

'You're on party-planning duty, though,' he tells me. 'And you'd better not avoid it like you're avoiding planning your wedding.'

'I'm not avoiding planning my wedding,' I reply, offended.

'OK, OK.' He laughs. 'Then you'll be gagging for this cake tasting as much as I am.'

'I am. Let's do this. And then we're going to have a sick party, and then you're going answer *any* question I ask you.'

'This cake better be worth it,' he replies.

Chapter 30

'We're supposed to be having a white Christmas this year,' Eileen tells us, making small talk as we wait for Debbie to show up.

'Cool,' Dylan replies, before laughing at his own choice of words. 'Literally.'

Eileen laughs, entirely charmed by Dylan. What woman isn't, though?

We're at the Bluebell Bakery in Kensington, waiting on Debbie to handhold us through our cake tasting – well, not *our* cake tasting, my cake tasting, but I'm not sure I'll be able to get Dylan out of here until he's in a coma.

It's a beautiful place, all decked out in lilac and white. The Christmas decorations are subtle, silver and white, with sparkles everywhere. There's nothing subtle about their cakes, though. They look beautiful – in fact they're practically art, and it doesn't matter where you stand in the room, it smells amazing, like icing sugar and buttercream.

Eileen escorted us through the shop and into the café where the tables were all full of people tucking into cakes and warm drinks, except for one free table at the back, reserved for *the De Lucas*.

With Eileen headed into the back to prepare our samples, Dylan beings to fidget like a little boy. He picks up the name card from our table.

'De Luca,' he says out loud. 'You're marrying an Italian?'

'I am,' I confirm.

'Mia De Luca,' he says out loud, to see how it sounds. 'Wait, are you Italian? With a name like Valentina?'

'No, I'm English. Valentina is my pen name. I grew up Mia Harrison,' I confess.

'That's nowhere near as sexy,' he concludes.

'I'll be sure to pass your feedback on to my parents.'

'Erm . . .'

We're interrupted by Debbie, who looks very confused.

'You're not the groom,' she says to Dylan.

'I'm not,' he replies, all smiles.

'You're Dylan King,' she tells him, just in case he might not be aware.

'I am.' He laughs. 'Mia, you told me she was good, you didn't tell me she was this good.'

Debbie somehow overlooks his sarcasm and takes a compliment from that, but her smile only lasts a split second.

'Well, what are you doing here?'

'Cake,' he replies simply. 'On the phone you said something about cake.'

'I thought that was Leo,' she says angrily, before tuning to me. 'Mia, you can't just bring a random man to your cake tasting. You're supposed to bring the groom.'

'Well, he's working today,' I tell her honestly. Well, so he tells me. Between all his overtime and his text from 'Amy', whom he gave his jacket to during a lads' night out, I'd be lying if I said my writer's brain wasn't in overdrive, daring to entertain the worst possible explanations. But I've always trusted Leo – he's never given me reason not to – so every time my brain wanders off in that direction, I yank it back. 'We're here, though, so we can get on with it or we can reschedule.'

We both stare at her blankly, Dylan with hope in his eyes.

As Eileen comes out with a platter of different cakes, I see Debbie roll her eyes.

'OK, fine, let's do this now,' she says, sitting down at the table.

'We're all set?' Eileen asks her.

'All set,' she replies reluctantly.

'So . . .' Eileen says excitedly. 'We've got your traditional fruit cake with white icing.'

Dylan scoffs in disgust, which lands him a dirty look from both Eileen and Debbie.

'Next,' he says with a flash of his cheeky smile.

'We've got a chocolate cake with chocolate frosting, salted caramel cake with a caramel drizzle, lemon cake with lemon drizzle, and finally, a selection of vanilla sponges with fresh fruit and whipped cream. Enjoy.'

Eileen disappears, leaving the three of us to our cake.

'Mmm,' I say, diving straight into the chocolate one. 'This is amazing. Dylan, try this.'

I delicately scoop up a little with my fork and hold it out for Dylan to try, holding my hand underneath to catch any crumbs.

'Shit,' Dylan says, banging his hand on the table. 'That's good cake, man.'

He stabs his fork into a square of salted caramel cake and shoves it in his mouth, whole.

'Mmm,' he moans, sounding like he's on the brink of an orgasm.

'*That* good?' I ask. Dylan nods, so I cut a little piece for myself to try. 'Oh wow, that's great. Do I have to pick just one?' I ask Debbie.

Now that I'm looking at her, I realise she's staring at us, a combination of disgusted and confused.

'What is happening here?' she asks me.

'Cake,' Dylan replies. 'Try some.'

'This is wrong,' she tells me. '*He's* here and something very important is missing.'

I smile and nod in acknowledgement.

'A cup of tea,' I say. 'Eileen, can we get some tea, please?'

'Right away, my love,' she says as she dashes past us with an armful of empty plates.

'What is it they do at weddings, where they feed each other cake?' Dylan asks, picking up a slice of vanilla sponge. It's two layers of vanilla cake with lashings of whipped cream sandwiched between them, and a big dollop on top holding a strawberry in place.

Dylan, clearly having seen too many wedding movies, squashes the slice of cake in the direction of my mouth, smearing it all over my face. The bit I do get to taste is phenomenal.

'Dylan,' I shriek in horror.

'Sorry.' He laughs. 'I get carried away when I have too much sugar. You want some, Deb?'

Debbie jumps to her feet. Only then do I realise everyone is watching us.

'Mia, I quit. You're ignoring my calls, you're refusing to book anything or tell me what you want, and now you're turning up with strange men and embarrassing me. This is the final straw. I'll be telling your mother exactly why I quit. I wish you all the best – but if you do get married, I'll be amazed.'

Debbie turns on her heel and storms out of the shop.

'Did she say she's gonna tell your mum on you?' he asks me.

'Yep,' I reply.

'No one likes a narc, Debbie,' he calls after her.

'Oops,' I say quietly, realising that everyone in the café is staring at us. Eileen is standing next to us with our pot of tea and two cups on a tray. Her jaw has dropped a little – I don't suppose she's had too many couples come in for a cake tasting that has ended like this.

'Oh, Eileen, you're here, great,' Dylan says. 'Can I get a four-tier cake, two tiers chocolate and two tiers salted caramel, please? Do we think that can be ready tomorrow?'

'The . . . the wedding is tomorrow?' Eileen asks.

'No, no,' Dylan replies. 'This is for me.'

'You just want a wedding cake for you?' she asks.

'Yeah. Well, not just me. I'm having a Christmas party tomorrow. I might let some people have some.'

The fact that Dylan wants to buy a wedding cake that isn't for a wedding is a concept too confusing for Eileen.

'That's quite short notice,' Eileen points out politely.

'I'll pay whatever it takes to get it made in time,' Dylan offers.

'I . . . I'll have a word,' Eileen stutters. She can't really argue with that, can she?

'You're getting a wedding cake for the party?' I laugh.

'It's just a cake, Valentina,' he replies. 'Anyway, someone needed to buy one. Even Debbie thinks you're avoiding planning this wedding. What's up? You not wanna get married or something?'

'Shut up and eat your cake,' I reply. Dylan happily obliges.

I don't think for a second that Dylan did this to sabotage my cake tasting. I think he was just being Dylan – a little drunk, a lot silly, having a laugh. He doesn't know what Debbie is like, or the problems she's been having with me, so why would a little cake mess drive her to quit? Maybe today was my fault, perhaps I annoyed Debbie too much, but it wasn't the deliberate act of sabotage people are going to assume it was. My mum is going to be so angry, and God knows what Leo is going to think – I mean, it does seem like something LA Mia would do. She's no stranger to making a mess with a wedding cake.

I'll just have to plan my wedding myself, all alone, which is what I wanted in the first place. Maybe I can wait until after Christmas, when things will be less stressful. And anyway, now I've got a Christmas party to plan at short notice. A showbiz party is always going to be awesome but, with Dylan promising me he'll open up about his personal life afterwards, it means the book I'm writing practically depends on this party . . . or maybe that's just what I'm telling myself so I get to have some fun.

Chapter 31

So it turns out that trying to get a sixteen-foot Christmas tree in through a front door before standing it upright in the hallway is actually quite a difficult task – one that took lots of manpower, skill and manoeuvring.

Dylan wasn't all that helpful. He just stood on the mezzanine, shouting instructions to the people doing the hard work, and I wouldn't exactly say they were helpful instructions, just random bursts of vague advice like 'lift it better, you mug'. Still, the tree is in, upright and decorated to perfection, if I do say so myself. In fact, the entire hallway, kitchen and living room all look fantastic.

It turns out Dylan hasn't put up any Christmas decorations for as long as he can remember – probably never, in this house – so he took a little persuading. I explained to him that if people thought they were coming to a Christmas party, they'd probably be expecting Christmas decorations. But then, once we started shopping for cool stuff, there was no stopping him, and now his house is a winter wonderland of twinkling lights, sparkly things, the delicious smell of festive nibbles and, of course, his four-tier chocolate and salted caramel wedding cake. He's even placed a little Santa figurine on the top, to make it festive.

Leo and I had a huge row earlier today and I can't get it

off my mind. I did tell Leo that I'd been to a cake tasting with Debbie, but I neglected to mention that she'd dumped me as a client. Well, I didn't want him thinking I'd done it on purpose, and I figured, once I started making my own plans, it would all work out just fine. Except Debbie called my mum and my mum called Leo, and now everyone knows everything and they're all mad at me. Leo seems to think I'm regressing back to being LA Mia who only wanted to have a good time, who didn't care about her relationships with her family or men. While I do feel like I've gained access to LA Mia's positive traits, I feel like a new and improved version now. I can't stress to Leo enough that I *do* want to marry him, because I do, but I don't know how to explain what's wrong with me. I'm trying to plan this wedding, but everything I look at, I don't want. I don't want a big wedding, in a big, fancy hotel. I don't want flowers. I don't want bridesmaids – hell, I don't even have any female friends to ask to be my bridesmaids. The thought of a first dance makes me want to walk in front of a bus!

Anyway, as Leo started getting on my case about the wedding, and the amount of time I'm spending with Dylan at the moment – supposedly to the detriment of my 'real life', whatever that is – something else that was on my mind just came angrily bubbling out of my mouth, before I had time to stop it.

'Who's Amy?' I asked.

'Amy?' Leo repeated back to me, a little taken aback by my question.

'Amy,' I repeated, like a broken record.

'She's one of the girls from work,' he said. 'Why?'

'Because I know you were out with her the other night, when you said you were on a stag do . . .'

'And how do you know that?' he asked.

'I saw a message on your phone and—'

'You've been checking my phone?' he asked me angrily.

I explained to him that, no, I hadn't been checking his phone, but that the notification came through while his phone was next to me and I saw it on the screen. But that wasn't the point. The point was that he said he was going on a stag do, so why was another girl wearing his jacket?

'Wow,' Leo said. 'I can't believe *you* don't trust *me*.'

'What does *that* mean?' I asked angrily. Of course, I knew exactly what he meant. He's talking about the fact I kissed another guy in the run-up to Belle's wedding, but that was not long after we met, before we'd even got together properly, days before I was supposed to be jetting back to LA – alone.

It's like Leo doesn't realise just what I gave up to be with him. My big house, the job of my dreams, hanging out with movie stars and sunbathing my days away. I loved my old life . . . but then I found Leo and I loved him more, so, without a fuss, I air-kissed my old life goodbye, and I'd do it again, but I just wish he'd realise how much I've changed for him.

Annoyed by him shifting the blame and more suspicious than ever, I escalated our argument.

'How to get away with cheating 101: project the blame onto your partner,' I said.

'Amy is one of the girls from work – the one who is getting married in a few months. I've told you about her before. The lads from work wanted to celebrate with her so we've been calling it a stag do. And I didn't give her my jacket, I left it in the Uber.'

'Oh.'

Things might not have been so bad, if he'd left it there.

'I talk to her, because she's been planning a wedding too. Except, she's been actually planning hers, not refusing to or having food fights with rock stars at cake tastings. Even Amy thinks it's weird, that you're not planning the wedding *at all*. She says she couldn't wait to plan hers. She thinks that maybe, deep down, you don't actually want to marry me . . .'

'Oh, so you and Amy talk about our private life together?' I snapped back. '*My* personal life? Awesome. Wait there, I'll go get you some bank statements to show her. Maybe give her my iCloud login. In fact, I think I've got my last smear test results somewhere . . .'

Getting nowhere by arguing, Leo went to work and I came here.

Now that the party is in full swing, I can see Dylan is having the time of his life. I am too. I did invite Leo along but it was a firm no – whether he had to go to work or not – because apparently I 'know' he hates showbiz types. Even so, I'm having a wonderful time. I've seen a few familiar faces – Charles, Mark and Mitch – who I recognise because I've met them recently, but then there are also people I recognise because they're incredibly famous, like Troy Reeves, who Dylan introduced me to over by the Christmas tree – apparently he's going to be doing a song or two later. The place is absolutely crawling with famous folk, industry people and an army of servers who are doing an excellent job of making sure everyone has a drink in their hand at all times.

I bought a new dress for the party, a rose-gold, sparkly dress with cut-out shoulders, teamed with a black pair of heels, rose-gold accessories and just a subtle hint of glitter hairspray in my big, long-blonde locks. When I went shopping with Dylan, who bought a grey pinstriped Vivienne Westwood suit (which he has paired with the most obnoxious Christmas T-shirt he could find in Primark), he was adamant that he pay for my stuff too. I wouldn't let him, which he didn't like – I think he's used to people just taking what they can get from him – but I think he likes the feeling he gets from being generous. Still, I really didn't feel comfortable letting him pay for a £600 dress, even if we are friends now.

A server removes the empty champagne glass from my hand, replacing it with a full one.

'Thank you,' I say. Well, I'm going to need it, seeing as how Dylan has signed us up for karaoke later, singing 'Baby, It's Cold Outside' together. Seems pretty unfair, I think, that he expects me to sing with him when he's a professional singer and I'm not.

A few more drinks and it will be fine, though. My shame will go out the window – well, it would if they were open, but it's freezing tonight and it's going to snow, apparently.

With a few drinks in my system, I grow braver and stupider, swiping Dylan's phone while he's not looking, ready to do something daft, but well-meaning. I flick through his contacts until I find Mikey King's number. It's Christmas, and it makes me sad that he and his brother aren't on speaking terms. Perhaps if I call him up and invite him to the party, he'll come along and build some bridges. I always read that Mikey was the smart, sensible one and Dylan was the hot-headed party boy, so maybe if I make the first move . . .

I punch Mikey's number into my phone, wandering into the office where it's quiet before pressing the call button.

'Hello?' a woman's voice answers.

'Hi, I'm after Mikey King,' I say as brightly and soberly as possible.

'He's asleep at the moment,' she tells me. 'I'm his girlfriend. Can I help?'

I hear a voice faintly in the background, but I could swear they said the name Nicole.

'Erm, no, it's OK,' I reply. She sounds a little suspicious . . . of the random girl calling her boyfriend on his mobile late in the evening – crazy, right? I'm sure I've heard Dylan mention the name Nicole before . . .

'Who is this?' she asks.

Before I have chance to make anything up, Dylan bursts into the room singing an expletive-heavy version of The Pogues' 'Fairytale of New York'.

I hang up quickly. OK, this wasn't my best idea. Thank God I didn't call his ex-wife too. I just need to mind my own business.

'Hey, there you are,' he slurs. 'I was looking for you, it's karaoke time.'

I follow Dylan back into the party room, slipping his phone

into his trouser pocket as I pass him.

I've never been one for karaoke, mostly because I can't sing, but Dylan assured me earlier that the fun in karaoke has nothing to do with whether or not you can sing – which is easy for the man with the multiplatinum-selling records to say. Then again, it might be the perfect way to let my hair down. I've been so stressed lately, maybe a bit of singing is just what I need.

I grab a champagne glass from the tray of a passing server and knock back the contents. If I'm going to do karaoke, I'm going to need some Dutch courage.

'OK,' I say, scrunching up my face as the alcohol hits. 'I'm ready.'

Chapter 32

'Valentina,' Dylan bellows from the mezzanine. I look up and see my new best friend practically hanging over the banister to wave at me. 'I just went to the loo.'

Everyone in the room laughs wildly at Dylan being Dylan. I just roll my drunk little eyes.

In a matter of minutes Dylan is downstairs, placing both hands on my cheeks as he slurs his words at me.

'I hope you know how fucking awesome you are,' he says.

'I hope you washed your hands,' I reply.

He laughs. 'Are you having fun?'

'I am,' I reply. 'Even though I sang, amped up, terribly, in front of musical royalty. It was fun.'

'You think three-fifths of the original One Direction line-up give a shit if you can sing?' he asks.

'It's the hottest three fifths, though. But it's cool,' I reply. 'I'm having a blast. I hope you are too.'

'I am, man. I am. Oh!'

Dylan gets distracted by two guys.

'Mia, meet Zander and Finn. Boys, meet Mia. These lads are my best mates,' he tells me.

I shake hands with Zander and Finn, who I recognise from

a band called Ganzás who I believe are currently still hanging around in the top-five section of the album chart, after their debut release was an absolute smash.

'Nice to meet you,' I tell them.

'I fucking love these lads,' Dylan tells me as he wraps an arm around them both.

'We love you too, dude. We love you too,' Zander says. 'We're going to a club. You guys wanna come?'

'Yeah!' Dylan shouts. 'Valentina, you coming?'

'Erm, OK, sure,' I say, giving in to peer pressure. Well, it's late, and even though Dylan said I could stay in one of his spare rooms, I don't much want to stay here without him, especially with him leaving while the party is still in full swing. It might be my responsibility to make sure no one does anything wrong and I don't want that kind of burden.

'Sweet,' Dylan says. 'Let's do this.'

Stepping outside the front door, I realise it's snowing.

'Wow, it's so pretty,' I say, watching as the tiny flakes float down, landing on Dylan's beautifully lit, long driveway.

'Don't worry, we're in the Range,' Finn says, unlocking his black Range Rover. 'Hop in.'

Finn and Zander get in the front while Dylan and I get in the back.

'I'm DJing,' Dylan insists, leaning into the front to grab the AUX cable.

'No way, dude, you'll put your own music on,' Zander says with a laugh.

'Oi, I've sold more fucking albums than you ever could,' Dylan chides him.

As we drive along the road, I snuggle into my heated seat. It feels glorious, but I'm hyped for this swanky club we're going to, that I'd never be able to get into without a few rock stars in tow.

I take my phone from my bag and see I have eight missed calls from my mum. Brilliant. There's also a message from her that says: *Need to talk you've done it this time. Stop trying to ruin Reading.* My mum has never been great at texting, so I'm going to assume a combination of anger, lack of texting skills and the ever-helpful autocorrect function has caused her to type 'Reading' instead of 'wedding' – then again, I wouldn't be surprised if she thought I had some kind of hidden agenda to ruin Reading. She's accused me of far stranger things in the past.

I decide to ignore her for now, instead opening the one message I've received from Leo. *Sorry about earlier. Have an amazing time and we'll figure this out later. I love you xxx,* it reads.

I begin typing a reply: *Having a great time, but miss you. I lo—*

My body is thrown forwards, only for a split second before my seatbelt does its job, grabbing my torso tightly, yanking me back towards my seat, which the back of my head hits forcefully. 'Merry Christmas Everybody' by Slade, one of the songs Dylan chose for the journey, is still booming loudly. The only thing louder is the ringing in my ears.

I look to my left to see Dylan clutching his chest as he takes off his seatbelt and climbs out of the car. Amid a cloud of white powder I see Zander and Finn fighting their airbags to do the same. I struggle to unfasten my own seatbelt before gathering with them at the side of the road.

I notice my ankle hurting as I limp over to where the guys are standing. I don't know exactly what happened but we've hit a tree head-on.

'Fuck,' Dylan says. 'Fuck, fuck, fuck.'

'What happened?' I ask.

Dylan, wincing in pain, wraps his arms around me and holds me close. I'm shivering, but I don't know if it's because I'm out in the snow wearing nothing but a tiny dress, or if it's because of the crash. I think it's both.

'Finn, dude, what happened? We're on an empty road. You hit some ice or something?'

'I . . . I think so,' he replies. There's an unsure look on his white, powder-covered face. 'I don't remember.'

'You don't remember?' I say. 'What are you, drunk?'

'No,' Finn replies quickly. 'Of course not.'

I was being sarcastic but suddenly we're all a little suspicious.

'Catch this,' Dylan says quickly as he tosses his iPhone in Finn's direction. Finn, who is appearing more and more obviously drunk by the second, doesn't even have time to look in Dylan's direction before the phone smacks him in the face.

'What the fuck is wrong with you?' he shrieks as he claps his hands over his mouth where the phone struck him.

'What the fuck is wrong with *you*?' I scream at him. 'You're driving us late at night, through a blizzard, and you're drunk.'

'It's OK, Mia,' Dylan assures me, rubbing my shoulders gently to keep me warm. 'I'll sort this.'

'We gotta make this go away, dude,' Zander says. 'Our careers are just getting going; we can't have a scandal like this. Dylan, the press will have a field day with you. And you . . .' Zander points at me. 'Doesn't look great for you, driving around at night with a bunch of musicians.'

I feel my eyebrows shoot up.

'Fuck you,' I say. 'Fuck you and your drunk-driving fucking bandmate.'

'Come on, Dylan, help us out,' Finn says. 'You can make this go away.'

Dylan looks at me.

'Dill, you can't just cover this up,' I say quietly. 'Look at you. I can see the pain on your face every time you move. My ankle is hurting – we both need to get to hospital and when we do they're going to ask questions.'

'She's right, man,' Dylan tells them.

It's so cold my teeth begin to chatter.

'We could say you were driving,' Finn suggests.

'Me?' I squeak.

'Yeah, you don't have as much to lose,' he replies.

175

'I'm drunk, not insured to drive this car and I don't even have a licence,' I tell him.

'Enough,' Dylan shouts. He pushes through his pain to grab his phone from the floor and dials 999, requesting the appropriate emergency services.

'I'm fucked,' Finn cries. 'Fucked.'

As the Ganzás boys panic about their future, Dylan leads me away from them and sits me down on a wall. Without a moment's thought he takes off one of his socks, fills it with snow and holds it against my ankle.

'Mia, I never would've let you get in the car if I'd known he was drunk,' he says seriously. 'I never would've got in myself.'

I place a hand lightly on his cold face. 'I know,' I assure him. 'This isn't your fault. And I'll make sure everyone knows it.'

'This is gonna be all over the fucking news,' he says with a sigh.

It's a weird night tonight, out here on this road, with no one around. He's lucky he crashed by a park, with no buildings or people around, or this could have been a lot worse. It's somehow simultaneously pitch-black and so light out, thanks to all the snow. It's falling so slowly and gently now, piling up on top of what has already settled, flakes landing in our hair and on our skin, holding their unique formations for a second or two before melting due to our slowly decreasing body heat.

I bend and extend the fingers on my left hand. It hurts a little. In fact it feels kind of swollen. I quickly remove my engagement ring and pop it in my bag. I would hate for my hand to swell up more, and for it to have to be cut off.

Perhaps it was because I've been drinking myself, but I can't believe I got in a car with a drunk person. How did I not realise? Even if he's only slightly over the limit or whatever, the limit exists for a reason.

The snow turns blue as the flashing lights approach us.

In a flurry of police officers and paramedics, I remember my phone flying out of my hand when we crashed.

I make a move for the car.

'Miss, please stay away from the vehicle,' a policeman informs me.

'I just need my phone,' I tell him.

'No, you need to go to hospital and get checked out,' he corrects me. 'We will have your phone brought to you when it's safe.'

Shit. I need to call Leo and let him know I'm OK. I just need to pray he doesn't find out about this from someone else before I get chance to tell him.

Chapter 33

Two months ago, if you'd told me I'd be lying here on this table, waiting for an X-ray after being involved in a car accident with three rock stars – one of them driving under the influence – I would've laughed in your face. Not even LA Mia had scrapes like this.

'OK,' the X-ray technician says, approaching me with her clipboard. 'I just need to ask you a few quick questions, then we'll get started.'

'OK,' I say softly, before answering her questions on autopilot. I want to get this over with.

'When was your last period?' she asks.

'Hmm?' I say, turning to look her in the eye.

'Your last period,' she repeats. 'Do you know when it was?'

'I'm not sure,' I tell her. 'I keep track of it in my phone, but my phone is still in the car.'

'Well, is there any chance you could be pregnant?' she asks.

'Erm . . . no, I don't think so.'

'Would you like to take a test?' she asks me. 'To be sure.'

I think for a second. We're more than halfway through December now, I think, and I definitely had my period just before Halloween because I remember the little jolts of anxiety I felt all evening, because I was wearing a white dress. So I'm expecting one just after Christmas, but did I have one in November? I'm not sure . . .

'Have you been trying for a baby?' she asks me.

'No.'

'Have you been practising safe sex?'

'I haven't been practising, I'm *really* good at it,' I joke awkwardly. 'There's no way I could be pregnant. Sorry, my head is just a little bit all over the place since the crash.'

'So long as you're sure,' she replies.

My mind does somersaults as I'm wheeled back to A&E. It's the middle of the night, but you'd never know being in here, where there are no windows and busy, wide-awake people everywhere.

I'm waiting to see a doctor, to get my results. I don't feel too bad. I'm just in pain with my ankle, my chest and my stomach. The doctor I saw thought it safest I be X-rayed to make sure nothing was broken, but she suspects it's just bruising. Still, I'll worry myself sick until the second it's confirmed.

From where I'm lying, I can see a small TV mounted on the wall. They've got some rolling news channel on, running a feature on how the homeless survive through Christmas. That's what you want when you're in hospital, right? Something to lift your mood . . .

'Back to our main story of the morning,' the reporter starts. 'For those of you just tuning in, we received word earlier today that pop mega star Dylan King has been involved in a car accident. It's being reported that, after a party at his house, he and two members of hot new band Ganzás – Finley Collins and Alexander Driscoll – got into a black Range Rover Sport, crashing not long after. We'll be bringing you more details as we get them. It is being reported, although it has not yet been confirmed, that alcohol may have been a factor in this accident. As we reported earlier, there was one other female passenger involved in the accident.

More on this story as it develops.'

'Oh shit,' I say out loud to myself.

'Shit indeed,' Leo says.

I am so happy to see his face and hear his voice, I immediately burst into tears.

'Leo,' I sob, holding my arms out for a cuddle. He gently obliges but his relief from seeing I'm OK soon dissolves into anger.

Before he gets to say anything, the doctor arrives.

'OK, Mia, so I have your results. Just as we suspected, no broken bones or anything like that. Just bruising to chest and stomach, as is fairly common for someone in an accident who is wearing their seatbelt. It's not very nice, it will hurt for a while, but obviously you're in a far better way than you would have been, had you not been wearing your seatbelt. As for the ankle, it's just bruising, no broken bones or dislocation. I'm thinking perhaps you hit it on something during the crash? Again, it will hurt, but the bruises should clear in a couple of weeks.'

I breathe a sigh of relief. 'Thank God,' I say. 'How are the others?'

'I'm afraid I can't discuss other patients with you, Mia,' the doctor tells me. 'But I've set the wheels in motion for letting you go home. Someone will be along shortly to get you out of that gown, sort out your pain relief and so on. Any questions?'

'No, thank you for everything,' I say.

'OK, I have to go. Please don't get in cars with drunk people in the future,' the doctor says sternly as he dashes off.

'Mia, what the hell were you thinking?' Leo asks me once we're alone.

'Leo, I didn't know he was drunk. I never would have got in a car with him if I'd known,' I insist.

'Could you not tell he was drunk?'

'He didn't seem drunk. But I'd only just met the guy, so I didn't know him well enough to be able to tell if he seemed drunk for him or not, y'know?'

'You didn't know him well, and yet you got in a car with him?' he replies angrily.

'Dylan, I promise you, I would never knowingly risk my life like that.'

'Leo,' he snaps.

'What?'

'Leo,' he repeats slowly. 'My name is Leo. Dylan is the one who nearly got you killed.'

'Shit, sorry,' I say, reaching for his hand. 'My head is all over the place.'

'Where is your engagement ring?' he asks, noticing it isn't on my finger.

'It's in my bag,' I tell him. 'I took it off. My fingers were hurting and kind of swollen.'

Leo runs his hands through his hair as he puffs air from his cheeks.

'Do my parents know?' I ask.

'No,' he tells me. 'I got the call at work and rushed straight over.'

Leo is wearing the navy-blue shirt and trousers he usually wears for work. I feel bad he's had to drive all the way here when I'm fine. Still, I need to get home, I suppose. I just hate to see this expression on his face – he looks so disappointed in me. I've only seen this look once before, before we got together properly, and it broke my heart then too.

'I know you're kinda mad at me . . .'

'Kinda mad at you?' Leo echoes. 'Mia, I'm furious. You could have got yourself killed.'

'I know, and I'm sorry,' I say, starting to feel like a broken record. 'But . . . please, I just need you to be nice to me. It's been a horrible night, I've been so scared . . . Can we do this later?'

'Shall I go get the car?' he asks. 'Bring it to the door so we don't have to trail you to the far end of the car park?'

'Please,' I say.

'Here's your phone, by the way. The police officer I spoke to gave it to me.'

'Thanks.'

'Back soon,' he tells me, heading for the door.

I unlock my phone and open up my calendar.

Several large tears roll from my eyes, which I quickly wipe away.

'It's the relief of being OK, isn't it?' says the lovely nurse who has been looking after me.

'Yes,' I lie.

She helps me down from the trolley and sits me in a wheelchair.

'Let's go get you your clothes,' she says as she pushes me.

'Can I ask you a question, please?'

'Of course,' she replies.

'I took a pregnancy test before my X-ray, just to make sure I wasn't pregnant,' I tell her.

'Sure,' she replies.

'It was negative, but I seem to have skipped a period. I just wondered what else can cause that.'

'Well, one missed period with no other symptoms isn't really anything to worry about. We all skip one at some point, usually down to lifestyle elements. Have you been stressed or dieting?'

'Both,' I tell her.

'Well, there you go. Try not to worry,' she reassures me. 'Wait and see what happens. If you skip another, maybe make an appointment to see your GP and get checked out. How old are you?'

'I'm thirty-three,' I reply.

'Do you have any kids?'

'No,' I reply.

'Well, like I said, wait and see what happens. I'm sure it will turn up.' She squeezes my shoulder reassuringly.

'Thanks,' I reply.

A first I was worried I *was* pregnant, but now I'm worried something might be wrong with me – I didn't even think about my fertility. I don't suppose anyone thinks about it until they need it, do they?

How have things got so messy so quickly? Leo is mad at me, my mum is mad at me – she'll be even angrier when she finds out about this accident. I don't know what's up with me at the moment, but if I don't figure it out soon, I'm going to drive everyone away.

Chapter 34

It's been a day of talking so far. Lots and lots of talking. First of all, I was woken up by a call from my mother who was, as I predicted, very, very angry. Not just angry, but disappointed. She can't understand why her 'thirty-three-year-old daughter', who she 'raised so well', could have 'got in a car with drunk men' and 'allowed one of them to crash'. Looking back now, of course I wish I hadn't got in that car, but it really didn't occur to me for a second that Finn might have been under the influence. Like, why would I assume a person would want to drive his own car while drunk? Risking his *own* expensive car and his *own* precious life. Why would that cross my mind?

Next up, she laid into me about Debbie. She wanted to know why I'm not taking my wedding planning seriously and why I would be so rude to Debbie. I tried to explain that I wasn't trying to disrespect her, but she wouldn't listen. Apparently, if I apologise to Debbie at the party tonight, she'll reconsider planning my wedding – but why would I want her to do that? I didn't want her in the first place, so I'm certainly not going to beg her to come back to me, after she flounced off.

Finally, my mum also wanted to confirm that I'll be in attendance at the family Christmas party tonight – I don't think anything less than a fatal accident (in which *I* died) would get me out of this family party.

Next up, I had to talk to the police about the accident. I told them everything I knew as Leo watched from the doorway. It was simple enough, telling them what I remembered, and they're happy Dylan and I had nothing to do with the crash, and that we got in the car in good faith. I'm not sure what's going to happen to Finn, but I imagine he's in big trouble.

I've also just finished up on the phone with Dylan, who called me to see how I was doing. He has similar injuries, but nothing more serious than bruising. Putting on your seatbelt when you get in a car is just one of those things you do, without really thinking about it, but it was those four seatbelts that saved our lives last night. Without them, who knows what would have happened. I will always, always remember to put my seatbelt on when I get into cars now, and every time I do I will be reminded that I am alive because of them.

Dylan also reminded me that he plans to honour his promise, and open up more about his private life. There are only a few days until Christmas now. I have a lot of information about Dylan, more than I need to write this book . . . except the important stuff. If I'm going to get everything I need before Christmas, I need to go now and get this last little bit of info so I can crack on, finish the book, and put all this business behind me.

I know I should probably rest up, and try and make things right with Leo, but he can hardly talk to me today. So I can stay here, in the doghouse, and maybe have a row if I'm lucky, or I can go and do my job – I know which one will benefit us more in the long run.

Moving hurts a little, but it's not a problem. I'm just quite stiff, which is making getting dressed a little tricky.

'What are you doing?' Leo asks from the doorway, wiping his paint-covered hands with an old rag. He must be doing something to the house. He's always doing something, not that we ever really have anything to show for it.

'I'm going to work,' I tell him.

He just laughs, angrily. 'Don't you think you should rest? And probably avoid that crowd for a while,' he suggests.

'It's work, Leo. You should probably avoid fires, but it's your job. And anyway, I'm nearly finished.'

'You were in a car accident that was his fault. Just take a day off, for God's sake.'

I stop what I'm doing and stare at him. I don't know what surprises me more: the fact he's blaming Dylan or that he thinks he can tell me what to do.

'This wasn't Dylan's fault,' I tell him. 'But even if it was, this is work. I need to finish this job so I can get paid and we can buy things like eggshell paint and six hundred pounds' worth of flowers.'

Leo shakes his head. 'Fine. Go. Don't forget the party tonight.'

'I won't,' I tell him. 'I'm going to take some stuff with me so I can get ready and head straight there.'

'So that's you out for the rest of the day?'

'Yeah . . .'

'OK, then,' he says dismissively, heading back downstairs.

For a moment I just sit on the end of our bed, thinking. Why is he so mad at me? I know I was in a bad situation, but it wasn't my fault, and I'm absolutely fine. No harm done. Why does he have to be mad at me? Why can't he just go back to loving me?

I get dressed, slowly and carefully, and apply my make-up. As well as my usual face-full, I've applied concealer and powder to my chest too, just where you can see my bruises above the top of my off-the-shoulder jumper. You don't realise how much damage seatbelts actually do you in the process of saving you. The bruises across my chest and my shoulder are huge, but definitely better than any of the alternatives.

I pick up my rose-gold dress from last night, considering whether or not to wear it tonight, only to see that the sequins have come off where my seatbelt was. Six hundred pounds, down the drain, just like that. I find another dress in my wardrobe, a black, sparkly bodycon dress that will be fine for tonight. It's a bit short for a family party, maybe, knowing how judgemental my lot are, but it has a high neck that will cover my bruises *and* it looks fabulous.

I scan an eye across my shoe collection. I'm not entirely sure I'll be able to get my bruised foot into a heel, but the only other kinds of shoes I have are trainers. I'll wear my sparkly gold Converse today and pick up some flat pumps before I head to the party – see, I can be sensible when I need to be.

'See you later,' I call out, as I reach the front door.

For five seconds I hear nothing, but then . . . 'Bye.'

If that's the way he wants to be, so be it.

Chapter 35

By the time I reach Dylan's house, my foot is really starting to hurt. There are a few cars outside his house, as always (a few belonging to him and a few belonging to staff). I'm relieved when Mitch answers the door immediately.

'Hello, Mia, how are you?' he asks considerately.

I raise an eyebrow. Mitch isn't all that friendly to people he doesn't deem important, which must means he thinks I'm one of them now. I suppose a drunken RTA was my initiation – I'm in the club now.

'Not too bad,' I reply. 'How's Dylan?'

Mitch smiles his best fake smile. 'Come in,' he says, ignoring my question.

Mitch shows me into the living room where a shirtless Dylan is lying flat out on the sofa, his chest bare so the world can see his bruises. His body is a mess, just like mine.

'Dylan, I'm doing everything I can,' I catch Charles, his publicist, explaining to him as I approach them.

'Do better,' Dylan insists. 'The press are having a fucking field day with this.'

'We've issued a statement saying you weren't driving – so has Finn, for all the good it's going to do him. People love to give successful people a hard time – you know this.'

'What about the tree people – are they still going?'

'Well, yes, some activists are still upset about the damage to the tree,' Charles replies. You can tell from his voice that he thinks it's ridiculous, that people are upset about a damaged tree when four people could've lost their lives if the accident had been worse. 'Forget about that for now. You were in a 2.5-tonne car – whatever it hit was going to be damaged. Be thankful it was only a tree, Dylan, seriously. I'll arrange for you to plant some in the New Year.'

'Hi,' I say, interrupting.

'Mia,' Dylan says, carefully pulling himself to his feet before hugging me. He's cautious of his own injuries as well as mine, hugging me gently, but I can feel the comfort he intended.

'I'll leave you two alone,' Charles says.

'How are you?' he asks, nodding towards the sofa. We sit down together.

'Not too bad. The drugs they prescribed for the pain are pretty great.' I laugh.

Dylan frowns. 'Yeah, they wouldn't let me have any,' he tells me. I look at him, shocked. Why on earth wouldn't they give him pain relief?! 'Because I used to . . . self-medicate.'

Oh, right. I supposed if you've had a drug problem before, *any* drugs will be a problem in the future – especially drugs that are as habit-forming as strong painkillers.

'It's OK,' he assures me, raising his glass. 'Dr Jack Daniel is helping me through it.'

I'm not sure self-medicating with alcohol is any better than doing so with drugs, but now really isn't the time or the place.

'I can't apologise enough, man. Seriously. I wish I'd never invited you.'

'I know,' I tell him. 'Please stop apologising.'

'We're fucking friends now; it's beyond the author/subject bullshit. I care about you, man. I feel sick that I put you in danger.'

'I care about you too,' I assure him. 'I don't blame you at all. I blame Finn, and he'll get what he deserves.'

'I hope they put him away, teach him a lesson. Although he'd never last in prison, would he?'

'Anyway, how about some work to distract ourselves?' I say brightly.

'Right, let's get this over with,' he says, topping up his glass before making himself comfortable.

'OK, so . . . your brother. Neither of you has ever spoken about what went on there, so . . . care to share?'

The only thing the general public knows is that Dylan and Mikey had a falling-out, which ended both their band and their relationship. No one knows why, and if Dylan were to reveal why in this book, it would pretty much cement its bestseller status.

'Everyone knows my marriage went to shit. I suppose I'll get into that next time – I can't do both today,' he tells me, which is understandable. 'So that relationship was short and wrong – it was hardly even a relationship. I married her for the wrong reasons. I didn't really do girlfriends – not my own at least.' He laughs.

I know those feels. I remember when I 'didn't do' relationships.

'The point is, I'm having casual relationships. I – and I admit this – didn't always treat girls all that well, so when I do meet a girl I like, I treat her like a queen. Like, look at me and you, man, we get on so well. I'm not gonna shag you and then show you the door.'

'Thanks.' I laugh, like he'd even get the chance, but I appreciate the sentiment.

'So, I meet this girl years ago and the first thing she does is insult me. It's great. She's like one of the lads so we become best buds really quickly and things stay this way for years.'

'Nicole?' I ask.

'Yeah,' he replies, surprised. 'How did you . . .?'

Suddenly, everything makes sense. I'm not even sure I need Dylan to finish the story.

'You've mentioned her a few times already,' I tell him.

'After my divorce, she saved my life. I left Crystal – that was her name – not too long after the wedding, around the time Nicole had broken up with her boyfriend. She was seeing – do you remember Two for the Road?' he asks.

I rack my brains but the name doesn't sound familiar. I shake my head. Probably something else I missed while I was in LA.

'They're another example of bands getting too big too quickly, going off the rails like Ganzás. So, Nicole and Luke, the drummer in Two for the Road, had this will they/won't they shit going on for months before they finally got together. She's an angel, man; he didn't deserve her. She helps him through his drug problem, gets his career back on track, and then he goes off on tour, gets addicted to smack, cheats on her. Swear to God, I wanted to murder him. So I leave Crystal and the kids, she leaves Luke, we're both in the shit at the same time – we decide we'll go on holiday together.'

'It's nice that you were there for each other,' I tell him.

'Yeah, it was fucking awesome. We did a sweet road trip across America. We flew to LA, first class, which means an open bar and a comfy bed. We didn't really know where we were going but we hired a convertible Mustang and just set off. We hung around Hollywood for a while. Man, that's a weird place – well, you'll know, you lived there.'

'It's definitely its own thing,' I reply.

'We didn't feel like we belonged there so, after we saw the sights, we hit the beach. It's just like it is on TV. Some local hippy told us we had to "cruise Route 1, dude, it's so sweet", so we headed north, and even though he was super-high, his advice was spot on. You gotta do that drive – Route 1 is something else. It's miles and miles of amazing views, and when you get to the end, San Francisco just kinda rises out of the mist.'

'Sounds incredible – I'm so jealous,' I admit.

'The last night there was so chilled out. We went for dinner and then we took one last late-night stroll, chatting and admiring the view. And I don't know why I did it – I wasn't really thinking – but I kissed her, out of nowhere, and she kissed me back, and I felt this part of my brain turn on, like a part that had never been accessed before. That kiss, it was like a punch in the fucking mouth; it was incredible. We went back to the hotel, kissed some more, and then we started taking each other's clothes off. No word of a lie, Mia, I was shitting myself.'

'Why?' I ask curiously.

'Honestly, I couldn't remember the last time I had sex sober – and I feel like an arsehole saying this, but I'd never given a shit about the other person, so long as I was happy, and then there I was, stone-cold sober, with my best friend. The pressure was unbearable. But we did it, and it was amazing. I woke up holding her the next morning and, just looking into her eyes, I saw everything about my life before Crystal that I missed. When I'm stressed I can't make music, but this woke me up. I was straight on the phone to Mikey, telling him we had to get to work on the new album as soon as I was back.'

I don't say anything; I just listen attentively.

'I don't think we were back in London twenty minutes before we see a copy of the *Daily Scoop*. They've got pretty much every bird I shagged while I was married dishing the dirt on me. I saw Nicole reading it and I saw this sadness all over her face – I swear to God, man, like she was disappointed in herself for sleeping with me. But then she laughs it off and tells me I never change, and that she'd never expect me to change. So our relationship is a nonstarter as far as she's concerned.'

'So, what did you do?'

'I fucking changed,' he tells me proudly. 'I'm not stupid. I just realised that I'm in love with my best friend – no messing around, I cleaned up my act. I quit getting pissed, I quit shagging girls, I get the band back in the studio and we make the best fucking album we've ever done, and it goes straight to number one.'

'Dylan, that's amazing,' I tell him, my smile beaming. Then, of course, I remember that this story all goes wrong at some point, because here we are.

'None of this shit was quick,' he tells me. 'Months later we're in Manchester, I think . . . maybe Liverpool. They call the band for a sound check but Mikey is nowhere to be seen. So I go to find him. I check the dressing room and I hear him in the shower, and when I go into the bathroom to tell him to hurry up, I hear noises . . . I storm in and there he is, with Nicole.' Dylan exhales deeply.

'Shit, Dylan, I am so sorry,' I tell him.

'So, I hit the roof, man. I mean, walking in on the girl I love with my brother . . . fuck me, it hurt. So I'm going mad and they're telling me to calm down . . . I stormed out. Never spoken to either of them since.'

I pull Dylan close, hugging him as tightly as I can without hurting him.

What a heartbreaking story. It's such rotten luck that the second he opens his heart, someone destroys it. I mean, I can see things from Nicole's point of view too – I'd probably feel the same in her position, like Dylan was just being Dylan. He missed his chance and it seems like he's worse than ever now.

'Was it this stuff that started the chain of events that landed you in rehab?' I ask.

He nods. 'And Mikey, perfect little Mikey, he's the favourite child, so the family support him. No one understands why I'm upset . . . I got pushed out. So it's just me now.'

'Listen, I completely understand,' I tell him. 'I didn't do relationships or feelings either. I was just lucky enough to let the right person in at the right time. And as for families, I'm the second-favourite child – of two children – so I get it.'

'But you've got your fiancé and you've got your family.'

'Just about,' I admit. 'It feels like they're both hanging by a thread at the moment. If I don't show up for this family party in a few hours, I'll be disowned for sure.'

'Family party?' he asks.

'The annual family Christmas party,' I tell him. 'It's this big, phony gathering of all our family and friends. It'll be shit.'

'Well, I don't have any family, and I don't have any friends,' he says.

'You have lots of friends,' I correct him.

'No, I have lots of hangers-on. Look at my "friends" – they're just people who work with me, or people who'll happily get off their nut and drive me into a fucking tree.'

I squeeze Dylan's hand. 'I'm your friend,' I tell him. 'I am. In fact, why don't you come to the party tonight?'

'What?'

'I told you, it's for our family and friends, and you're my friend. It *will* be shit, I'm warning you now, but you should come.'

'OK,' he says, cheering up. 'Thank you.'

'You're welcome,' I reply. 'Did I mention it will be shit, though?'

He laughs. 'Thank you for giving a fuck about me,' he tells me. 'It's been a while since anyone did that.'

Dylan pulls himself to his feet and heads upstairs to get ready – he wants to make sure we're not late. I actually think he's excited.

I wonder if I should call ahead and let people know he's coming. I don't just think it will do Dylan good to go to a non-showbiz party, but it will do my family – and Leo – good to meet the person I've been spending all this time with, and to realise he's not the monster the media make him out to be. Sure, he's got his issues, don't we all, but if he truly cleaned his act up before then I'm sure he can do it again. He just needs the right support. I get how he feels, I really do, because when I was alone in LA it was easier to go on a bunch of dates than it was to accept that I had no family around me, and no real friends. It's hard to make friends as an adult – no one warns you about this growing up. That's why so many people stick with their childhood best friends, I think, even when their lives go off in different directions, because making a friend you can trust as an adult is so hard.

I think I'll keep Dylan a surprise and just turn up with him. I think everyone will like that.

Chapter 36

The Christmas party, as always, is at the Mercer Hotel, in their function room. We've been having it here for so long, I think they give our family a discount now. I'm surprised my parents aren't pushing for me to have my wedding here actually.

'Aw, it's kinda cute,' Dylan says as we walk into the function room.

The room looks perfectly festive. Tables are scattered around the edges, with a little decorative Christmas tree in the centre of each. They've got good lighting game here, with twinkly stars in the ceiling, and a large, kaleidoscopic disco ball, bouncing different colours around the room.

On the stage there's a Michael Bublé tribute act who, despite looking nothing like the man himself, is belting out perfect covers from his Christmas album. Still, you can't have it both ways, can you? You can be born looking like a singer or you can have a voice that sounds like theirs, but the chances of having both are slim. Best you get the guy who sounds like Bublé, rather than someone who looks like him but can't sing to save his life. Well, for this sort of thing anyway.

'You've got a big family,' Dylan observes.

'I guess, but I couldn't name most of them. A lot of the people here are just family friends. Oi, Hannah,' I say, noticing my cousin walking little Angel across the dance floor on her feet.

My cousin looks up at me but then she notices Dylan next to me. I'd say she was perfectly frozen, were it not for the slow, rhythmic blinking of her eyes.

'Dylan, this is my cousin Hannah,' I say as we walk over. 'Hannah, this is—'

'Dylan King,' she blurts, sighing. I've never seen my cousin lose her cool before. I'm not sure if she's dumbstruck, starstruck or lovestruck – maybe a combination of the three. 'Hi.'

'Hello,' he says, the cheeky smile of his ever-present.

'Is Leo here yet?' I ask her.

'Not yet,' she replies, looking at Dylan instead of me. 'He went to Gran and Granddad's to help out with something first.'

'Oh, OK,' I reply. 'Well, I'm going to go and introduce Dylan to some more people. If you see Leo, let him know I'm here.'

She nods, watching us as we walk away.

'Are all your family big fans?' He laughs.

'Probably just my cousin – don't get excited,' I warn him. 'Shall we get a drink?'

Dylan nods. 'Just an orange juice for me,' Dylan tells the barman. I fire him a surprised glance. 'I don't want to peak too soon.'

I really appreciate him behaving.

'Mia . . .' I hear my Auntie June's voice from behind me.

'Auntie June,' I say brightly. 'Hello.'

She scrunches her face at my enthusiasm to see her. 'All right, Mia. No one likes a sarcastic person.'

'Hello,' Dylan says to her politely.

'Hello,' she replies. 'You want to be careful talking to this one.'

My Auntie June points me out to Dylan with her eyes.

'You know what happened to her last night? She was in a car accident. She's been going around with *musicians*.' My auntie says the word 'musicians' like they're a terrible crowd to be in with, like drug dealers or the mafia. 'Last night, they all pile in a car, drunk, and smash into a wall. It's a miracle she's alive.'

'It was a tree,' I correct her.

'It was bloody stupid,' she replies, like it doesn't matter either way. I suppose it doesn't.

I find it funny, that she doesn't recognise Dylan. June isn't the kind of woman who is up-to-date with pop culture anyway, but I suppose Dylan doesn't look very rock-starry tonight. He looks normal – normal, but great. He's wearing black trousers and a white shirt with a black waistcoat. He's got his shirt buttoned up and his sleeves down to cover his tattoos. It might just be my imagination, but I feel like he's trying to keep his inked hands hidden too. He looks really smart; he's scrubbed up nicely.

I, on the other hand, am wearing the LA Mia dress I picked out earlier. The short, dark and sparkly one (which is probably how I'd describe LA Mia). My engagement ring keeps catching on it; in fact, it's really starting to bother me. Were I the superstitious type, I might think LA Mia was trying to send me a message, showing me that my old life is comfortable and my new one is just getting in the way. That's daft, though, right?

'So, are you someone's plus-one?' my auntie enquires. 'You want to watch yourself around this one – nothing but trouble. She's been known to steal men – taken men.'

'I'm right here, you know,' I point out.

Dylan just laughs.

'Mia,' my mum says as she and my dad approach us.

'Mia,' my dad says.

'Birth mother, sperm donor,' I say jokily, greeting them in a way I feel is as warmly as they greeted me.

'Oh, hello,' my mum says, noticing Dylan. 'This is your musician friend?'

'Dylan King, nice to meet you all,' he says, shaking hands with all three of them.

'Excuse me for a moment,' my auntie says, darting off as her cheeks flush.

'Well, it's nice to meet you too,' my mum says.

'I brought you a Christmas present,' he tells her. 'A case of champagne for the party. I had the bar staff put it on ice. Let me know if it's not enough – I can get more.'

'Well . . .' my mum starts, touching her hair nervously. 'That is so very kind of you.'

Of course she's charmed. She's female.

'Now, just a second . . .' my dad says. 'You weren't taking very good care of my daughter last night now, were you?'

'Wow,' I blurt. I don't think I've heard more than eight different words from my dad since the Nineties. It gives me a fuzzy feeling in my heart, to hear him looking out for me like this. He might be the strong, silent type, but it shows that he does listen, and he does care.

'I'm watching you, young man,' my dad warns him, pointing at him.

'OK, down boy,' I say, laughing it off awkwardly. 'Thanks, though.'

'I'll go and tell the rest of the family you brought a guest,' my mum says, ushering my dad away. I imagine the next time she comes over, she'll leave my dad at the other side of the room.

'Ooh, look, there's my granddad. You have to meet him,' I tell Dylan, taking him by the hand, dragging him across the room to where my grandparents are.

'Hello,' I say brightly.

'Hello, Mia,' my gran replies, her gaze immediately falling to my feet. 'I see you thought trainers were a good idea.'

'Gran, I was in a car accident. My foot is all messed up – did you expect me to turn up in stilettos?'

'If I know my granddaughter like I think I do, yes,' she replies.

'I heard about the crash,' my granddad says. 'Horrible business. You OK?'

'Just bruised,' I tell him. 'I'll be fine.'

'Are you OK, son?' he asks Dylan.

'Me?' Dylan asks, surprised. 'Bruised too, but that's all. We were both so lucky.'

'You were,' my granddad says. 'Good to hear you're both OK. It just goes to show, you can't trust anyone.'

I smile at him. He's the first person who hasn't blamed us.

'Where's Leo?' I ask. 'Hannah said he was with you guys.'

'He nipped home to get changed,' my granddad says. 'We had a bit of bother with the water; he took a look for us.'

'Oh, OK,' I say. 'Well, I'll go introduce Dylan to some more people. See you in a bit.'

We're halfway back across the empty dance floor when Dylan stops me.

'I'm beginning to think you've made this fiancé up.' He laughs.

'Oh no, you've figured me out. Nothing gets past you,' I say sarcastically.

'He pretty handy then, your fiancé?'

'Handy?' I repeat back to him.

'Yeah, you know, like a manly man who does jobs and shit,' Dylan explains.

I cackle. 'That's like something my gran would say – "Ooh, that Leo's handy".'

'All right, all right,' he says. 'It sounds like he is.'

'Shit,' a voice booms over the PA system. Everyone stops what they're doing and looks at the stage, where Fake Bublé has stopped mid-song. He was in the middle of 'Holly Jolly Christmas' – the backing track is still playing in the background.

I hear a gasp at his language – I'd put money on it being my gran.

'Sorry, sorry,' he says into his microphone, composing himself. 'But . . . you're Dylan King.'

Suddenly all eyes are on Dylan, and with most of the people here knowing who he is, the room comes alive with chatter. Standing with him in the middle of the dance floor, I look around at the crowd. I feel like I'm in a scene from *The Walking Dead*, stuck in the middle of this room, surrounded by zombies who are about to swarm us.

'You have to sing a song,' Fake Bublé insists.

'Erm, isn't that what we're paying you for?' I remind him.

'It's fine.' Dylan laughs. 'You'd be surprised how often this happens.'

Dylan, bless him, climbs up onto the stage and takes the microphone from Fake Bublé. They confer with each other quietly before Fake Bublé goes off to change the backing track.

'Hello, ladies and gentlemen,' Dylan says into the mic, ever the professional. 'My name is Dylan King and I guess I'm going to sing a song for you.'

Everyone cheers.

'On one condition,' he adds. 'Mia?'

'Huh?'

'Come on, Mia.' He holds out his hand. 'Ladies and gentlemen, give Mia Valentina a big round of applause.'

I slink over to the stage to ask him what he's doing, only for him to extend a hand to pull me up.

'Dylan, what are you doing?' I whisper, standing onstage next to him. I'm a writer, not a performer – always have been, always will be.

'So, Mia and I do a mean rendition of "Baby, It's Cold Outside",' he tells the room full of my nearest and dearest. 'Music, Bublé!'

As the long intro plays I try and talk him out of it. No one wants to hear me sing. He isn't having any of it, though, and once the intro is up, I know I have no choice but to play along.

In my head I'm channelling my inner Cerys Matthews, attempting my take on her husky voice. I probably sound nothing like her but, I have to admit, I'm having fun. I might be imitating a star but Dylan is just Dylan, with a voice that is unmistakably his. Like, if someone were to play you a Dylan song you'd never heard before, you'd just instantly know it was him. I guess that's why he's a star and I'm not. Another way you can tell he's a performer is the easy choreography he's ad-libbing – the way he holds his microphone, the way he dances with me, the way he works the crowd.

We finish our song to a huge cheer from the crowd. I feel my cheeks blush a little, even though I know they're cheering Dylan and not me.

'Can . . . can I sing a song with you?' Fake Bublé asks him.

'Sure you can, man.' Dylan laughs. 'Your choice.'

Fake Bublé excitedly hurries over to the mixing desk to pick a song, before hurrying back.

'It's not a Bublé song,' he tells us. 'I hope that doesn't shatter the illusion.'

'I'm sure it will be fine,' I assure him. I don't think he has anyone fooled.

I carefully climb down from the stage as the pair start their duet of 'You've Got a Friend in Me' by Randy Newman and Lyle Lovett.

The first person to catch my eye is Leo. He looks amazing, in his black shirt that looks fit to burst under the stress caused by his broad shoulders and bulging biceps. One thing that has, without a doubt, not even come close to wearing off over the last four years, it's my attraction to Leo. I still fancy him so much, and tonight, as always, the second I clap eyes on him, I want to rip his clothes off. One of my favourite things is when I'm set to meet him in a public place somewhere, and I'll spot him before he spots me, and I'll just stare at him, unable to believe my luck.

I remember one time he was in town having his hair cut, so I walked to meet him. As I hit the town centre I turned a corner and came face to face with a man who took my breath away. It all happened in a split second, but I felt this overwhelming attraction – which I hadn't felt for anyone other than Leo since the day we met – and the only feeling that hit me harder than this attraction was guilt, that I was checking out some random man in the street. Then I realised it was Leo, with a new, shorter haircut, and I felt not only relief that I hadn't checked out a stranger, but great to know that I was so, so attracted to my own boyfriend. I thought this stuff was supposed to wear off but I can't ever imagine that happening with us.

I smile, excited to see him, just like I always am, but then I see the unimpressed look plastered across his face, a look he can't seem to hide, and then I remember he's mad at me.

'Hey,' I say, approaching cautiously.

'Hey,' he replies. 'How are you feeling?'

'Not too bad,' I tell him. 'Just achy.'

'I saw your duet,' he tells me, nodding towards the stage.

I laugh awkwardly. 'Yeah . . . I didn't really want to, but I didn't want to ruin the fun,' I tell him.

'Sounded like it was a regular occurrence for you and your buddy Dylan,' he says.

'This was only the second time.' I laugh. 'And I feel like it has a shelf life. No one wants to hear this song for at least eleven months after Christmas.'

'Why did you bring him?' he asks.

I feel the muscles in my face tense up. 'He doesn't really see his family and it's Christmas and, well, we're friends now, you know? And I don't have too many of those.'

'You're friends?' Leo repeats back to me. 'I thought he was just a job?'

'You have friends at work, right?'

'It's not the same.'

'It's not different either,' I point out.

Leo sighs. 'I just don't know how you can be friends with him,' he says.

'You don't know him,' I point out. 'He's a good person.'

'Is he just misunderstood?' Leo asks sarcastically.

'He is actually,' I reply. 'What's your problem?'

'No problem here,' he replies. 'You must really like him.'

'I do really like him,' I reply quickly, but then I pause and backtrack. 'Well, you know, not like you're implying I do, just as a friend.'

'Did you take your engagement ring off before his party?' he asks me, seemingly out of nowhere.

'What? No! I took it off after the accident. I was scared they'd need to cut it off if my finger swelled up,' I insist.

'OK,' he replies. 'I'm going to go get a drink.'

Shit. Does Leo really think there's something between Dylan and me? Because, of course there isn't. We're just friends, and what Leo forgets is that I've always got on with men better than women, and I've always had male friends (that's why I can't find a bloody bridesmaid to save my life), and it's never been a problem before. I am perfectly capable of having a male friend I'm not at all romantically interested in, and it offends me that he thinks otherwise, especially after we've been together all this time, after I've changed my entire life just to be with him.

I do a lap of the room, but with Leo giving me the silent treatment, propping up the bar, and Dylan onstage forging a bromance with Fake Bublé, I realise I have no one to talk to.

When the song finishes, Fake Bublé pinches himself, remembering that he is a professional, here to do a job.

'It's been an honour, sir,' he says, offering Dylan a hand to shake.

'You're welcome, man,' Dylan says, pulling him in for a hug. Fake Bublé can't hide his happiness.

'While we're between songs . . .' my mum says, making a beeline for the stage. Please, God, no one give that woman a microphone. She gestures at Fake Bublé, who hands over the mic without a fuss. 'I just wanted to say how wonderful it is to have everyone here. You all show up year after year, and it's just so wonderful to see you all. Thank you to Dylan, for that impromptu performance – and for the champagne,' she says, raising her glass.

'If everyone wants to make sure they have a glass . . .'

Waiters and waitresses rush around the room, hanging out glasses of fizz. I look over at Leo, who turns a glass down, gesturing at his small glass of what looks like a neat spirit from where I'm standing.

'Merry Christmas,' my mum says, raising her glass.

'Merry Christmas,' everyone echoes.

As torturous as this annual event is, my mum is right; it's nice when everyone gets together, and the fact that we can fill a room with people who love each other – no matter how crazy we drive each other sometimes – is a big deal, and something to cherish. If my *near* near-death experience has taught me anything, it's just how precious life is, and I don't want to waste another second of it on bad terms with Leo.

'Hey,' I say as I approach the bar. 'You not fancy the champagne?' I'm making casual conversation, just to get us talking.

'I don't want anything from him,' he replies, pointing at Dylan.

I watch as the barman clears the empty shot glasses from in front of him.

'They're never all yours,' I say in disbelief.

'Why not?' he asks.

'Because, for a big, buff, bloke, you get really pissed really quickly.' I laugh.

'Not like your buddy, Dylan, huh? What did you call him the other day? A high-functioning alcoholic?'

'Someone say my name?' I hear Dylan laugh awkwardly behind me.

Unsure what else to do, I make polite introductions.

'Leo, this is Dylan. Dylan, this is Leo.'

'It's good to finally meet you, man. I've heard a lot about you,' Dylan says, offering Leo his hand to shake.

Leo just laughs. I can't believe he's being so rude and embarrassing me like this. I've spent so much time banging on to Dylan about what an incredible fiancé I have, and here he is, acting like a stroppy little kid. Well, fine, if he wants to be childish, I'll show him childish.

As Fake Bublé launches into a cover of 'Have Yourself a Merry Little Christmas', a few couples make their way onto the dance floor.

'Do you want to dance?' I ask.

Leo scoffs at me hurtfully, as though to say 'as if', but then he realises I'm talking to Dylan and his face falls.

This clearly isn't Dylan's first time at the rodeo.

'Erm, is that a good idea, Mia?' he asks quietly.

'Yes,' I reply confidently.

'You wanna cut in, man, you just give me a shout,' Dylan tells Leo as I drag him towards the dance floor.

I take Dylan's hands and place them on my hips before wrapping my arms around his neck.

'Look, I'm usually down for a bit of trouble-causing,' Dylan starts, slow dancing with me. 'But . . . I mean, that's what this is, right? You're trying to make him jealous?'

'I don't know what I'm doing,' I admit. 'All I know is that, since the accident, he won't talk to me. He's so mad at me, he's struggling to look at me.'

'Give him time,' Dylan insists. 'He'll come to his senses. I mean, look at you. You're amazing.'

'Thank you,' I tell him sincerely.

Before I know what's happening, Leo is pushing between us, grabbing Dylan by the back of his shirt, escorting him towards the door.

'Leo, Leo . . .' I say, hurrying after him. As he stops to open the door it gives me a few seconds to catch up, but I get too close too quickly and Leo accidentally bumps both me and Dylan as he opens the door. We both wince in pain, the slightest touch having a huge impact on our tender bodies.

'Look at you,' Leo says once we're out in the hallway. 'Look at both of you, all bashed up, crying in pain every time you move.'

'Leo, we were in a car accident,' I remind him angrily. 'I'm sorry we don't all have the same muscle mass as Superman.'

'That's my point,' Leo snaps back. 'That's what I'm so angry about – that you were in the accident in the first place.'

'Listen, man, you've gotta believe me, there's no way I would've let Mia anywhere near that car if I'd known Finn was drunk,' Dylan insists, approaching Leo.

'No, you listen, *man*, Mia is my fiancée – *mine*. She's my world. And you might not give a shit about your family, or your own life, but you don't fuck around with other people's.'

I appreciate what he's saying, but the territorial, aggressive way he's saying it is making me uncomfortable. And those remarks can't be making Dylan feel very good about himself.

'I think we all just need to calm down,' I say.

'Calm down?' Leo says. 'Mia, you could've died.'

'I know,' I tell him. 'Don't think it hasn't been at the back of my mind all day, every second I was on the train, every time I crossed the road.'

'So, what are you still doing around him?' Leo asks me. 'Why have you brought him here?'

'Because he's my friend,' I say, slowly and loudly so he can absorb it.

Leo just looks at me for a second. 'You need better friends,' he tells me, storming off.

'You were right about him, he's a regular Prince Charming,' Dylan jokes once we're alone.

'I really don't know what's wrong with him at the moment. I'm sorry he roughed you up,' I say.

'Ooh, that Leo's handy,' Dylan says in a woman's voice. 'I fucking felt how handy he is. He picked me up like I was a fucking pillow. He might be a dick but, with muscles like that, I can see why you're with him.'

I laugh. I hope he's joking.

'I don't suppose it will be easy to find a hotel so last-minute that isn't extortionate, but I don't really want to go home. Can I stay in one of your guestrooms, please?' I ask.

'Of course you can,' he replies. 'Your bed is still made up from last night.'

'Thanks,' I reply. 'Can we get out of here now?'

'Sure. I'll call for my car.'

Chapter 37

I was woken up this morning by a sharp pain in the lower left part of my abdomen. Typical, I thought, that I'd finally get my period when I'm staying in someone else's house – a male, who absolutely won't have anything in his bathroom to help me out. But when I got up and went to the bathroom there was no sign of it so I did what anyone would do – I started googling whether or not having a glass of champagne on top of my painkillers had damaged my stomach. When that didn't really turn up any information to make me feel better, in my increasingly anxious state, I started googling missed periods and the potential causes. As one search term led to another I found myself on a very scary article about fertility.

I don't know if it's my age or my friends or what, but Facebook has been pushing its baby agenda on me in recent weeks. That's what it feels like, anyway. I haven't been able to help but notice that all of the sponsored content I'm seeing is about pregnancy and babies – so why wouldn't I think they were trying to tell me something? First up, I started seeing ads for baby blogs and mummy forums. Next it was serving up fertility trackers. Finally, this week, they sent me the biggest hint yet: an ad for a sperm bank. It's like they thought: OK, let's just remind this girl that babies are a thing that people her age are having – like, maybe she forgot. When that didn't work they figured: clearly she doesn't know how to get pregnant, or she'd be doing it, right? So they showed me fertility tracking apps and stuff. But now they've finally figured out why I'm not reproducing – because I'm missing that one vital ingredient, and if I can't source any on my own, I might as well order some online, right?

With my womb on my mind, I started googling the fertility of thirty-something-year-olds, and I really wish I hadn't.

This morning I read all about a study which concluded that, by the time a woman turns thirty, she's lost ninety per cent of her eggs. *Ninety!* And this number declines so quickly that, by the time you're forty, you've only got three per cent of your eggs left. I suppose I'd never really given it much thought, but I had no idea it was so hard to conceive in your thirties. Now I'm panicking because I feel like I was so stubborn for so long, insisting I didn't want to get married and that I didn't want a family, and now here I am, wanting both of those things, and seemingly unable to have either.

My fertility might be out of my hands, but my unexplained reluctance to plan this wedding is all me. Leo talks about wanting to be a dad so much; if I can't give him kids, it wouldn't be fair to marry him, would it? That's what he wants from life. It's important to him. It's kind of unfair that men have their entire lives to have kids and women just have this window (*and* they have to do all the hard work bringing them into the world) – but that's being a woman, right? It's not easy.

I stare into my coffee cup until a voice snaps me out of it.

'Morning, Mia,' Mitch says chirpily.

'Morning,' I reply. 'Do you live here?'

He laughs. 'I don't. I know I'm here a lot. I came in early to see Dylan this morning. He's written a song he wanted me to hear.'

'Dylan is up? It's not midday.'

'And he's written a song! Do you know how long it's been

since he's written a song?'

'That's great,' I tell him. 'Where is he?'

'He's in the living room. I'm sure he won't mind being disturbed.'

I grab my coffee and head off to find him. I walk into the room just in time to catch the last few lines of a beautiful ballad he's penned.

'Wow, Dill, that's amazing,' I tell him.

'It's not really finished,' he says, sounding the tiniest bit embarrassed. 'But I felt inspired. I haven't felt inspired in a long time.'

'I'm so proud of you,' I tell him, and I mean it. I know how rough he's had it; it's amazing that he keeps going.

'How are you?' he asks.

'I'm panicking about running out of eggs,' I tell him honestly.

'We can get more eggs,' he replies, but then he clocks the look on my face. 'Oh, *those* eggs. Lady eggs.'

'Sorry, I was just reading some dumb article and I probably should have gone home last night.'

'It's OK,' he replies. 'It's not weird that you're thinking about having kids. Most people want kids.'

'You didn't?' I ask.

'We getting into it already?' He laughs. 'Go on, get your Dictaphone. Let's get this over with.'

'Are you sure?' I ask. 'This really is the last bit of information I need from you, then we're done, and I can write the book.'

'I have mixed feelings about that fact,' he tells me. 'But yes, I'm sure.'

Dylan and I settle down on the sofa with my Dictaphone for our final session. I think I'm going to miss hearing his stories. Not just because they're interesting, but because of the way he tells them. He's a born entertainer.

'Where shall I start?' he asks.

'Start with when you met your ex-wife,' I suggest.

'So, I don't actually remember meeting Crystal Slater,' he

starts. 'Looking back, she was the kind of girl I would've slept with – blonde and desperate to shag someone famous.'

I can hear just how negatively he feels towards her in his voice already.

'One day she reaches out, tells me she's eight months pregnant with twins, tells me they're mine, tells me she's got the conception on tape, she's threatening to go to the press with it . . . I figure I'm screwed. I have all these PR experts telling me just how bad this is, so . . . I feel so stupid now . . . because I want to do the right thing by these kids, I marry her. I do it for the kids, to cut down on bad press and because I think there's this scared girl about to have two babies she didn't plan for and it's all my fault.'

'Your intentions were good,' I tell him.

'So, I pull out all the stops, money no object, to give her the wedding she wants, and then she has the babies and . . . she changes. It's like she hates me, man. She doesn't wanna be around me; she kicks me out of *my* bed. So, I'm not proud to admit it – and I swear, I did want to make this marriage work – but I started sleeping around again. My life was just so miserable. I started drinking more too. Do you really think I'm a high-functioning alcoholic?' he asks me, quickly steering us onto a different topic, one I wasn't expecting.

'You do drink too much,' I tell him. 'Well, like, you drink too much at inappropriate times.'

'Do I really, though?' he asks.

'What's in that mug?'

'Point taken,' he says. 'Anyway, things get worse and worse and they finally come to a head and I tell her I want a divorce. She says fine, because the kids aren't mine anyway. She says she just wanted some rich idiot to bleed dry.'

'What?'

'So, when she said she had a video of the conception, I just kind of took her word for it, and when I mentioned a DNA test before the wedding she got really upset and offended – I felt bad, man. I wasn't there when they were born. I missed it; I was off partying. Don't look at me like that,' he says, even though I didn't realise I was.

'I didn't want kids, didn't want to get married. I only spent a few days over Christmas with them before I had to go off on tour. So, few months after Char and Lamb are born – and don't say anything about their names because I had no say in them at all – she's suddenly saying they're not mine, we're getting a divorce, she's not gonna let me see them . . . I tell her I don't care, I want to take care of them. Like, I didn't want them generally, before they were born, sure, but I'm not a dick. She gets the DNA test done, literally throws it in my face and . . . they're not mine. She doesn't know who their dad is, but figured I'd be the best shot at giving them a good life so she said it was me. I figure, we leave my name on the birth certificate and that way, sure, they've got a bad mum, but I can still pay for the best care for them. So they go to a fantastic preschool; they have the best nannies taking care of them. I look like the villain who doesn't see his kids, but surely it's more important they're taken care of?'

'Man, marriage is nothing but trouble,' I say. 'My life was so much easier before I entertained the idea.'

'Same.' He laughs.

'People need to know the real you, Dylan. You have to let me include this in the book.'

'You think I like playing the villain? The bastard who doesn't want anything to do with his kids? Of course I don't.'

'OK, but when they're old enough, they'll read this book and see what you did for them, and whether they're your blood or not, they might want to reach out to you, to thank you for giving them the best start in life.'

Dylan thinks for a second.

'Well, OK, put it in the first draft, and I'll have a word with Charles and the publishers and we'll see what everyone agrees is a good idea.'

'OK,' I say, turning off the Dictaphone before clapping my hands. 'So, we're done.'

'Wow,' he says. 'I knew we'd run out of stuff to talk about eventually, but . . .'

'I know what you mean.' I laugh. 'We'll keep in touch, though, right?'

'Course we will,' he replies.

'Well, I'll go get my stuff,' I tell him. 'Then go home and face the music.'

'Come to Paris with me tonight,' he blurts as I reach the living-room door.

'What?'

'Come to Paris,' he says. 'I've got this thing tomorrow; I'm flying there late tonight. You deserve a break, and a thank you for all your hard work. You got the job finished when no other writer would. I'm flying on a private jet, bit of work tomorrow, back the next morning. It'll be cool.'

Oh God, I'm so tempted.

'I don't think my family will be happy with me, pissing off to Paris, just for fun, a few days before Christmas.'

'So, tell them it's for work. Pretend we didn't just have this conversation and this is your last chance to get information out of me.'

I think for a second. That could work. Well, things have been so shitty recently. My anxiety has been creeping back . . .

'I can't,' I tell him. 'I'd love to, but I can't.'

'You going to go home and smooth things out with your fella?' he asks.

'Yeah,' I reply. 'In fact, I'm going to go call him now.'

I head upstairs, close the bedroom door, sit down on the bed and take a deep breath before calling Leo. After several rings, he picks up.

'Hello?' a female voice answers.

'Erm . . .'

I move my phone away from my head to check that it was Leo I actually called.

'Mia?' she says.

'Erm, yeah . . .'

'Sorry.' She giggles. 'Leo is just finishing screwing something and then he can talk.'

I'll bet he is.

'Mia, hey,' he says coolly, sounding mad at me still, but mindful of the fact he has company.

'You got a secretary now?' I ask.

'Amy is here. She's helping me with furniture.'

'OK?' I reply, although it sounds more like a question than a response.

An awkward silence follows.

'Can you go somewhere so we can talk, please?' I say calmly.

'Sure,' he replies.

I wait a few moments for Leo to go into a different room.

'OK,' he says.

'First I find out you were on a "lads' night" out with her, then I find out she's got your jacket, then she's texting you . . . After all that, do you really expect me to believe that, after you and I have a huge row, you just decided to invite her over to build furniture with you?'

'Why, Mia? Because you think that when people fall out they just go off and sleep with someone? That's something LA Mia would do.'

'This term "LA Mia" needs to die now, because there is no LA Mia or UK Mia, there's just Mia, and this is me, and you seem to have a problem with it,' I reply.

'Amy is here helping me build furniture because there's something I wanted to get finished before Christmas, but . . . do you even care? Do you care about the house? The wedding? Do you care about me? You're the one who didn't come home last night,' he points out.

215

'I figured you'd want some space,' I tell him. 'And I slept in one of Dylan's five spare bedrooms – one that you were perfectly happy for me to stay in the night before – one that we were both invited to stay in the night before.'

'Yeah, I was fine with it when I thought he was looking after you. Not trying to kill you or shag you.'

'Dylan isn't trying to shag me,' I squeak, before quickly adding: 'He isn't trying to kill me either.'

'Mia, don't you see the way he looks at you? He came to your family's Christmas party, for crying out loud. Who does that if they're not interested in someone? And he just flashed his cash and everyone fell at his feet. I was pushed right out.'

'Leo, that isn't how it was at all.'

'And then you singing your little duet with him, dancing with him, defending him when he nearly got you *killed*.'

'OK, Leo, listen, you need to calm down,' I insist.

'How can I calm down when the woman I love doesn't want to marry me?' he asks.

For a moment, I'm silent.

'Leo, of course I want to marry you – I said yes, didn't I?'

'You did – but why? Every time anyone mentions the wedding to you, you change. Anytime anyone tries to plan any element of it, you make excuses. In five months, you haven't made one arrangement – you haven't even made any decisions, let alone any bookings.'

'I'm busy with the book.'

'. . . the book,' he says in sync with me. 'Yeah, you're always busy with the book. But I don't think that's it. I don't think you want to marry me. I want to get married, I want to have kids – you told me you wanted the same things, so if that's not true, what are we even doing?'

My breath catches in my throat. I love Leo so much, but he's right. I have been avoiding planning this wedding, and I can't explain it, but maybe it is because I don't want to get married.

And as for kids . . . I'm not sure that's going to be my decision, not if Mother Nature says no.

'Mia?' he says. 'Do you want this wedding to go ahead or not?'

I open my mouth to reply, but no words come out, just shallow breaths in quick succession.

'You can't say yes, can you?' he says.

'I . . .'

'Mia, are we even engaged anymore?' he asks. 'Because I don't think we are.'

'You're dumping me?' I squeak. 'You've got Amy there, answering your phone, and you're dumping me days before Christmas?'

'Look, I was busy putting something together, but I did tell Amy to answer my phone. I wanted to give you a scare, to see if you cared about me,' he confesses.

'What the fuck, Leo?'

'Mia, look, I'm not dumping you.'

'No, you're just testing me,' I reply angrily.

'I want to marry you, but I want you to want to marry me too. And I don't think you do. So stay there for a while if that's what you want, but figure out what you want before you come back, because I won't wait forever.'

'Oh, yeah, sure I'll stay here and you stay there, in my home, playing house with Amy,' I reply angrily, before hanging up the phone in a temper.

How dare he test me like this? I don't know if Amy is helping him with his screwing or not, but letting her answer the phone to see how I reacted is ridiculous. He knew it would upset me and for what? So he could feel less insecure?

Well, if he wants me to stay away for a few days and figure out what I want then, fine, I'll do it, but I might as well do it from Paris.

Chapter 38

I can finally tick flying in a private jet off my bucket list.

From the outside the jet seemed small . . . well, small compared to the massive passenger plane I'm used to nipping back and forth across the Atlantic in. But inside, it was massive. I was expecting a narrow cabin with a few seats either side of the aisle, not the mobile luxury apartment I stepped into.

I expected more people but it was just me and Dylan. He said his backing band were making their own way there, and that Mitch would be accompanying them. It felt like a huge waste, there being so much room on the jet, but it was kind of nice having it to ourselves. Not only did it have sofas, a TV, a bed and a kitchen with all the bells and whistles you could hope for, but there was also a bathroom with a massive bath in there. The flight only took thirty-five minutes but I was so comfortable on my cream-leather sofa, sipping champagne, that I jokily asked the pilot if we could go around the block.

It was pretty late when we arrived so we went straight to the hotel and then straight to our room. We're staying at the luxurious five-star Hotel du Petit Fleur. Dylan told me he always stays here, and that it 'used to be the house of some emperor or some shit'. I found the tourist information he offered up adorably hilarious.

He looked so serious as he said it. I also felt fiercely jealous that he has a 'usual' hotel in Paris, for all his regular trips.

I say 'our' room, but we're staying in the penthouse suite, which actually boasts two bedrooms at opposite ends of a huge living room. Just in case the huge floor-to-ceiling windows weren't enough, they open out onto an impressive balcony with a postcard-perfect view of the Eiffel Tower. Even though I was tired when we arrived last night, I still found time to Instagram the perfect skyline. If this trip is anything, it's a good way to raise my Instagram profile again.

I woke up this morning and stretched out fully in my bed, and, even in full starfish formation, I couldn't even reach the sides. It was glorious and, just when I thought this hotel couldn't get any better, there was a knock at my door and waiting behind it was breakfast. I'm afraid to even begin to consider how much Dylan must have spent on a trip like this, but I feel very fortunate to be invited. I know burying my head in the sand isn't exactly the smartest thing I can do right now, but if Leo thinks he can kick me out of our house for a few days to 'think about what I've done'... well, if he thinks I'm just gonna sit around being upset, he can think again. Ever since I regained my self-confidence, and became more like the girl he fell in love with in the first place, I've seen him panicking. Why doesn't he want me to be happy? I don't know, but if he can test me, then I can test him. Let's see how *he* copes without *me*.

Today, Dylan joined me in full-blown tourist mode, visiting all the sites Gay Paree had to offer. It's been a blur of a day, vising museums and taking selfies in beautiful places.

Annoyingly, Leo has been on my mind all day. Tugging at my heart, all day long, has been this feeling, this thought, that I wish he were here, enjoying it with me.

My favourite moment of the day came when we visited the Arc de Triomphe. We headed into the underpass with the intention of coming out under the arc; however, somehow we wound up heading into the underground walkway and then coming out the way we went in. I'm not sure how exactly we got turned around, but I couldn't stop laughing. When we finally made it out of the arc end of the tunnel, I was blown away by how crazy the traffic was around the roundabout; it was lawless. Bikes and motorbikes were weaving in and out of stationary cars, and when the cars weren't stationary they were nearly crashing into one another.

My second-favourite part of the day was the incredible four-course dinner we just enjoyed at Le Marguerite restaurant, the highlight of which was the crème brûlée – my God, every last calorie was entirely worth it.

'I still can't believe Leo was OK with you coming,' Dylan said as he polished off the last of his dessert, scraping every last bit out with his teaspoon.

'Well, he didn't exactly let me,' I confessed.

'Oh,' he replied.

'In fact, I probably shouldn't have come,' I said. 'He thinks I don't want to marry him.'

'And do you?'

'It's not a conversation for now,' I said, before quickly trying to change the subject.

Now we're on our way to what Dylan keeps calling my surprise. I don't know where we're going, but he's currently leading me through the breathtakingly beautiful Jardin des Tuileries. It looks gorgeous at night. I'd love to stop and take pictures, but Dylan says we have an appointment. Well, I suppose it's evening now, and he does keep saying he has his work thing later, although I feel like he's being purposefully vague about what it actually is.

'OK, eyes closed for the last stretch,' he insists.

'You want me to close my eyes?' I ask. 'In Paris, in the street, at night, you want me to close my eyes?'

'Yes.'

'I can't argue with that.' I laugh.

With my eyes closed I have to rely on my other senses for clues as to where we are. The first thing that hits me is the warmth, moving from outside in the cold December air to inside where the heating is cranked. The next thing that hits me is the smell: it's a beautiful, sweet vanilla scent, subtle but delicious. Classical music is playing, but none of these things gives anything away about where we are. I'm so intrigued, but I said I'd close my eyes so I'm keeping them tight shut.

'OK, open them,' Dylan says.

I open one eye slowly, then the other, before twirling around on the spot.

'Wow,' I say. 'Wow.'

I am in the middle of the most beautiful bridal boutique, surrounded by rails of dresses, all laid out ready for me to look over. Other than Dylan and me, there's only one other person here.

'Hello,' she says. 'My name is Sylvie.'

'Hi,' I reply.

'Your friend says you would like to try on some dresses?'

I look over at Dylan who gives me an encouraging nod.

'Come on, Mia, you're not gonna find dresses like this in the UK. If this doesn't get you excited about getting hitched, nothing will.'

He's got a good point.

'OK,' I say. I mean, I'm not even sure my fiancé still wants to marry me, but when in Paris, right?

'I could make some suggestions,' Sylvie suggests. She's a very tall, very slender lady with a sharp, dark, inverted bob that's so perfectly sculpted I can hardly believe it's real. I love her French accent – it makes her seem effortlessly sophisticated, unlike my Kentish accent that is more Kelly Brook than Coco Chanel. 'Or you could just browse?'

'Erm, I think I'll just browse,' I tell her. 'Thank you.'

'Of course,' she replies. 'I'll give you some privacy.'

'Am I a genius or what?' Dylan says. 'All this time people have been trying to make you plan your wedding, they never thought to show you a few dresses to get you excited.'

'You are a genius, Dylan King, congratulations.'

I browse one rack, then the next. It's only on the final rack that I find a dress I love. It's an ivory ball gown with a sweetheart neck and a sheer lace insert from the bust to the waist. I think the thing I love about it the most is the cascading skirt with horsehair trim. I admire the dress on its hanger, unsure I'm even worthy of trying it on.

'Is that the one?' Dylan asks.

'It's stunning,' I tell him. 'Just . . . wow.'

'Perhaps this is more of a winter dress,' Sylvie points out. 'Mr King said your wedding is in the summer.'

I sigh. I'm so crap at this wedding stuff that, even when I do think I've found the dress of my dreams – the first wedding dress I've looked at that I didn't find disgusting – I'm wrong.

'So what?' Dylan laughs. 'It's a dress. It's a wedding dress, she's having a wedding. You go out in that thing in winter, you'll freeze. I think you should try it on.'

'Really?' I reply. Sylvie looks visibly repulsed by our blasé attitude towards wedding-dress culture, but . . . it is a beautiful dress. Why is the world so insistent that weddings have to be done a certain way? It's my day, so why can't I just do what I want and be happy?

'Yeah, I'll step out. Try it on.'

'OK,' I reply excitedly. I don't even deserve to be in the same room as this dress, let alone try it on.

I slip off my cocktail dress and slip on the most beautiful wedding dress I have ever seen in life – on or off-screen – and, somehow, I look amazing in it.

'Whaaaat,' I exclaim, loud enough for Dylan to hear me.

'Can I come in?' he calls from the other side of the door.

'Yeah, come in here,' I reply. 'Someone needs to see me in this dress. It's like some kind of witchcraft. I actually look good in it – well, except for the seatbelt bruises that make me look a bit like a zombie.'

'Wow,' he says. 'I mean . . . just . . . wow. Mia, you look incredible.'

'I know, right?' I laugh. 'I just want one of these for sitting around in my house while I'm writing.'

I examine the price tag on the hanger.

'Oh, wait, no, I don't,' I correct myself. 'This thing costs a house.'

Dylan laughs. 'I'll buy it for you,' he says.

'Yeah?' I laugh. 'I'll take two of them then. Do you think they have it in black?'

'I'm serious,' he says. 'We'll call it a work bonus.'

'Shut up,' I reply. 'Dylan, don't be crazy.'

Dylan takes me by the hand and leads me over to the wall of mirrors, twirling me around in front of them.

'Mia Valentina, you were born to wear this dress, and you deserve to be with someone who can buy you expensive things.'

I stare at myself in the mirror and, as I look myself up and down, my engagement ring catches my eye as the light bounces off it. My modest little engagement ring, which was everything I wanted. Suddenly, everything makes sense.

'Oh my God,' I blurt. 'I don't want to get married.'

Dylan takes me by the hands. 'Mia, are you sure?' he asks.

'I'm so sure,' I tell him. 'This has just confirmed it.'

Before I have chance to explain, Dylan moves in to kiss me.

'Whoa, Dylan, what are you doing?' I ask.

'I thought . . .'

I wiggle free from his embrace. 'Wait, it's, like, 9 p.m. What work do you actually have tonight?'

'Look, don't get mad,' he starts slowly and cautiously, holding his hands out in front of him. Why do I think he's used to women attacking him? 'I don't actually have work, I just wanted to bring you to Paris. No funny business, I promise. You've worked so hard on this book, and, you know, the whole nearly-getting-you-killed thing. I just wanted to do something nice.'

'So . . .' I shrug my shoulders theatrically.

'So, I figured if you really did want to get married, showing you the best dresses on the planet would get you excited, and then you said you didn't want to get married and . . .'

'Oh God, Dylan, I am so sorry. I just . . . I realised something. I know why I've been putting off planning this wedding, and it is because I don't want to get married. Well, I do, but I don't.'

'I want to apologise for misunderstanding the situation,' he says, wincing with embarrassment. 'But I still have no idea what you're talking about.'

'So, all my adult life I've thought weddings were stupid – I'd rather attend the Red Wedding than a white wedding. There was no way I ever wanted to get married. And then I met Leo and fell in love, and I thought I'd changed my mind. But I haven't changed my mind . . . well, not about weddings anyway. I do want to marry Leo. I just don't want the big white wedding everyone has been pushing me into.'

'I see,' Dylan says sadly. 'Shit, I'm sorry, Mia. It's just . . . I haven't got on with anyone this well since . . .'

'It's OK,' I assure him. 'You told me yourself I reminded you of Nicole. But listen, just because you fell in love with your friend before, doesn't mean you have this time. I know you're probably so scared of missing your chance at happiness again.'

'Fuck, I'm mortified.' He laughs. 'I got it so wrong.'

'So, I'm going to get out of this dress, we're going to go to a bar, have a drink, sleep and then, tomorrow, we'll pretend this never happened. Cool?'

'Cool,' he replies.

Poor Dylan. It's probably been so long since he had someone genuinely care about him, no wonder he got his wires crossed. And I don't know what I was thinking, jetting off to Paris with him when my fiancé is at home, thinking I don't love him enough to marry him. It's all going to be OK, though, because as soon as I explain myself . . . well, Leo knows me better than anyone else in the world, so he'll understand. I hope . . .

It feels good to know how I feel finally. I do want to be Leo's wife; I just don't want to get there via a big, fat wedding.

Chapter 39

If there's one thing that does not get better with age, it's hangovers. My God, why are there rabbits burrowing in my brain and how do I get them out, ASAP?

Dylan and I went for one drink last night, just to clear the air before we flew back home today. It was all going well, until Dylan got a phone call . . .

'Oh, shit. Mikey is calling me,' he said, glancing down at his iPhone as it vibrated on top of the bar.

Shit, I thought to myself. This couldn't be because I called Nicole the other night, could it? I blocked my number and I never gave my name . . .

It turns out that Dylan's unmistakable singing voice was easy to hear in the background of the call – I really didn't think that through – even if he was drunk and not exactly nailing the lyrics.

As the call went on, I could tell from Dylan's face that I was in trouble. Not only did the expression on his face change, but the way he looked at me changed. Up until now, he'd always looked at me like he cared about me, but last night, he looked so angry. He didn't even reply to Mikey, he just hung up on him.

'I can't believe I opened up to you, and you started meddling,' he said, calling me out in the busy bar. 'You called Mikey?'

'Dill, I was just trying to help you, Mikey and Nicole work things out,' I explain, but it was no good. He stormed off. That's when I decided to have a few drinks, to try to take my mind off what an absolute mess I've made of everything. How have I managed to push the two men closest to me so far away?

I grab my phone from the bedside table. The first thing I notice is that it's only 6 a.m. The second thing I notice are the eighteen missed calls from my mum. Shit, something must be up.

I sit up quickly, so quickly it actually feels like my head spins, and call her back. She answers almost immediately and the first thing I notice is the noisy background – it's only 5 a.m. there. Where is she?

'Listen, Mia, I don't want you to panic,' she starts, but I'm panicking before she's finished her sentence. 'Keep nice and calm.'

'I'm calm,' I lie.

'There was an incident at your gran and granddad's house. They're both OK, but your granddad is hurt. He's in the hospital.'

'Oh no. He's OK, though?'

'He's going to be just fine,' she assures me. 'The thing is, the fire brigade had to be called and, well, Leo got hurt too.'

'What? How? Is *he* OK?'

'I obviously don't know the full story with Leo, no one will tell me anything, but I heard he's having an operation this morning.'

'Fuck,' I blurt. My mum doesn't say anything, clearly forgiving of my profanity during this stressful time. 'I'll be right there.'

I rush into Dylan's bedroom without knocking. 'Dylan, wake up,' I say, shaking him lightly. 'DYLAN.'

Dylan looks at me for a second and smiles, before remembering that we fell out last night. His face falls again.

'Dylan, listen, I need to get home. My granddad and Leo have been in some kind of accident.'

'Shit,' he replies, sitting up quickly. 'Listen, I'll make some calls. Take my car, take the jet. I'm thinking I'll spend Christmas here anyway.'

'Thank you. Thank you so much,' I say, hugging him. 'You're an amazing man. I'm so sorry for last night. My intentions were good, I swear.'

'I know,' he replies. 'I overreacted, I guess. I was embarrassed and . . . Leo is lucky to have you.'

'Maybe give Mikey a call back,' I tell him. 'And Nicole. Make up with them, spend Christmas with them. Life is short.'

'Maybe,' he says. 'See you around, Valentina.'

'See you around, King.'

Chapter 40

Being in a complete state of panic, the return journey on the private jet wasn't quite so magical. Neither was the trek from the airport back to Kent.

I hate hospitals; I always have. They make me think of illness and death, and after my last little visit a matter of days ago, I was really hoping I wouldn't have to set foot in one for a while. And yet here we are.

'Mum,' I say, hurrying towards her along the corridor.

'Mia,' she says, grabbing me and hugging me. I can count on one hand the number of times my mum has hugged me as an adult. My God, it feels good. 'Your granddad is this way.'

I follow my mum along the corridor, towards the ward where my granddad is.

'Any news about Leo?' I ask, petrified something is really, seriously wrong with him.

'Don't worry,' my mum assures me. 'I've spoken to Maria. She says he's broken a couple of bones. He needed surgery to put them right, but he should make a full recovery. She's going to let me know when you can go and see him.'

I exhale, finally, after what feels like two hours of holding my breath.

'What the hell happened?' I ask.

'I'll let your granddad tell you himself,' my mum says, nodding towards his bed.

'What the hell have you been up to, hey?' I ask, trying to sound upbeat, but seeing my little old granddad here in a hospital, with his arm in a sling and forehead stitched and bloody, breaks my heart.

'I'm fine, I'm fine,' he insists. 'Just a knock on the head and a dislocated shoulder.'

'What happened?' I ask, stroking his hand lightly.

'I couldn't sleep. I was in a lot of pain with my knees, so I went to sleep downstairs, in my chair,' he explains. 'Anyway, I woke up a few hours later and the room was full of water, with more pouring in by the minute. Your gran was fast asleep upstairs. She didn't want to help me.' I love that he always finds time to crack a joke. 'So I called the fire brigade and then, er . . . well, I don't know. I woke up here.'

'Turns out your granddad took a tumble and fell under the water, he couldn't get back up.'

'Oh my God,' I gasp. 'Granddad, you could've died.'

'I could've,' he agrees. 'Until a brave fireman came in and saved me. Picked me up, got me out to the paramedics, apparently. I've no recollection of this, although I hear he broke his leg in the process.'

'Leo,' I say.

'They say he insisted he went in,' my mum tells me. 'He's a good man.'

'I know he is,' I reply. 'So, what caused this?'

'A bloody burst water main,' my granddad says. 'Ran down the hill and down our driveway, filled up the house in no time.'

'Shit.'

'Language,' my gran says, waking up in the chair next to my

granddad's bed.

'Sorry, Gran.' I smile.

After my mum receives a message from Maria saying Leo is out of surgery, and that she's going home to get changed while we wait for him to wake up, my mum and I hurry to his bedside. We arrive in the room where Leo is recovering. A nurse is fussing around him, doing various tests.

'Are you his fiancée?' she asks. I nod.

'His mum told me to expect you. She's gone home to get some things for him but you're welcome to wait here until he comes round.'

'Thanks,' I say, curling up in the big armchair in the corner of the room.

'Do you want me to stay with you?' my mum asks.

'I'll be fine,' I tell her. 'Thank you for everything.'

'Don't mention it,' she replies. 'You're still my little girl.'

I feel a tear escape my eye, which I quickly wipe away.

I look over at Leo, in his hospital bed, and he seems so helpless and yet he looks like he's sleeping so peacefully.

I would spend hours, sometimes even full nights, worrying about him doing his job, and in a way I was right to, because he *has* had an accident. But if there weren't people like Leo doing this job, there wouldn't have been anyone to save my granddad's life last night. Leo isn't just my hero, he's everyone's hero. On the plane, on the way over here, when I had no idea what had happened to him, I was so scared I'd never get to tell him how I felt, that he'd die thinking I didn't want to marry him. Now all I want him to do is wake up so I can tell him as soon as possible.

*

You know that feeling when you wake up and you know you've been asleep, with your head at a funny angle and your mouth wide open? Ouch.

I straighten my neck and wipe my chin with the back of my hand as I get my bearings, remembering where I am.

I look over at Leo's bed. He's awake and sitting up. My God, it's so good to see him.

I rush over to him, hugging him so tightly it makes my chest hurt.

I release him and look into his eyes, and for a moment neither of us says a word.

'You just couldn't handle not being the centre of attention, could you?' I joke. 'I have an accident, you just have to go and have an even more impressive one.'

'Oh no, you see right through me,' he says sarcastically.

I hold his hand tightly. 'Thank you for saving my granddad,' I tell him.

'Just doing my job,' he says. 'Anyway, he's practically my granddad too. You never need to thank me for looking out for our family.'

I smile. Then I cry. 'Leo, I should have come home. I'm so sorry.'

'I'm sorry for so much more than that,' he tells me. 'I was feeling insecure and I didn't know how to tell you.'

'Have you seen yourself?' I ask him. 'You have nothing to be insecure about. Your abs have abs.'

Leo laughs. 'Yeah, but I don't have endless money. I can't give you the lifestyle you had before. Not like Dylan could . . . I guess that's why I got so jealous, seeing you and him getting on so well. He could give you your old life back.'

'Leo, I don't want my old life back,' I assure him. 'Skinner offered me my old job back and I said no. Sure, I thought about it, fantasised about it even, but I told him I don't want to go back to LA and there's no negotiating or expensive gift basket that can change that. I knew that, if I told you, you'd tell me I should go.'

'I just want you to be happy,' he says. 'And since you took this new job, you've been happy again. Happier than you were at home with me.'

'Yes, it's been nice going out to work, and yes, I've enjoyed the perks of hanging out with Dylan, but I realised something while I was away. You're absolutely right. I have been putting off planning this wedding, and you were sort of right about me not wanting to get married . . . I love you so much and I want to be married to you, but I don't want a big white wedding. I'm sorry. It's just not me and the thought of having to go through with it has been terrifying me. And then, well, I got myself into a little bit of a state because my cycle is a bit messed up and I googled eggs and I don't have that many left and—'

'What have I told you about googling things?' he says.

'That it's smart?' I reply, knowing full well that isn't the answer. 'I know, I know, and I know I probably have nothing to worry about but . . . It all sounds kind of stupid now but I guess I worried that if I couldn't give you a wedding and I couldn't give you kids . . . I should've been honest with you.'

'Mia, listen to me, OK?'

I nod.

'I don't care about any of that stuff – not one bit of it. All I care about is you, and whatever does or doesn't come with that package is fine by me. You should've just said you didn't want a big wedding. Do you think I care about that stuff?'

'Everyone was pushing me towards it,' I tell him. 'And then when Belle came over and told me no one in the family would be a bridesmaid for me I realised I didn't have anyone to ask. And then all the other stuff that followed, it just wasn't me.'

'You should've asked Rory and Iwan.' He laughs.

'I should've just spoken to you,' I reply.

'So, how about we elope then?' he suggests. 'Forget the wedding stuff, forget the family. Let's just do things how you want to do them.'

'What, like, on a beach in Hawaii, just the two of us?'

'That could be arranged,' he replies with a smile.

'We should probably wait until your bone has healed.'

'Bones,' he corrects me. 'My fibula *and* my talus.'

'All right, all right, don't milk it.' I laugh. 'Here's the thing, though. I don't think our family would be very impressed with us if we got married without them.'

'Probably not,' he replies. 'But who cares?'

'I do,' I tell him. 'Let's come up with something together, that makes everyone happy.'

'I'd love that,' he tells me. 'And I love you.'

'I love you too,' I reply. 'Now, when can we get you out of here?'

Chapter 41

The Valentina-De Luca household is finally looking festive, after I spent hours this morning making it so.

It's Christmas Eve and Leo is coming home today, so I've spent the day tidying up and putting up Christmas decorations. I just want everything to be perfect when he gets here.

I'm just moving the last few bits from the living room when I hear my phone ringing. For a minute I worry it's the hospital, telling me they're not letting Leo come home for some reason, but then I realise it's Skinner calling.

'Hello,' I say brightly. 'I can't talk right now, unfortunately.'

'I won't keep you long, Mia,' he assures me. 'I'm just calling to give you the best Christmas gift of all time.'

'Go on.' I laugh. 'I hope it's not more cheese. There was so much cheese in those hampers I'll be feeding it to my grandkids.'

'No more cheese, just good news and bad news. Bad news, Savannah has had some kind of stress episode and she's been signed off sick.'

'Oh no, that's awful. I'm so sorry to hear that,' I tell him sincerely.

'Good news, you hold all the cards now,' he tells me. 'I need you, Mia. No one else can write this movie, so, what if you were to work remotely?'

'What, work from here?'

'Sure,' he replies. 'Why not?'

'Erm, that would be wonderful,' I tell him. 'Wow, this really is the best Christmas gift ever.'

Well, maybe the second best, after Leo coming home, but I don't think my boss will appreciate the mush; he'll just tell me to save it for the movie.

'OK, I'm going to go enjoy the holidays with my family, and you do the same,' he tells me. 'You start work in the New Year.'

'Thank you,' I tell him. 'Happy Christmas.'

Once I'm off the phone I have a little squeal to myself. It finally feels like everything is falling into place.

'Hello?' I hear my dad call from the hallway.

'Hey, Dad, thanks for bringing him home,' I say as he wheels Leo in.

'No trouble,' he says. 'But I've got to get straight off. Your mother needs a pie for tonight. Christmas Eve, so of course she does.'

I laugh, kiss him on the cheek and thank him for all his help. Then, once Leo and I are alone, I tell him about my great work news.

'That's amazing,' he tells me. 'Congratulations.'

'Thank you,' I say, smiling widely.

'I should probably give you your present then. It might help,' he says.

'Ooh, yes, please,' I reply.

'Wheel me to . . . the secret room,' he says dramatically.

'Oh my God, I've been desperate to see in this room forever,' I squeak.

'Well, it's all yours,' he says. 'Take a look.'

I open the door slowly and peep my head inside. 'Oh . . . my . . . God.'

'Do you like it?' he asks.

I step inside the room and twirl around, taking in everything it has to offer.

Leo has built me the most stunning office. It's white and kind of minimalist, but then there's such beautiful detail and intricate little finishing touches that I love, that really make the room special.

On one wall is a canvas print of each of the books I've written; on the other main wall is a huge bookshelf, already stocked with all the books I own, with an awesome sofa built into it. A cute little nook for curling up and reading books in.

'Leo, this is just . . . wow.'

'See, you thought we weren't making progress, didn't you? But I've been spending all my time getting this done for you. This is why I asked Amy to come over and help, along with two other guys from work. I probably should have mentioned that. I'm sorry.'

'Forget about all that,' I tell him. 'This room is perfect. You're perfect.'

'No one is perfect.' He laughs. 'You're the closest thing to it I've ever met, though.'

Chapter 42

As I stroll along the beach in my dress I marvel at how, no matter how much changes, this beach always stays the same. I know that whenever I come to Cornwall and stay at the beach house, everything is going to be exactly as I left it, beautifully familiar.

My dress may not be the dream dress I tried on in Paris, but I like it. It's a long, floaty ball gown – in cream, not white. If there was one thing I was sure of, it was that I didn't want a white dress.

It's a year, almost to the day, since Leo popped the question here on the beach and, in an hour or so, we'll finally tie the knot in front of our family and close friends. Well, we met here, he proposed here, so it makes sense that we get married here too.

I'm just killing time, strolling along the beach until it's time to do this thing. We may not have observed many traditions, but one thing I do want to make sure is that my hubby-to-be doesn't see me before the wedding. Not because I think it's bad luck, but because I want to blow him away with this dress.

I'm heading back in the direction of the house when I spot an old friend walking along the beach.

'Oi, Chris,' I shout in a rather unladylike fashion.

Chris the lifeguard is another thing that doesn't change about the beach. He'll probably still be here when he's eighty.

'Hey, I know you,' he says, his Australian accent bringing back so many memories from when we met. 'It's, erm . . .'

'Mia,' I tell him.

'Mia, right. From the big house.'

'That's me,' I reply. 'Where's Jay?'

Chris's face falls. 'He passed away a few months back. Still can't get used to not having him follow me around everywhere.'

'Oh, I'm sorry,' I say. I know how much he loved that dog.

'He had a good life,' he says. 'I don't pick up nearly as many chicks without him.'

'So, I was here last year and you jogged straight past me,' I tell him.

'Did I? Sorry,' he says. 'Surprising, really, you're still a babe.'

Amazing that, last year, when I wasn't all dolled up, he didn't even look twice at me, but now, because I look like the old Mia again, he's turning on the charm.

'I'm getting married today,' I tell him.

'*You* are?' he asks. 'Wow. I wondered why you had so much skin covered up. Who's the lucky fella?'

'You've met him, actually,' I tell him. 'Leo, from when we met.'

Chris's eyes widen. 'Well, I'm happy for you,' he tells me.

'Thanks,' I reply. 'I'm happy for me too.'

Chris laughs. 'Well, have a good one,' he says, jogging off.

I smile to myself before carrying on with my walk.

I feel my phone buzz from inside my tiny handbag. It's Dylan to tell me that he's nearly here and he's bringing his new girlfriend to meet me. He's been seeing her for two months now and he's never seemed happier, plus he's back in touch with Mikey, so maybe I'll get to meet him one day too. I don't think he's lonely anymore, which makes me happy. He says he has me to thank for that, but I don't know. I feel like I learned a lot from him too.

As I approach the beach house I adjust my dress. Were it not for the big skirt, I think my bump might be showing today, and no one other than Leo knows I'm pregnant yet. Well, I feel like if my gran knew I'd got knocked up before I got wed, she'd give me a lecture on how I'm doing things in the wrong order, so I'm biding my time before I tell them, and then I just need to go around stealing all their calendars . . .

Standing on the decking I look into one of the downstairs rooms and see Leo there, looking incredible in his blue suit. As I watch him nervously pacing around I just gaze at him lovingly and stroke my tummy with my hand. I finally have everything I never realised I wanted, and it feels amazing.

If you enjoyed *Never the Bride*, why not try *Here Comes The Ex*? Another uplifting and laugh-out-loud romantic comedy from Portia MacIntosh! Available now.

Keep reading for a sneak preview of *Here Comes The Ex* . . .

Chapter 1

Now

I've never been one for inspirational quotes. You know the ones, they constantly pop up on your Facebook news feed; white text on a colourful or scenic background, usually shared by some distant cousin, old school friend, or random acquaintance you don't remember befriending – shared because it's just so damn profound and relatable.

'Don't be a woman that needs a man, be a woman that a man needs' emblazoned across a sunset, as though the two are somehow related, or the famous 'Marilyn Monroe' one: 'If you can't handle me at my worst, you don't deserve me at my best' which I really don't think anyone should subscribe too, because it basically translates to: 'If you don't put up with me when I'm being a bitch, you don't deserve me when I'm being nice.'

As much as I hate these quotes, I saw one today that felt very apt (not that I felt the need to hit the share button though). It said: 'The friends you make at university are your friends for life' and that one must be true because if it weren't, I wouldn't be driving down a dark country lane in Norfolk, on my way to my old uni friend's wedding.

I alternate concentrating on the road with scanning the darkness for signs of life. One of my colleagues told me there was a lot to see in Norfolk, but not here, not tonight. There is absolutely nothing to see here.

It did cross my mind, to make an excuse – I have to work, I'm having dental surgery, I'm on holiday – but these days people book their weddings so far in advance, they don't even give you the chance to come up with an excuse that is both polite and gets you off the hook. I had to RSVP to this thing almost two years ago. Can you imagine being engaged for two years? I can't even imagine having a boyfriend for two years. That's probably why I'm so anxious about this wedding tomorrow.

Matt, the groom, is one of five people I shared a house with in Manchester during my third year at uni. It's been ten years since we all graduated and five years since we all saw each other last.

For the most part, we've always been the worst kind of millennials. With the exception of Ed, who is more than making up for our collective shortfall with his four children so far, we all stumbled into our thirties unwed and childless. The rest of us are contributing to a country with an aging population and a declining birth rate, because we're all way too busy with our jobs and our lives, and it's just so easy to think we can put off these things until later. But as my mum keeps reminding me, I'm losing daylight, eggs, and the figure to bag myself a decent man – all of which sound like something from a bygone era, or a sci-fi movie with a dystopian future for women. But when my mum was my age – 31 – she'd already had me and my sister, so I guess you can't blame her for thinking I'm wasting my life. The problem now is that it's so easy to compare myself to my uni friends. We all had the same start in adult life, we all got degrees and then we went off into the world (well, I didn't go off anywhere, I stayed in Manchester) and we all got jobs in our fields. Relationship-wise, we're all at very different stages. But while Ed is married, Matt is getting married tomorrow, Zach and

Fiona are engaged (yes, to each other), and Mark (or Clarky, as he's more commonly known to those who tolerate him) has a girlfriend, I am still single. I'm not sure that counts as a stage. I don't really feel like I've left the starting line yet.

I glance at the digital clock in my car. The red glowing numbers tell me that it's nearly 10.30 p.m. So much for saying I'd arrive early and have a drink with my old friends. I'm sure everyone will be in bed by now, so that they can be up early for the wedding tomorrow.

I notice car headlights in my rear-view mirror – the first sign of life I've seen on this road and I'm not sure if it puts me at ease or makes me feel nervous. I've seen too many horror movies, I think.

The lights grow bigger, brighter, and they appear to be heading straight for me. As the car gets too close to mine, I speed up a little to try and put some space between us, but the car behind only goes faster.

As my speed increases, so does my heartbeat and my breathing. I feel my hands begin to sweat, but I daren't adjust the grip on the steering wheel that I'm holding so tightly, I can see my knuckles turning white.

It all happens so quickly. Suddenly the car behind – a red sports car with a private plate – pulls out from behind me, moving onto the other side of the narrow country road to overtake me, before speeding off ahead.

I loosen my grip as I watch its lights grow smaller and smaller until they disappear.

Finally alone again, I puff air from my cheeks. What an arsehole, driving like that on a lonely country road at this time of night. I don't care where he has to be, no one is in that much of a hurry that they have to drive so recklessly. I suppose I ruined his fun, sticking to the speed limit in my Polo that's seen better days.

The thumping in my chest slows down around the time I spot the Willows Lodge Hotel floodlit in the distance. Thank God. At least when I leave in a couple of days, I'll be driving in the daylight.

Drivers like that are almost always nocturnal, aren't they? No sign of them during the day and then, under the cloak of darkness, they come out in their ridiculous cars to drive like maniacs. I could just about tell that it was a man in the car – a man with too little in his pants and too much in his bank, if you ask me.

I pull into the hotel car park, turn off my engine and breathe a sigh of relief. I'd say thank God I'm here, but I'd rather be anywhere else. Well, apart from car wrapped around a tree courtesy of someone who is overcompensating for something.

I give myself a brief internal pep talk to try and psych myself up (You can do this, Luca. You're a strong, independent woman, Luca etc). I'm not sure it works, but I get out of my car, grab my hold-all from the boot, and make my way across the floodlit gravel car park.

As I walk between the parked cars, I can't help but look over my shoulder every now and then. It feels so lonely out here, with no sign of life anywhere. The only sound I can hear is from the stones crunching under my feet as I walk – at least I'd be able to hear footsteps, if someone were to try and creep up behind me.

I remind myself to keep my imagination in check, but it doesn't matter. Something distracts me. I'm almost at the hotel entrance when something catches my eye: a red sports car. It's not the same one that sped past me, is it? I hover a hand over the car and feel heat radiating from its hot body. And then there's that number plate, that tosser private plate that makes me hate this guy already.

Maybe it's because I'm all frazzled over this wedding business or maybe it is because he genuinely scared me, but I do something completely out of character from me. I take a pen and a piece of paper from my bag, and I write a note.

I'm not usually the kind of girl to write: 'no one is impressed by your driving or your car' on the back of a receipt before placing it under the windscreen wiper. In fact, it's so unlike me to do something like this that I quickly grab my bags and retreat to the safety of the hotel, before anyone sees me.

As I check in, I notice a little sign on the counter advertising homemade red velvet cake. That's exactly what I need to take the edge of a rubbish evening.

'Is it too late to get some cake?' I ask the receptionist. 'There might be some left,' she replies. 'If you ask in the bar.'

The receptionist points to a small, empty looking bar in an adjoining room.

Another thing that is out of character for me is hanging out in bars on my own, but I can't really face going to my room just yet, and some cake would be lovely. I might even have a drink too. A quick nightcap, just to relax me little. Then I'll go to my room, climb into my bed, and get a nice early night in preparation for the big day tomorrow. I do have a tendency to be late, but I absolutely cannot do that tomorrow – I want my friends to think at least one thing changed since the last time they saw me.

Acknowledgements

Thanks so much to Sophia, George and the rest of the team at HQ for all of their hard work on my books. You're doing such a fantastic job.

Thank you to my lovely readers for taking the time to read and review my books. It means so much to me.

Finally, thank you to my incredible family (Joe, Joey, James, Kim, Pino, Aud & Darcy) for all of their support – I couldn't do it without you.

Dear Reader,
We hope you enjoyed reading this book. If you did, we'd be so appreciative if you left a review. It really helps us and the author to bring more books like this to you.

Here at HQ Digital we are dedicated to publishing fiction that will keep you turning the pages into the early hours. Don't want to miss a thing? To find out more about our books, promotions, discover exclusive content and enter competitions you can keep in touch in the following ways:

JOIN OUR COMMUNITY:
Sign up to our new email newsletter: http://smarturl.it/SignUpHQ
Read our new blog www.hqstories.co.uk

𝕏 https://twitter.com/HQStories
f www.facebook.com/HQStories

BUDDING WRITER?
We're also looking for authors to join the HQ Digital family!
Find out more here:
https://www.hqstories.co.uk/want-to-write-for-us/

Thanks for reading, from the HQ Digital team